To Scotland, With Love

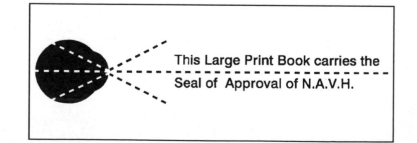

This Large Print Book carries the
Seal of Approval of N.A.V.H.

TO SCOTLAND, WITH LOVE

KAREN HAWKINS

THORNDIKE PRESS

An imprint of Thomson Gale, a part of The Thomson Corporation

Detroit • New York • San Francisco • New Haven, Conn. • Waterville, Maine • London

THOMSON

GALE

TM

Thorndike Press® Large Print Basic.
The text of this Large Print edition is unabridged.
Other aspects of the book may vary from the original edition.
Set in 16 pt. Plantin.

LIBRARY OF CONGRESS CATALOGING-IN-PUBLICATION DATA

Hawkins, Karen.
    To Scotland, with love / by Karen Hawkins.
        p. cm. — (The MacLean family series ; #2) (Thorndike Press large print basic)
    ISBN-13: 978-1-4104-0402-2 (alk. paper)
    ISBN-10: 1-4104-0402-1 (alk. paper)
    1. Large type books. 2. Scotland — Fiction. I. Title.
PS3558.A8231647T6 2008
813'.54—dc22   2007039345

Published in 2008 by arrangement with Pocket Books,
a division of Simon & Schuster, Inc.

Printed in the United States of America on permanent paper
10 9 8 7 6 5 4 3 2 1

This book is dedicated to Nate V. N.
for introducing me to such wonderful,
incredible, and life-changing wonders as
the magic of sailplanes,
the questionable wisdom of
the BBC's *The Office,*
and the hilarity that is
Karaoke Night at Big Daddy's.

CHAPTER 1

Aye, I believe in the MacLean curse. If ye'd seen the blinding white lightning and heard the roar of thunder over MacLean Castle on a clear summer morn as I have, ye'd believe it, too.

> Old Woman Nora from Loch Lomond
> to her three wee granddaughters
> one cold evening

"Argh! Bentley! Where are you?"

The yell echoed through the morning air, over the loud clops from the horses and carts that were just beginning to stir in Mayfair, London's most fashionable district.

Startled, Gregor MacLean stepped back from the ornate door of Oglivie House and glanced up at the open third-story window.

It was far too early for drama. Well, it was too early at *most* domiciles. At Oglivie House, drama was never out of fashion.

Gregor bit back an impatient sigh and

stepped forward, rapping the knocker hard. The Oglivies were silly, extremely emotional, and far too given to excitement. Nothing could have brought him to this door except their one and only daughter, Venetia. Calm, logical, and rarely indulging in unseemly displays of emotion, Venetia easily offset her parents' sad tendencies. In fact, during his years of friendship with Venetia, Gregor had discovered only one flaw: a disturbing inclination to become overly involved in the lives of others.

"Bentley!" Mr. Oglivie's voice rang out louder than before, a hint of a sob at the end.

Gregor rapped on the door yet again. The quicker he collected Venetia for their morning ride, the quicker he'd be away from the brewing madness.

The door flew open, the usually impassive butler gasping a relieved sigh. "My lord, I am so *glad* — you can have no idea — it's been a horrible morning and —"

Gregor walked past the incoherent butler. At Oglivie House, something as small as the chef quitting or a misplaced bracelet resulted in scenes worthy of the stage, complete with ranting, raving, accusations, and weeping. He knew from long experience that the best way to deal with such distractions was to ignore them. "I've come to take Miss Venetia for our morning ride. I assume she's ready?"

Overhead, a thump rattled the crystals on the chandelier.

Gregor frowned up the stairs before saying uneasily, "Is Miss Venetia awaiting me in the breakfast room? We should make haste to reach the park before the fops arise and clog the pathways."

Bentley's brow wrinkled. "But, my lord, Miss Oglivie isn't —"

A loud crash sounded from upstairs, followed by an unmistakable yell: *"Bentley! Order the carriage!"*

Gregor cut a hard glance at Bentley. "What were you saying about Miss Oglivie?"

The butler's eyes teared up alarmingly. "She's missing, my lord, and we don't know where to find her."

"What?" The word snapped through the air.

Bentley wrung his hands. "Yes, my lord. Miss Oglivie apparently left the house quite early this morning, and no one knows where she went." The butler glanced warily up the stairs, then leaned forward to add in an undertone, "She left a note for Lord Oglivie and he has been in a taking since he read it."

9

"Do you know what the note said?"

Bentley shook his head regretfully.

How odd. It was quite unlike Venetia to —

A door slammed above, then Mr. Oglivie appeared on the landing and ran down the stairs. Though usually the most elegant of men, he wore a long white night rail, his robe loose and streaming about him, his feet bare, his hair in a white, unkempt fluff around a precariously tipped nightcap.

"Bentley!" Oglivie waved a crumpled paper over his head. "Did you not hear me? We must — Venetia cannot — she might be — Oh, no!" His voice caught and he sank to the bottom step and dropped his head in his hands. "What shall I do? What *shall* I do?"

Gregor eyed Venetia's father, unmoved. Oglivie had once taken to his bed for a week over the loss of his prize poodle, certain his dog had been abducted for ransom. Of course, the dog had shown up a week later, bedraggled but happy, having taken up with some amorous three-legged mutt. The resulting pups were as hideous as expected.

Venetia's mother was cut from the same cloth, dismissing servants on a whim, declaring herself to be dying whenever she had a headache, going into a decline if an acquaintance unknowingly slighted her, and enacting Cheltenham tragedies at the drop of a hat.

Gregor couldn't count the scenes he'd witnessed, none of which he'd allowed to affect him. Why waste one's strength on mere emotion? Things always sorted themselves out, usually without anyone's help.

Despite Mr. Oglivie's piteous sobs, Gregor doubted that Venetia was in any danger. More than likely, she'd merely forgotten their promised ride and had gone for a walk. She'd send him a note when she returned, and all would be right with the world.

Whatever the truth, Gregor decided it was time for him to make his exit. "Mr. Oglivie, I bid you *adieu.* You obviously need privacy in your time of distress, so I will leave you n—"

"No!" Venetia's father held out an imploring hand. "Lord MacLean! I beg of you — for Venetia's sake, if not mine! She —" He gulped as if the words were caught in his throat, his gaze desperately seeking Gregor's. "Please," the older man said, his voice cracking, his eyes wet with tears, his tone strained to a mere thread. *"Please* help me find her."

Something in Oglivie's face chilled Gregor's heart. There was genuine terror in his gaze.

Suddenly both cold and hot, Gregor snapped, "What's happened?"

"She — She —" Oglivie dropped his head back into his hands, a sob ringing through the foyer.

Gregor's hands fisted at his sides. Outside, thunder suddenly rumbled, the wind rattling against the windowpanes. He strode toward the stairs, his boots sounding sharply on the marble floor as he came to a halt before the older man. "Oglivie, *what about Venetia?*"

Mr. Oglivie lifted his head. "She's gone, MacLean! Abducted! And all because of me!"

The sentence hung in the air, a living, breathing fear. The wind lifted again, more furious and colder than before as it whistled around the closed door and chilled their ankles, ruffling the edges of Lord Oglivie's night rail.

"How can this be your fault?"

Oglivie's lips quivered. "Because he — he — told me he wished to run off with Venetia and I — I — I encouraged him, thinking she might find it romantic. I never thought he'd do it without her knowledge. I thought —"

"What's his name?" Gregor asked, his jaw so tight it ached.

12

"Ravenscroft."

Gregor had an instant image of a young man with a weak chin and an overeager manner. "That *whelp?* You encouraged *him?*"

Oglivie flushed a deep red. "He seemed genuinely taken with Venetia and she was always pleasant to him —"

"She's pleasant to everyone." His gaze locked on the note in Oglivie's hand. "Is that from Venetia?"

His eyes swimming with tears, Oglivie handed over the note.

Gregor scanned it.

Oglivie's voice quavered. "You must understand, MacLean. Lord Ravenscroft wished to marry her, but she's so shy and —"

Gregor crushed the note between his fingers. "Bloody hell!" The note was written in Venetia's distinctively looping scribble. It said simply that she was accompanying Ravenscroft to attend her mother in Stirling 'as requested.' The fool must have told Venetia that her mother was ill.

Mr. Oglivie rubbed a trembling hand over his eyes. "I can't believe he did such a thing! I thought he was a fine, outstanding —"

But Gregor had already turned on his heel and was striding toward the door.

13

"MacLean!" Oglivie jumped up and followed Gregor onto the doorstep, not noticing that a mere hour ago it had been clear and springlike, while now the cold wind blew with a ferocity that ripped off his nightcap and sent it tumbling down the road. Shivering, he said over the wind's howl, "MacLean, where are you going?"

"To find your daughter." Gregor took the reins of his horse from a waiting footman and threw himself into the saddle.

"But how? You don't know where to begin!"

"I've heard that Ravenscroft lodges on St. James Street. I will start there."

"But when you find them? What will you do then?"

"Whatever I damn well have to," Gregor said, his face grim. "In the meantime, wait here and keep your mouth closed. No one can know she's gone."

"But —"

"*Closed*, Oglivie. That should keep you occupied until I return." Without waiting for a reply, Gregor turned his horse and galloped away.

Oglivie crossed his arms against the frigid wind, unable to look away from MacLean's rapidly disappearing figure. "What have I done?" he whispered, tears streaming anew. "Venetia, my darling girl, where *are* you?"

Miles away, in a rented carriage that raced over a deeply rutted road, young Lord Ravenscroft held his wounded hand against his chest. "You *cut* me! I'm bleeding like a stuck pig!"

"Do not overstate the facts, if you please." Swaying with the wild ride of the coach, Miss Venetia Oglivie pulled her handkerchief from her reticule and wiped off the pin of her pearl and silver brooch. "I did not cut you — though had I a knife, I might have been tempted to do more than stick your hand with my brooch pin."

Ravenscroft stuck his knuckle into his mouth. "Whatever it was, there was no call for it."

"I warned you to cease making a cake of yourself."

"I wasn't making a cake of myself! I was merely saying that I love y—" Ravenscroft gasped as Venetia raised the pin once again, his eyes wide as if she held a dagger.

She lowered the pin and sighed. "Really, Ravenscroft, these missish vapors are not the least attractive."

"Missish vapors? Venetia! How can you say —"

"That's *Miss Oglivie* to you," she said firmly.

Ravenscroft scooted down the seat, away from the glimmering pin. "Look, Vene— I mean, Miss Oglivie. I — I — I am sorry if you think I was out of line in declaring myself —"

"You were grossly out of line, especially in these sad circumstances."

He blinked uncertainly, hanging on to the leather strap that hung overhead as the carriage bumped over a deep rut. "Sad circumstances?"

Venetia eyed her companion for a grave moment. "Have you forgotten why we are traveling over this horrid road at such a dangerous speed? My poor mother is ill."

"Ah, yes. That." Ravenscroft tugged at his cravat as if it had suddenly tightened about his throat. "Your mother. I suppose I was . . . not precisely forgetful, for that would never do, but I was, ah, overcome — Yes! I was overcome by passion and forgot your mother." He added hastily, "But only for a moment! I quite remember now that we're going to visit your poor mother at your grandmother's house in Stirling."

Venetia supposed she shouldn't be surprised at Ravenscroft's scattered memory; he wasn't the sharpest quill in the pot. But something whispered that things were not right. Something she couldn't quite put her finger on. "Perhaps we should stop at the next inn and see to your hand."

Ravenscroft shook his head vehemently. "No. We can't stop."

She regarded him through narrowed eyes. "Why not?"

"Because . . . we'll be late. And it would make more sense to wait until it's dark."

Venetia frowned, her suspicion rising even more. She should have asked more questions before leaving, but when Ravenscroft had burst into the breakfast room that morning, a note clutched in his hand, desperation on his young face, she hadn't thought at all. Written in her father's hand, the note requested that she immediately go with Ravenscroft to assist Mother.

Used to Mama's tendency to think every twitch a death spasm and Papa's unerring ability to avoid responsibility, Venetia had found the request inconvenient but not odd. So she'd changed out of her riding habit, hastily packed a portmanteau, and swiftly dashed off a reassuring note to Papa that she'd do as he'd bid, before climbing into Ravenscroft's carriage.

Of course, it would not do to worry until she'd seen Mama for herself. It was a pity, though, that the burden of escorting her had been placed on Ravenscroft, Papa's newest "project." Papa thought of himself as a champion of the downtrodden, which meant that every once in a while, he'd attempt to help some poor lost soul navigate the tricky waters of the ton. Papa called it his great social experiment, though Venetia privately thought he simply enjoyed the extravagant compliments that Ravenscroft gratefully showered upon him.

Early this morning, as they were madly dashing from London, Venetia'd felt sorry for poor Ravenscroft for getting embroiled in her family's mad contretemps. But after sitting in the carriage for more than two hours, she had serious doubts about him. Something — she wasn't certain what — was not as it should be. He seemed exceedingly nervous, and kept sticking his head out the window as if expecting that someone was following them.

Venetia was many things, but stupid was not one of them. When she attempted to question Ravenscroft about the circumstances that had led Papa to request they fly off to Mama's side, Ravenscroft stuttered and stammered a mishmash of unrelated explanations and excuses that left her with a headache.

She unhooked the leather curtain to look outside. They were traveling far too swiftly for safety. The horses were fairly sprung, so they'd have to stop soon to change them. When they did, she'd refuse to continue until Ravenscroft answered her questions. If he refused to do so, she'd take refuge with the landlady and send word to London for her father to come for her.

Her plan in place, Venetia shivered at the cold wind and latched the curtain back into place. She settled back against the squabs and cast a disparaging eye over Ravenscroft. Though twenty-two years of age, he seemed much younger. He was thin and lamentably short-statured, a fact he tried to conceal by adding buckram wadding to the shoulders of his coats and heels to his riding boots. He possessed watery blue eyes and no chin to speak of, but what he lacked in looks and comportment he made up for in enthusiastic flattery — which was why Papa thought Ravenscroft could do no wrong.

Venetia grabbed the edge of the seat as the carriage slid around a bend in the road. "Ravenscroft, we are traveling too fast for this road!"

"Yes, but, ah, if we go fast, we'll get there . . . faster."

Venetia frowned, but before she could ask

another question, the carriage rocked violently as it hit an especially deep rut, and for a second, they were tossed into the air. Venetia slammed back onto the seat with a gasp. "Ravenscroft, we are going much too fast!"

He stuck out a foot to press against the corner, trying to wedge himself firmly into place. "We can't slow down," he said, in the tone of a mutinous child. "Your mother is expecting us."

"If we have an accident and turn over, we won't get there at all!"

Ravenscroft's mouth turned downward, but he didn't answer.

Miffed, Venetia tugged at the carriage blanket that was over her lap. She was bruised, tired, and quite out of sorts. Plus it was getting colder as they traveled north, much colder. So cold, in fact, that it made her think of Gregor.

Gregor. Oh blast, she hadn't left him a note! By now he'd be at Oglivie House, wondering where she was.

Venetia closed her eyes, clinging to her seat as the carriage bumped and swayed along. Gregor MacLean was her best friend. He knew all of her foibles and shortcomings, her passions and disappointments, and she knew his. She trusted his solid good sense. What would he tell her to do right now?

Most likely, he'd deliver a thundering scold about her impetuosity in going off with Ravenscroft. Gregor never did anything to help anyone. In his skewed opinion, everyone should help themselves. It was only the weak who needed assistance.

Venetia thought Gregor was a bit naive, which wasn't surprising the way the ton feted the man. It wasn't just because of his good looks; it was also because of the mysterious rumors that swirled about him — rumors that he and his family held the secret to raising the winds, unleashing storms, and loosening thunder upon the heads of their enemies. People said that centuries long ago, Gregor's family had been cursed. When they lost their temper, storms rose — wild, uncontrollable storms that could destroy everything in their paths. Because of this, all of the MacLeans struggled to maintain their tempers.

Sighing, Venetia reached over and unlatched the leather curtain to stare outside again. When she'd first met Gregor all those years ago, she'd heard the rumors but hadn't believed them. Over the years, though, she'd seen the curse in action — which was why these rapidly gathering clouds and the chilling air made her think of Gregor.

Perhaps he'd discovered her missing and was even now riding to her rescue. She savored the picture of Gregor astride a white horse, galloping hell-for-leather to save her, his green eyes gleaming with . . . irritation.

Her shoulders sagged. That's all Gregor would feel if he was ever put into the position of coming to her rescue — irritation and a great sense of disgust that she'd been foolish enough to be tricked into an impropriety.

Disheartened, she latched the curtain back into place and sat back in her seat with a thump.

"What's wrong?" Ravenscroft asked, his face going pale. "Did you see someone? Are they following us?"

"No," she said shortly. "No one is following us." She crossed her arms, holding the carriage blanket a bit tighter, and regarded her companion with a steady gaze.

Ravenscroft pasted a smile on his face that looked as comfortable as the prince of Wales's corset. "Well!" he said brightly, "I daresay it's colder today than I've ever felt it to be in April. Don't you think so, Ven—"

"*Miss Oglivie,* if you please."

His smile froze. "Miss Oglivie, of course."

"Thank you. And yes, I do think it's colder than any April I've ever seen, which is yet another reason why we should stop soon."

"But we'll lose time, and —"

"Ravenscroft, I don't think you understand: it's a matter of personal comfort."

"Personal com—" He blushed. "Oh! I didn't think — that is, I didn't realize that you —"

"Really, Ravenscroft, do not make this more embarrassing for me than it already is. I need to stop and that is that."

"Of course! I'll ask the coachman to halt as soon as we reach Torlington. That's a mere half an hour away."

She nodded and turned away from him, wedging herself into the corner to combat the severe swaying of the coach, and hoping for some silence.

To her relief, Ravenscroft settled into his place opposite hers, grabbing the seat with both hands to keep from being bounced into the air at every dip in the road, his chin sunk into his cravat. He looked exactly like a sulky schoolboy.

The minutes flew, the carriage jolting, the wooden body creaking and straining, as Venetia prayed that they'd make it to Torlington without toppling into a ditch.

Closing her eyes, she said a swift prayer that she could force some answers from Ravenscroft at the next stop.

Until then, prayers were all she had.

At this same time, a tall, elegant figure stepped out of White's Gentlemen's Club, settled his hat to shield his eyes from the falling snow, and waited as his carriage made its way up the crowded street to where he stood.

A moment ago, Dougal MacLean had been on the verge of winning a considerable sum playing whist. Then an idle glance out the window had caused him to exclaim aloud, toss down his cards, and leave so quickly, his companions were still blinking in surprise.

Dougal glanced up at the thickening snow and frowned. Only one thing could make it snow like this in April: the MacLean curse. It caused storms to gather whenever a Mac-Lean grew angry, yet varied within each of them. Gregor, always cold and in control, produced storms of ice and snow. Lots of snow. Masses of snow. More snow than London had ever seen. Which was why Dougal had to find his brother, and quickly.

St. James Street was filled with scurrying

people hunched against the wind, all of them staring at the rapidly falling snow with astonishment. The carriage arrived, the footman jumping down to open the door. Just as Dougal put his foot onto the step, he caught sight of a large figure coming through the snow. Unlike the other souls on the street, this one did not seem to mind the icy air. In fact, he almost seemed to relish the snow powdering his bared head.

"Gregor!" Dougal called.

As he drew near, Dougal saw the whiteness about his brother's mouth. "I must ask a favor of you," Gregor said. "My horse is at the end of the street. Can we —" He nodded toward the carriage.

"Of course." Dougal looked at his footman, who dashed off to collect Gregor's mount. Soon the coach was rumbling down the street, the horse trotting behind.

Gregor slanted a hard look at Dougal. "Someone has absconded with Venetia Oglivie."

"Good God! Who would do such a thing?"

"Ravenscroft."

"That pup? He wouldn't have the sand."

Gregor's gaze was icy green. "That *dead* pup, once I'm through with him. He tricked Venetia into leaving town with him."

Venetia had left with the man of her own

volition? Dougal regarded his brother from beneath his lashes. Venetia and Gregor had been friends since childhood, for so long, in fact, that even the gossips in town had ceased to comment on their morning rides and easy camaraderie. Was her association with Ravenscroft something more? "Do you think Venetia and Ravenscroft —"

"*No.*"

Dougal raised his brows as a raw wind rocked the coach and screeched along the ground.

"She was *tricked*," Gregor growled.

Dougal looked at where the wind was forcing snow through every crack on one side of the coach and wisely said, "Of course she was tricked. Venetia would never do something as impulsive as eloping, even if she was madly in love with someone."

The wind rocked the coach like the slam of a fist.

Dougal winced. "Gregor, please! We'll be blown off the road."

Gregor gripped his knees and took a deep breath, trying to relax. "If you wish to stay on the road, then stop making such asinine statements. Venetia did not elope. Ravenscroft told her that her mother had taken ill in Stirling. Ravenscroft's servant told me of the bounder's plans: how they are to travel to Gretna Green, how he will tell her the truth of their situation once they are far enough from London that she can't turn back. How he has massive debts and was to meet Lord Ulster for a duel this morning, but didn't show."

"The coward!" Dougal shook his head. "You must have offered Ravenscroft's man plenty of gold to get such information."

"Fortunately for me, the weasel has a dislike of being held by his ankles out of an open window."

Dougal grinned.

"Ravenscroft plans on crossing to the North Road at the juncture above Pickmere and hopes Venetia won't notice."

"Won't notice? A road she's traveled many times before?"

"Ravenscroft is not the most intelligent of men. Which will make his death all the less missed."

"Gregor, if you do something rash, it will cause a scandal and Venetia could end up paying for it. It would be better to retrieve her and bring her back unscathed, and deal with Ravenscroft later."

"I will, but only if things haven't progressed too far."

Dougal's expression darkened. "You think that slack-jawed fool might take advantage of her?"

Gregor's hands fisted at the words, his heart thudding so loudly his ears rang. "If Ravenscroft wishes to live, he'd better not place so much as a finger upon her head."

"I can't believe he thinks to get away with this."

"It gets worse: Ravenscroft's servant thinks the idiot plans on fleeing England to avoid the duel and his debts."

"With Venetia in tow? Bloody hell!" The carriage rumbled to a stop and a footman quickly appeared to open the door. Gregor and Dougal stepped out and walked toward the portico of Dougal's London home. As soon as they were out of hearing of the servants, they stopped on the walkway, ignoring the swirling snow. "What can I do to help?" Dougal asked.

"Go to Oglivie House and stay with Venetia's father until I bring her home. He's distraught and out of control. If he tells even one soul that she's missing and how it came to be, the damage to her reputation will be irreparable."

"I'll hold him at pistol point if I must." Dougal paused, his gaze locking with his brother's. "Can you save Venetia?"

Gregor glanced up at the swirling snow, the wind seeping through his clothes. Already the snow was beginning to pile up in places. "I don't know," he said, the words torn from his lips. "I may have placed the one obstacle in my path that even I cannot overcome. This storm . . ." A sick feeling clutched at him at the thought. Damn his temper.

"Nonsense," Dougal said briskly, pulling his collar more tightly about his neck. "If the snow slows you down on horseback, it will slow down a carriage even more. I daresay it will give you an advantage, when all is said and done."

Relief flooded Gregor. "You're right. I hadn't thought of that."

"There'll be time enough for thinking once you're on your way. I have horses posted along the North Road. That will help." At Gregor's surprised look, Dougal shrugged. "There's a woman I occasionally visit when London seems dull. If you need to use one of my mounts, do so."

"I don't know how to thank you."

Dougal gave him a small smile. "Just find Venetia."

Gregor nodded, then strode back to the carriage, where the groom stood with his horse. Within seconds, he was thundering down the street.

Ice and snow lay thick upon the road, and

he took heart in Dougal's words about the storm slowing Ravenscroft's carriage. But that was the only bright thought he could find.

Hold on, Venetia, he thought, urging his mount onward. *Hold on.*

CHAPTER 2

Proud men oft think 'tis a sin to admit to any wrongness; proud women oft think the same thing. Aye, lassies, pride travels o'er the line as divides the sexes with so little effort!

Old Woman Nora from Loch Lomond
to her three wee granddaughters
one cold evening

Eight miles north of London, Lord Ravenscroft was facing the dismal fact that his life was ruined. A scant two years earlier, he'd arrived in London certain he was soon to find his fortune. He was handsome, fairly well set, and of a decent lineage.

However, none of his obvious attributes guaranteed him the invitations and attentions he thought should be his. He had letters of introduction from his dear mama, who once had enjoyed relative success in society before she married his father, but he quickly discovered that though she might have been considered a beauty in her day, she'd disappeared from sight upon her marriage, and no one had given her an instant's thought since. Her letters did him little good.

He also had a friend — or *thought* he had a friend — in one Mr. Philcourt, who'd offered to sponsor Ravenscroft at White's. Unfortunately, the offer, made so generously near a well-filled punch bowl at an entertainment in York, never came to fruition. Indeed, Mr. Philcourt conveniently seemed to forget he'd ever met Lord Ravenscroft and seemed to avoid him at various functions.

Daunted but unbowed, Ravenscroft had refused to give up either his social aspiration or his desire to be *somebody.* Still, things did not get better. Oh, he was invited to some events, but none lofty enough to make him feel as if he'd arrived.

The whole business put him into a fit of the sullens, and some people who had formerly been polite began to turn and hide at his approach. Lord Ravenscroft grew more determined to garner notice, and what had been a pale, inauspicious beginning grew worse each day. It truly seemed that the longer he was in London, the more slights he was forced to endure.

Someone clearly had decided he was a man of little sense, no address, and less importance, which was preposterous. He had more than his fair share of brains; his mother, God rest her soul, had always told him so. And he was certain he had address, for he'd been the darling of York society. As for importance, why, his family was descended from Bloody Jack Ravenscroft, the first highwayman who'd also possessed a title. That was nothing to sneer at!

Unfortunately, once a note was struck, it was difficult to erase; only a solid fortune would overcome the established picture society had of him. So, desperate and with little to lose, Ravenscroft began to gamble. Unfortunately, the mediocrity of his fortune didn't allow much room for blunder, and in the space of a week of increasingly desperate wagers, he managed to lose most of what his blessed mother had left him.

Though he was not a man of powerful intellect, it didn't take Ravenscroft long to realize he'd made a· mistake, one that couldn't be undone. Which was why he'd finally realized that he had only one option left: marry an heiress.

Of course, not being completely accepted into the ton, Ravenscroft didn't know any heiresses. He was on speaking terms with only one lady of quality, Miss Venetia Oglivie, the daughter of Ravenscroft's one and only friend in the ton. He knew from something Venetia's father had said that, though not wealthy, he planned on putting quite a bit into his daughter's dowry, a fact Ravenscroft only recently remembered. And a good-sized dowry, attached to a wife already clasped close to the bosom of the fashionable set, would put Ravenscroft exactly where he wanted to be.

He could almost see the stack of invitations on his breakfast tray each morning, Venetia beaming lovingly at him across the table as they planned their daily amusements among the haute ton.

And it was true love, Ravenscroft thought, looking across the carriage at his beloved, who was wrapped neck to toe in a fur-lined pelisse, a lined bonnet tied over her curls, and a thick blanket covering her lap.

But not even Ravenscroft, who was desperately in love (as well as needing access to his beloved's fortune), could pretend that her gray eyes were regarding him with anything other than irritation.

"Ravenscroft, when are we going to stop? You've yet to ask the coachman to slow down and look for an inn."

"We'll stop soon. I promise."

"So you said thirty minutes ago."

Ravenscroft had started to say something when the gleam of her brooch caught his eye. It peered malevolently at him from the collar of her pelisse. He rubbed his hand reflexively and said plaintively, "I'd ask the coachman to slow down now, but I fear we'll get caught in this snow."

She gazed at him with suspicion. He had imagined they'd pass the trip laughing and talking and sharing stories of their youth. Not once had he thought she'd be so suspicious.

The carriage hit a deep rut, and Ravenscroft had to scramble not to fall across the seat into Venetia's lap.

"We are going too fast," she announced, glaring at him. "If you do not do something about it now, I will."

"But we really should press on while we can, before the snow builds up. You would hate having to stay the night at an inn. Why, what if your mother worsens through the night and dies? I'd wager then you'd wish we'd pressed ahead!"

"That's the third time you've suggested that my mother might be at death's door."

Blast it, why *hadn't* he just told her that her mother was dying instead of simply ill?

Venetia would have been much more malleable then — though perhaps not in the mood for a marriage proposal. "Your mother is quite delicate, so naturally I worry."

"Mother? *Delicate?*"

Ravenscroft was not certain, but it sounded as though his beloved had accompanied that statement with a decided snort.

"Mother is as hardy as they come. Besides, none of that matters right now. Rap and tell the coachman to slow down."

Ravenscroft eyed her sullenly.

Her hand went to her brooch.

"Oh, very well! But I must say I think you're overreacting."

He rapped on the ceiling to alert the coachman, then leaned out the window to converse, the wind whipping away the sound of his voice.

Venetia shivered as the cold air entered the carriage. In her entire life, she could think of only one other time when it had snowed in April, and that had been because of Gregor.

Venetia frowned, again wondering if he had caused this weather. It was possible, but only if he lost his temper, which he rarely did. Besides his older brother, Alexander, Gregor was the MacLean most in control of his temper.

Surely the storm was a fluke. She turned her attention back to Ravenscroft, who seemed to be having some sort of altercation with the coachman. Finally, Ravenscroft withdrew into the carriage, tacking the leather curtain back in place, his face red from the wind.

"There. I did as you asked."

There was a loud "Hie!" and then the carriage was off even faster than before, rocking wildly.

"You didn't tell the coachman to slow down at all! You told him to go faster!" Venetia accused.

Ravenscroft was too busy trying to keep his seat to answer.

With a loud huff of frustration, Venetia raised herself and knocked hard on the roof of the carriage.

An answering knock was heard, and the coachman slowed the carriage, the rear wheels sliding back and forth before they regained control.

"Venetia! What are you doing?" Ravenscroft cried.

"I am making certain we reach Grandmama's house alive."

"But we *must* go faster! We cannot creep along at this pace!" He banged his fist on the carriage roof.

There was a questioning knock in return, a hesitant tempo that made Venetia breathe a sigh of relief. "See? The coachman thinks it a poor idea. We should maintain this pace and —"

Ravenscroft banged heavily once again, louder and more forcefully. Instantly, the carriage sprang to a faster pace, throwing them both back into the seat. They rounded a curve in the narrow road, and the back of the carriage swung wildly for a moment before righting itself.

Venetia braced her feet on the edge of the seat across from her, struggling to remain upright. "You are mad! What on earth is wrong with you?"

Ravenscroft sank into his seat, his chin almost to his chest as he clung to the leather strap by the door. He looked pale and was perspiring, despite the cold.

Venetia refused to feel sorry for him. Maybe she could escape, toss herself out the door. She flipped back the leather curtain to see blinding snow whipping by. She could barely make out the outlines of trees and fences, a small inn, and a long stone wall before she refastened the curtain. She'd break her neck if she attempted to jump.

Which left her with Ravenscroft and his increasingly bizarre behavior. "Ravenscroft, please. Let's just stop for a moment and get some hot tea and discuss this like adults who —"

The carriage swung to one side, careening madly before suddenly tilting up, then the whole world slid sideways. Venetia slammed into Ravenscroft, who rammed into the carriage door. They seemed to hang there, mashed against the latched door, until, with a loud snap, something broke — and then there was nothing but white and cold wind.

Gregor pressed a coin into the innkeeper's rather grimy fist. "When did you see them?"

The innkeeper rolled the gold coin between his fleshy fingers, his heart beating a little faster at the sight. Suddenly, it didn't seem like such an imposition to stand in the snow and talk. " 'Twas an hour ago, no more."

Gregor smiled grimly. He was catching up.

The innkeeper shook his head. "The carriage tore through here like the hounds of hell were after it. And in this snow, too. We all stared, we did, to see it slidin' along at such a pace."

"It didn't stop?"

"Not here, though if I was a bettin' man, I'd say they'd stopped at the White Swan in Tottingham. They've room to stable twice't the horses I can."

Gregor swung back up on his horse. "Thank you for the information, my good man."

The innkeeper nodded, watching as Gregor wheeled his horse and rode down the road, far faster than was wise in this weather. There'd been a grim look to the man's expression that had not boded well for the occupants of that carriage, and for a moment the innkeeper felt sorry for them. But the feel of the metal coin in his pocket soon turned his mind elsewhere, and, with a large smile, he entered his inn and called his wife to show her their good fortune.

Venetia found herself lying on her back, staring up into the swirling snow, the damp flakes tickling her lashes and cheeks. She was positively freezing, thanks to the snow that had been forced down her neck upon her impact with the ground. She gingerly moved her limbs, relieved when she felt only a dull throb in her head and a bit of an ache low in her back.

"Miss Oglivie?"

Venetia turned to find Ravenscroft digging snow from one of his ears. Behind him, she saw the lopsided carriage, half in the ditch, one wheel splintered into a thousand pieces. The door she and Ravenscroft had been thrown against was gone, the gaping doorway pushed full of muddy snow.

"Miss Oglivie — Venetia — are you injured? Did you —" Ravenscroft's voice crackled with strain as he struggled through the snowdrift to her side.

Allowing him to assist her, she struggled to her feet. "I am fine, but the horses? How are they?"

Ravenscroft turned a gloomy face her way. "They're as well as can be expected."

"Aye," said the groom, hobbling over. "They were fine until the bloke here made me spring 'em!"

Venetia's impatience bubbled to the surface. "I agree. He should be shot for being in such a ridiculous hurry. Ravenscroft, see what your impatience has caused —" She caught sight of her companion and frowned. A thin trail of blood ran down his forehead and disappeared into the neck of his cravat. "You're bleeding."

Ravenscroft touched a hand to his forehead, pulled it away, and looked at the red drops. He gasped, his eyes rolled back into his head, and he fell into a dead faint, facedown in the snow.

Venetia looked at him with disgust. "Lovely. We've a broken carriage *and* a broken Ravenscroft." She glanced at the coachman. "We should at least turn him over so he can breathe."

"If ye say so, miss," the coachman said grudgingly, helping her do so.

The swirling snow was thickening even as they stood. "Unhitch one of the horses, please. I shall ride to the inn we passed not a mile back."

The coachman gawked. "But ye're a woman! And there's no proper saddle!"

Venetia tucked her pelisse collar more securely about her throat. "I can handle a carriage horse, with or without a saddle. Come, we must hurry."

"Very well, miss. If ye say so." He started to turn to the horses, but then paused to look back at Ravenscroft. "Do ye think his lordship is dead?"

"Heavens, no! He's just a —" Silly boy. Fool. Idiot. There weren't words. "He will be fine. Stay with him until I return."

Hearing the note of steel in Venetia's voice, the coachman finally did as he'd been instructed, and Venetia was soon on her way to fetch help.

"Aye, we seen them." The man rocked back on his heels, looking through the snow at Gregor. "Raced past here about twenty minutes ago."

Gregor fished a coin from his pocket. "They didn't stop to change the horses?"

"No, though they should have. The leaders looked winded." The groom handed the reins of a large bay mare to Gregor.

He climbed up on the newly saddled horse. "Take good care of my horse. I shall return for him in a day or so."

"I will, guv'nor! See if I don't."

"Thank you. This bay looks to be a good one."

"Heart o' gold and strong as an ox. Not fast, but she'll carry you through this weather without complaint."

"Excellent." Gregor tossed the coin to the groom, whose eyes widened when he realized it was gold.

"Thankee, m'lord!" But he spoke to the snow; Gregor was already pressing on, his head bent against the wind and snow, his jaw firm.

The groom patted Gregor's exhausted mount. "I don't know who he's after, but

I'm glad it ain't me."

The wind whipped Venetia's pelisse and skirts and seeped through her gloves. The snow fell so heavily she could barely see the road now. Jacobs tossed his massive head, sending a shower of wet snow onto Venetia, who sputtered and wiped it from her face. If this weather was indeed caused by Gregor, then something was seriously amiss. He was her dearest friend. If something was wrong, she should be there for him. Another reason to find a swift way out of this mess, let alone her concern for her mother.

Papa had certainly made Mama's case sound desperate. But then Papa made *life* sound desperate.

Venetia sometimes wished her family was a bit less dramatic. Thank goodness Gregor laughed at them frequently; it helped her keep her perspective.

She smiled slightly and patted Jacobs's neck. "Gregor has a sharp wit. Unfortunately, it cuts as often as it tickles." Not that she minded; she gave as good as she got. Besides, Gregor was good company. He was a bruising rider who could keep up with her in the field, had a sharp sense of humor that usually matched her own, and possessed a well-informed mind. Best of all, he didn't force one to listen to inane conversation. If he had something to say, he said it. Otherwise, he was perfectly content with a peaceful silence now and then.

It didn't hurt that he was also amazingly, painfully, incredibly handsome, even with that intriguing scar down his cheek and jaw. One of Venetia's friends had once confessed that she'd dreamed of tracing that scar with her fingertips, kissing him as she did so — such silliness. An odd warmth flashed through her.

The faint outline of a building arose through the dim snow. Relieved, Venetia urged Jacobs on, and they soon trotted through the stone gate and into the yard. The two-story inn appeared snug, the fogged windows covered with white lace curtains, while welcoming clouds of smoke poured from every chimney.

Venetia swung down when she saw the hostler hurry from the stables, his eyes wide with surprise. In a remarkably short time, Venetia was standing inside the inn's common room beside a warm fire, a cup of hot tea between her numbed hands, telling her story to the inn's proprietors, Mr. and Mrs. Treadwell.

Venetia was glad to hear that there were two rooms available; a widow and her companion occupied the third guest chamber. No sooner had Venetia mentioned that their coach had overturned than Mr. Treadwell, a small, thickset man with a twinkle in his eyes, had bundled up and was on his way to the rescue, not pausing for details.

Mrs. Treadwell, a tall, angular woman with wiry gray hair that refused to be contained in a neat bun, instantly began to prattle about how nice it was to have so many guests under their humble roof. She eyed Venetia up and down, sizing up the cost of the ermine-lined pelisse and soft doeskin gloves. "My, ye must have come straight from London, to have such fine things!"

"Yes, we did. We're —"

"We?"

"Yes, myself and —" Venetia blinked, suddenly realizing how awkward it might appear for her to be traveling alone with a single man. "My — ah — brother and I are traveling to my — our grandmother's house."

Mrs. Treadwell's gaze cleared. "That's nice, to be sure. Mr. Treadwell and I don't believe in turning away anyone, especially in weather such as this, but we won't support none of the elopers as use this road, neither."

Venetia frowned. "Why would elopers use

46

this road?"

"Law, child! Surely you've heard of Gretna Green? All the elopers wish to travel the North Road!"

"Of course I have heard of Gretna Green, but this isn't —" Venetia's gaze fell on the snow-covered road. They'd begun on the right road when they pulled out of London. But as it had grown colder, and she'd become more distracted by Ravenscroft's odd behavior, she hadn't looked out the window long enough to notice that the familiar landmarks that marked the road to Grandmama's were not in sight. It was entirely possible that they had crossed over to the North Road. But why —

With an almost audible click, it fell into place. They weren't going to Grandmama's at all. Instead they were on the North Road, headed for Gretna Green. She was being abducted — and by *Ravenscroft,* of all people!

Venetia's knees wobbled. Fortunately, there was a bench behind her, and as her knees buckled, she sat hard.

Mrs. Treadwell's brows rose. "Miss! Are ye well?"

Venetia's mouth opened, but no words came out. Her heart thudded thickly in her ears. A dull sickness tightened about her stomach.

"Ye look a mite pale. Are ye well?"

Venetia forced herself to find her voice. "I don't know. I suddenly feel a bit dizzy."

The innkeeper's wife clicked her tongue sympathetically. "Ye're pale as a ghost, miss —" She paused, her bright eyes fixed on Venetia. "I'm sorry. I didn't hear your name?"

Venetia smiled thinly, rage surging though her. "I'm sorry, I should have introduced myself. I am Miss —" *A name. I need a name.* "West." She continued quickly, "I am still quite chilled. Do you think I might have some more tea?"

"Oh, lawks! I'll run and put on a fresh pot. I daresay yer brother will want a warm cuppa when he arrives, too."

All Venetia wanted was to box Ravenscroft's rather large ears, but she murmured agreement as her hostess left the room. The second the woman was gone, Venetia sprang to her feet and paced furiously. Blast it all, what was Ravenscroft thinking? She had no desire to wed, and he could hardly have thought to force her to. There were too many people who would rush to assist a woman who was screaming wildly, and scream she would.

Even Ravenscroft couldn't be that foolish.

She paced back and forth, more and more furious as the minutes passed. When a commotion arose out in the innyard, she flew to the window to see a rickety cart pull in. Mr. Treadwell, bundled until he appeared twice his size, rode in the front seat, with Ravenscroft wavering beside him. The hostler sat behind with the luggage, holding the reins of the limping carriage horse.

Venetia's fingers curled into fists at the sight of Ravenscroft. She hurried to open the front door, only to find Mrs. Treadwell tramping down the hallway before her.

Mrs. Treadwell threw open the door just as Mr. Treadwell assisted Ravenscroft from the carriage. Ravenscroft's legs folded as he climbed down from his seat, and it was fortunate Mr. Treadwell was there to catch him. Had it been Venetia, she wouldn't have bothered.

"Bring the lad here!" Mrs. Treadwell ordered. Her husband obligingly lifted Ravenscroft to his feet and carried him in.

Mrs. Treadwell hurried to slam the door, closing out the frigid air. "Lord, the lad looks frozen through!" She readied a chair by the fire. "And his head! Lor', that's a nasty wound."

Ravenscroft blanched, though his teeth clattered too much for him to reply.

Venetia whispered to Mrs. Treadwell, "Pray do not mention his wound; he has already fainted once for that very reason."

"Oh!" she whispered back. "He's one of those, is he?"

"Among other things, yes."

Mrs. Treadwell's lips twitched, but she only nodded.

Ravenscroft huddled before the fire, his teeth clacking. "C-c-c-cold!"

"Aye," agreed Mr. Treadwell stoically. "Don't think I've ever seen it this cold in April in all me days."

Venetia forced herself to stop imagining her fingers around Ravenscroft's thin throat. "The horses — how are they?"

Mr. Treadwell said, "A strained fetlock, 'tis all. My hostler is looking after that one now. Yer coachman is bringing t'other two."

Ravenscroft shivered. "What a h-h-horrid experience!"

"Yes," Venetia said shortly. "For *all* of us." She turned to the innkeeper. "I know an excellent poultice for a strained fetlock. Do you have bran, barley, and some oats?"

The innkeeper beamed. "Aye! And some honey, too, if you are making the poultice I'm thinking of."

She managed to smile in return. "Yes. I shall mix some up and —"

"Nonsense," Mr. Treadwell said stoutly. "I'll take care of the horses. You stay here with the young man —"

"Her brother," Mrs. Treadwell interjected.

"Well, I'm glad to have ye both here, Miss —"

"West," Venetia said, sending Ravenscroft a firm glance.

Ravenscroft blinked woozily. "But —"

"Oh, dear! You are quite muddled, aren't you? I'm not surprised, being tossed from the carriage as we were. Mrs. Treadwell, do you have anything for his head?"

Mrs. Treadwell clicked her tongue. "Poor thing. The tea should be ready. I'll make a nice chamomile head wrap, too, to help clear his thoughts." She smiled kindly on him, then took Venetia's arm and led her away to whisper in a low voice, "I'll slip a bit of laudanum in yer brother's tea. After he's relaxed a bit, we'll wrap up his noggin and get him fixed up right and well."

Venetia nodded, though the only thing wrong with Ravenscroft's noggin was that it was empty.

As Mrs. Treadwell whisked herself from the room, Mr. Treadwell tightened his muffler around his throat. "I'll go see to the horses. Yer man should be here soon with t'other two." He paused to eye Ravenscroft. "Can ye take care of yer brother by yerself?"

Ravenscroft's eyes opened, and he flicked a confused glance toward Venetia. "B-b-bro —"

Venetia gripped his arm.

"Ow!"

She pinned a smile on her face, acutely aware of the innkeeper's sharp gaze. "There, there! I am sure you hurt everywhere, but one must not complain."

"Complain? But —"

Venetia used her nails this time.

"Argh!"

"His poor head!" She moved in front of Ravenscroft yet left her fingers tightly wrapped around his arm, nails at the ready. "Mr. Treadwell, I wish *I* could take care of the horses. I am certain they would not complain near as much."

The innkeeper chuckled. "Call Mary if'n ye need anything." With a nod, he left, his boots clomping down the hall.

The second the door closed behind the innkeeper, Ravenscroft regarded her sullenly. "You told them we were brother and sister!"

Venetia released his arm. "Yes. Unlike you, I have no desire to court scandal."

Ravenscroft rubbed his arm. "You left a mark!"

"You're fortunate that's *all* I did. Ravenscroft, I know what you were doing. This is the North Road, and we were not on our way to my grandmother's."

Ravenscroft's shoulders slumped. "Oh."

"Oh? Is that all you can say?" She put her fists on her hips and glared. "My father doesn't know of this, does he?"

"Yes. No. I mean, I hinted to him —"

"So *you* wrote that letter? And signed his name to it?"

"Yes. But you wrote him a note and told him you were with me before we left, so he won't be worried, if that is your concern."

"He will be worried when I don't appear at Mama's side!"

"He won't know that right away."

"Yes, he will. My mother and father write every day. They send one of the servants to carry the letters. By tomorrow, my father will know that I did not arrive."

Ravenscroft shook his head, then winced and grabbed his head. "Oh! It hurts so."

Venetia didn't move.

He peeped through his fingers, then sighed and dropped his hands. "You don't feel the least bit sorry for me, do you?"

"No," she said shortly, although he appeared absurdly youthful with his hair over his brow, his nose and cheeks red from the cold, his lips pressed into a pout.

He sighed. "You must allow me to explain. I have good reason for all this. You cannot know, you cannot understand how I — oh, bloody hell!" He dropped from his seat to his knees, grasped her hand, and kissed it wildly. "Miss Oglivie — Venetia — I love you!"

Her face hot, Venetia twisted her hand free and quickly stepped out of reach. "Do *not* do that!"

Ravenscroft remained on the floor, his arms outstretched. "But I must, for I love you. I even *eloped* with you!"

"Had I known this was an elopement, you would be alone."

"But you have always been so nice to me!"

"I am nice to everyone. Ravenscroft, I am going to say this as plainly as I can. I don't love you, and I will never marry you. Not now. Not ever."

Ravenscroft dropped his arms to his sides. "You *must* marry me. You are with me. Alone. In an inn. You are ruined."

"I don't see why . . ." Her voice trailed off as realization sank into her stomach with cold surety. If word of this reached London, she would indeed be ruined. Blast it, that

54

was unfair! She enjoyed London society and its amusements immensely. Now, they might be gone forever.

Suddenly, the events of the day seemed too much. She whirled away and went to stand at the window, her mind in turmoil. Perhaps she could return to London before anyone realized she was gone. But how? Only a madwoman would travel alone in such weather.

What a horrid coil! She was stuck. Completely stuck. How she wished Gregor were there. Whatever else he might be, he had a good head on his shoulders, and he never panicked or grew emotional.

For a wild instant, she imagined that the thick snow parted to reveal a tall, black-haired man on a white horse, his multicaped coat dusted with snow, his curly-brimmed beaver hat shading his green eyes from the wind and cold.

The image faded; Venetia stared morosely out into the snow.

"We must come up with some sort of plan," Ravenscroft announced in a loud, petulant voice.

She didn't turn to look at him but was certain he was attempting to appear senatorial. She bit back a frustrated sigh. Really, he was too much like her father, full of useless emotion, not a drop of common sense in his body.

"Venetia," he said dramatically. "We —"

"Miss Oglivie." She paused. "Actually, you should call me Miss West."

"Won't everyone think that odd if I'm your brother?"

She sighed. He was right. She was going to have to allow him that familiarity, at least. "Oh, blast you, very well."

"Venetia!" he said triumphantly. "Allow me to assure you I plan on making this right, whatever it takes."

Venetia closed her eyes against a sharp comment and began counting to ten.

As she hit four, Ravenscroft suddenly said, "Good God!"

Something in his voice cut through her irritation, and she opened her eyes to see a most welcome sight through the window.

Climbing down off a large bay, his coat and hat powdered with snow, his face set in stern lines that only made him appear more handsome, was Gregor MacLean.

CHAPTER 3

Och, me lassies, I wish't I could tell ye that
the path to love is full of flowers and gentle
breezes and pretty phrases. Sometimes
'tis, but sometimes the path travels through
barren lands o' harsh rock and icy winds.
If ye make it through that, then ye'll find
the flowers and gentle breezes, and yer
hearts will speak the pretty phrases and
more, lassies. Ever so much more!

Old Woman Nora from Loch Lomond
to her three wee granddaughters
one cold evening

"Why — that's MacLean!" Ravenscroft said
in a bright voice.

Gregor? Here? How could that be? Her
heart gave the oddest jump, her breath
caught in her throat. Venetia smoothed her
skirts nervously, her breath short, her skin
tingling oddly. It must be relief that someone had come to help. *It's just Gregor,* she

reminded herself. *It's nobody special, just —*

She heard the front door open, heavy footsteps on the wood floor, then Mrs. Treadwell's startled voice approached. A deep voice murmured answers to the innkeeper's wife's questions, and then the door flew open.

Gregor stood in the doorway. Except for the blazing heat of his eyes, one would almost think him a statue. But those deep green eyes, framed in thick, dark lashes, burned with an inner fury that made her want to take a step back. He turned to Mrs. Treadwell and said in a voice tinged with caustic wit, "Thank you for showing me the way to my errant charges. I shall make certain that Mr. and Miss West are kept well in hand."

"Indeed, my lord, they've been no problem at all," Mrs. Treadwell said, sketching a curtsey. "In fact, I was just making a bit of tea for the two of them."

"They don't deserve tea."

With something remarkably like a simper, Mrs. Treadwell curtseyed once more and returned down the hallway. Gregor closed the door behind him and entered the common room.

Venetia clasped her hands before her. Gregor's face was flushed with the cold, but his lips were almost white — from the cold or his temper, she could not say.

The gaze he threw at Ravenscroft, full of cold outrage, should have sent that young lord into a flurry of fear. But Ravenscroft, ever the eager puppy, saw neither the censure in the blazing gaze turned his way nor the thin-lipped regard he was being subjected to. All he saw was a well-connected acquaintance come to save them all.

"Ravenscroft, you bloody fool," Gregor said, sneering.

Venetia's pleasure at seeing him evaporated. She'd thought his arrival meant an improvement in her circumstances, the presence of a trusted friend whose calm sense would help them navigate their way from this rocky shore of circumstances. Instead, he faced her and Ravenscroft as if they were less than the mud beneath his boots.

It was almost too much. She was suddenly achingly tired, aware of a vague soreness in her body from her tumble from the carriage. She leaned against the window seat, rubbing her arms to remove the chill, her eyes blurring with tears.

Pressing her lips together, she fought the wave of unfamiliar emotion. Good God, she was no vaporish miss to weep merely because Gregor didn't appear pleased to see her. The thought made her stiffen. Why, the ass hadn't even bothered to ask how she was! Had he no manners at all?

Chin set, she wiped her eyes and turned a cool gaze toward Gregor. "We are glad to see you, too, MacLean. I trust you had a lovely journey from London."

He barely glanced her way, his attention fixed solely on his original quarry. "Well, Ravenscroft? Have you nothing to say for yourself?"

Ravenscroft dropped his outstretched hand; his eager expression faded. "Lord MacLean! I don't know — that is, what do you mean by — how can you —"

"Sit down, whelp."

The younger lord stiffened and said in an awful voice, "I beg your pardon?"

"You heard me. Sit down, and let me think. I came to see what is to be done to rescue the two of you from this mess. A pity you've run your carriage aground."

Ravenscroft's face burned redder. "That was an accident."

"It was foolish of you to continue in this weather. And to be pressing the horses —" Gregor's gaze suddenly turned to Venetia. "I would have thought that you, at least, would have known better."

Venetia stiffened. The annoyingly superior glint in Gregor's green eyes set up her hackles even more. "I objected to traveling at such a dangerous speed. I also asked to stop, since the weather was worsening."

"That's true," Ravenscroft interjected. "She was against it all."

Gregor lifted a brow. "Then you not only abducted Miss Oglivie, but you put her life in danger by not heeding her advice."

Ravenscroft's hands balled into fists at his side.

Venetia realized her own hands were fisted. Why, oh, why had she thought Gregor's presence would *help?*

Ravenscroft sputtered, "There is no need for that! Miss Oglivie and I aren't in a mess of any kind. In fact" — he stuck out his chin — "we are doing perfectly well."

He cast a pleading glance at Venetia. She almost winced at Ravenscroft's desperation, though she completely understood it. For years, she'd witnessed Gregor burn impertinent servants, encroaching mamas, brazen fortunehunters, and clinging fashionmongers with his cutting green gaze. But never once, in all the years of their friendship, had he turned it on her. Now that he had, she didn't like it, not one bit. His coldness sparked a flicker of staunch pride and something else, something hot and impatient, that simmered through her. Something that made her refuse to bow before his imperious manner, something that made her blurt out, "Really, Gregor, I don't know what you think you're doing, riding to our rescue. We are fine. We were just saying how lovely it was to have found this snug inn during such a horrendous snowstorm." Her gaze narrowed on Gregor. "It's so *unusual* to see a snowstorm in April, don't you think?"

Ravenscroft didn't seem to catch the accusation in her tone, for he nodded vehemently. "Exactly! It's most unusual, or I'd have planned things differently." He paused, then added stiffly, "Not that we need any help now, do we, Miss Oglivie?"

Gregor took in Venetia's disheveled appearance, a look of obvious disbelief on his face. "Oh?"

It was a "That's a falsehood, and you know it" sort of "Oh?" which didn't sit well with Venetia at all. "Yes," she said in a firm tone. She couldn't stand the way he was looking at her and Ravenscroft as if they were the silliest creatures on earth.

Gregor scoffed at those he called "the weak-kneed and the weak-willed," an attitude she'd always found insufferable.

They'd had plenty of arguments about it, too. However, things had changed in this instance. She could not stand the mockery she saw in his eyes, and suddenly it was imperative that Venetia not appear incapable, no matter the cost. Though Ravenscroft's silly plan had been a setback and had foolishly led her to wish for a rescue, she'd be blasted if she'd let Gregor know that. "You wasted your time coming here," she sniffed. "I'm not certain why you bothered."

Gregor unbuttoned his long coat and pulled it off, tossing it onto a chair in the corner of the room. "Your father sent me and begged me to return with you posthaste."

"But it is *his* fault this happened to begin with! He encouraged Ravenscroft."

"No matter what your father did, *you* were the one who was so foolhardy."

"Oh!" Venetia fumed. "I did nothing wrong!"

"No, she di—" Ravenscroft began again.

"Oh?" Gregor said without taking his gaze from Venetia. "Did you or did you not willingly climb into a carriage with an unknown man?"

"I know Ravenscroft!"

Ravenscroft opened his mouth, but Gregor

spoke over him. "You *barely* know Ravenscroft."

"I know him well enough," Venetia huffed.

Ravenscroft dropped his head into his hands.

"Then tell me about him," Gregor said. "Explain his circumstances. Explain how you both came to be overturned in a carriage on the North Road."

Venetia glanced at Ravenscroft, who didn't even look up. She took a deep breath. "I don't have to explain myself to you or anyone else. Ravenscroft is a — a fine young man who — ah — is quite well spoken," she said, trying not to remember that less than ten minutes ago she'd wished the poor young man at the bottom of a very deep snowdrift. "He has been nothing but gentlemanly since we left London." *More or less.*

Gregor's brows lifted. "Except for the fact that he abducted you —"

"I was going to marry her!" Ravenscroft said, though no one looked his way.

"— lied to you —" Gregor continued.

"I told her the truth, once we were here."

"— and has kept you imprisoned ever since —"

"I did not!" Ravenscroft said, his face now as red as his waistcoat. "Had it not been for the snow, we would have been married and

64

on our way to the continent by now!"

Venetia's mouth opened, then closed. "The continent?" There was a decided squeak to her voice.

Gregor smiled. "I thought you knew the, er, gentleman?"

Venetia ignored him. "Ravenscroft, what is this about the continent?"

Ravenscroft sent a resentful glare at Gregor before answering, "I was going to tell you, but I wasn't sure when to say something and if, perhaps, it wouldn't be better just to wait until —"

"Oh, for the love of Zeus, just spit it out," Gregor said impatiently. "Explain why you wished to travel to the continent right on the heels of your surprise nuptials."

Ravenscroft stiffened. "There are many reasons."

"We just want the real one."

"Perhaps I like Italy."

Gregor crossed his arms, his broad chest framed by his powerful arms. Beside him, Ravenscroft appeared even younger and more narrow-shouldered than usual.

"Ravenscroft," Venetia said, "why the continent? You aren't fleeing because of debt, are you?"

"No! Of course not!"

"It's worse than mere debt," Gregor said.

Ravenscroft glowered. "Look, MacLean," he blustered. "My lord, I know you don't mean to insult me, but —"

"Come, come, cub! Of course I mean to insult you."

Ravenscroft's mouth opened. Then closed. "You *mean* to insult me? On *purpose?*"

"Yes. I find your company unbearably tedious and your actions in regard to Miss Oglivie selfish. Therefore, I do not bother to speak in a polite tone, or even in a polite manner."

The younger lord drooped as if his bones would no longer bear his frame. "Oh. I see."

Venetia stamped her foot. "Ravenscroft! Do not let Gregor beat you down in such a way."

The young lord's cheeks reddened. "I am not allowing him anything. I was merely attempting to understand, that is all."

"He is insulting you. If I were you, I would be furious."

Gregor's low voice drawled with an amused undertone. "I believe she would have you challenge me to a duel."

Venetia whirled to face him. "I do not believe in such idiocy, and you know it. I was merely suggesting that he stand up for himself."

"It's no matter. If Ravenscroft challenged

me to a duel, I fear I would have to stand in line and await my turn."

Venetia frowned. "What?"

Ravenscroft suddenly came to life, gulping as he spoke. "Lord MacLean! Perhaps we should discuss this elsewhere —"

"No," Venetia said, her gaze narrowing on Ravenscroft. "Is there something you have not told me?"

"Yes — no — a very *minor* thing, to be sure."

"What is it?"

Ravenscroft winced. "Venetia, don't —"

Gregor grinned, pulled a chair into the center of the room, sat down then crossed one booted foot over his knee. "Continue," he invited.

Venetia placed her hands on her hips. "Would it kill you to be of assistance?"

"I put my neck at risk traveling here in this weather to do just that, but you informed me that I was not needed." He shrugged. "So I might as well enjoy myself."

"That is no excuse to make things worse."

"I beg your pardon," Gregor said with that devastating half grin that made her stomach warm in the most annoying way. "How could I possibly make things worse?"

Venetia hated it when Gregor was right. She forced herself to turn to Ravenscroft.

"You might as well get this over with. Lord MacLean is not leaving until you've aired everything."

Ravenscroft sent a resentful glare to Gregor, who threw up his hands and said with a laugh, "Don't look at me like that; *I* am not the one challenging every male within earshot to a duel."

Venetia ignored Gregor, which was not easy to do, as he was leaning back negligently in his chair, his wet boots thrust out across the rug, making it difficult for anyone to walk anywhere. In his wet clothes, his black hair a bit curly from the dampness, his green eyes sparkling with amusement, he was devastatingly handsome. Even the scar on his left cheek seemed attractive, secretive, hinting at potential danger.

"Well, Ravenscroft?" Gregor quirked a brow at the younger man. "Will you tell Miss Venetia your plight? Or shall I?"

"Oh, I will tell her," Ravenscroft said in a voice so sulky that it quite put Venetia out of patience. "First of all, Miss Oglivie, you must realize that no matter what, *no matter what,* I am here because I love you madly."

"And?" Gregor prompted.

"And I had to leave the country because of a duel I was to fight."

Venetia blinked. "I beg your pardon?"

He sighed, his shoulders sagging beneath the buckram wadding that padded them. "What happened was — It wasn't my fault, but last week, Lord Ulster and I were playing cards at White's. He accused me of cheating, and I —"

"Were you?" Gregor asked.

"No," Ravenscroft said sharply. "I dropped a card on the floor. I bent to retrieve it without thinking, and Ulster had the . . . the *gall* to suggest I was not playing a fair hand!"

Gregor's brows rose. "In the middle of a game, you picked up a card from the *floor?*"

"Well, yes! I'd dropped it and hadn't noticed it, and I know I shouldn't have, but it was a queen, and I particularly needed . . . That's not to say that if I had it to do over again, I might —"

"Bloody hell." Gregor looked at Venetia, his eyes shimmering with humor. "You really wish to wed this fool?"

Ravenscroft's hands fisted, his face flushing a dark red.

Venetia ignored him. "I never said I wished to marry anyone, MacLean. I only said Ravenscroft had been a gentleman. Or so I'd thought."

"He is quite fun to watch," Gregor said thoughtfully, looking at Ravenscroft. "Much like having a pet monkey."

"My lord!" Ravenscroft stepped forward, his eyes blazing in anger.

"Sit down," Gregor said in a bored tone.

"My lord, I cannot allow you to —"

"*Sit down!*" This time, Gregor's voice thundered, his eyes the dark green of an angry sea. Outside, a crashing echo lashed through the air.

Ravenscroft's butt hit the chair, a stunned look on his face.

Venetia's heart pounded in her throat. Gregor rarely became angry. In the many years they'd been friends, she could count on one hand the number of times he'd lost his temper.

And now he was angry with her, something she'd never thought to see happen, and it rattled her in ways she'd never imagined. *It's just Gregor,* she told herself, trying to calm her thudding heart. *I've known him forever.* Yet somehow that didn't reassure her as it once might have.

She clasped her hands. "Ravenscroft, pray continue with your story. Ulster accused you of cheating, and —"

"I had no choice. I challenged him to a duel."

"Who won?" Venetia asked.

The young lord bit his lip, saying in a very

quiet voice, "No one."

Venetia leaned forward. "I beg your pardon?"

He cleared his throat. "I said no one. We — we have not yet met."

Venetia considered this. "When did this incident occur?"

"Three days ago."

Three days ago. Just before he'd come to steal her away and — She fixed her gaze on him. "*That* is why you wished to go to the continent."

Gregor's soft chuckle punctuated Ravenscroft's wince.

"You see, my love?" Gregor asked calmly, though something tight snapped beneath the surface. "I not only saved you from an unwelcome elopement but from a grim life on the continent, the wife of a banished man."

A flame of anger flashed through Venetia. "Let me get this straight, Ravenscroft. You not only tricked me into accompanying you by claiming that my mother was ill, but you planned on taking me with you into a life of hiding on the continent?"

"Well . . . yes. I thought you'd like it."

She was going to explode. "You thought I'd *welcome* such a thing? Living from country to country, never returning to

England —"

"We would be able to return!"

"When?"

"Once Ulster could be persuaded to drop the charges."

"And how would you get that accomplished?"

"I — I thought perhaps your father —"

"You thought my father would undertake to beg for your return to England?"

"Your father likes me!"

"And so does my mother. But *they* would not be the ones living with you on the continent, would they?"

"No," Ravenscroft said in a sulky tone. "I didn't think they would mind assisting their son-in-law, though."

"I'm sure *they* wouldn't have minded being banished, either. Indeed, I am certain *they* would have thought it a grand adventure, hiding from the constable, registering at low inns under assumed names. As much as I love my parents, no one would ever think they possess the smallest bit of common sense. *I,* however, would have been greatly put out by the entire mess."

Ravenscroft leapt from his chair. "Ven— Miss Oglivie, truly, I didn't think you'd object! I hear it is beautiful in Italy! There are villas and shops and all sorts of amusements —"

"And how, pray tell, would we afford these villas and shops and amusements?"

Ravenscroft looked desperately around the room, finding nothing but Gregor's amused gaze and Venetia's indignant one.

"What sort of lovely plans did you have laid? Have you purchased a house, perchance?" Venetia pursued.

"Ah. No. I didn't really have the funds —" He caught sight of Venetia's expression and hurried to add, "I am certain something would have presented itself!"

"I don't know why I thought you were going into this unprepared," Venetia said calmly.

Ravenscroft looked relieved, but Gregor knew Venetia better.

She was a wrathful goddess — her gown mussed and crumpled, her hair a tangled mess upon her head, but her gray eyes flashed silver, her smooth skin flushed with passion. Gregor had gone through agony since this morning. Venetia's disappearance had forced him to admit something rather uncomfortable: the *necessity* of their friendship. He not only enjoyed having Venetia in his life, but he *needed* her. Facing the prospect of possibly never seeing her again, or at least not in the same easy circumstances they'd always enjoyed, had sparked his fury like nothing else ever had.

Worse, as the hours had passed, he'd imagined her fearful and upset, alone and frightened. Then he'd come upon the wreckage of their carriage, buried in the snow. His entire body had frozen for a moment, too shocked to accept the sight of the splintered wood and what it might mean.

He'd been frantic in a way he'd never been before. Of course, it was merely a protective instinct, nothing else, but still . . . the feelings had been immediate and overwhelming.

Which was why when he'd followed the path of the cart to the inn and discovered Venetia there — not broken and bloodied, but warm and snug, a sparkle in her eyes as if she'd actually *enjoyed* her "outing" with Ravenscroft — a new emotion had lodged itself in Gregor's breast, one he didn't recognize. One that had set off his frayed temper yet again.

For some reason, seeing her flare at Ravenscroft went some way toward soothing Gregor's temper. She was magnificent! Grinning to himself, Gregor leaned back and waited.

Ravenscroft, ever eager to think things were in his favor, was nodding. He took

Venetia's hands in his. "I am not the sort of man to rush into things without thinking them through. Of course I have a plan, one that has taken into account every exigency."

Venetia's gaze flickered from Ravenscroft to the window, where snow swirled outside. "Really?"

Gregor bit his lip to keep from laughing.

Ravenscroft clasped her hands more tightly. "Indeed, my dear! After marrying, we were to go to Italy via France."

"How? That would cost a bit."

"No need to worry your pretty head over that. I have quite a sum put away to pay for the trip."

"We were to travel in the best of style, I presume?"

He looked a little uneasy, but his smile remained in place. "Not the best, of course. But well enough."

Gregor cleared his throat. Both Ravenscroft and Venetia turned toward him. "I know something of crossing to France. How much money did you bring?"

Ravenscroft colored. "Enough."

"More than twenty pounds?" Gregor asked gently.

There was a frozen moment, and then Ravenscroft nodded. "Of course."

The whelp didn't have ten, if he had a

pence, Gregor decided. Still, he would show the lad some mercy. "Providing you have twenty, you will find crossing the Channel quite comfortable. You can have a private cabin and meals, with your luggage, horses, and carriage loaded and unloaded."

There was a moment's pregnant pause, then Ravenscroft said, "And if I have less?"

"If you have ten, you might get a private cabin but will have to provide your own meals and load your own belongings. Of course, since you did not inform Miss Oglivie of your flight, I daresay she has very little luggage, anyway."

"Very little," she said in a resentful tone. "Ravenscroft, I can see from your expression that crossing is much higher than you thought. Did you make any inquiries at all before you began this mad bolt to Italy?"

Ravenscroft glared. "Yes! I made all sorts! People say it is remarkably inexpensive to live over there —"

"It had better be, since you don't even have enough for passage over. How were we going to live once we arrived? If you were planning on my parents assisting us, you do not know their circumstances, for they are forever living at the edge of their means."

"No, no! I would never ask such a thing! I thought, once we arrived, we would find a pretty little cottage in a vineyard. And once there —" Ravenscroft straightened, his expression beaming. "Once there, I am going to write a book!"

The clock on the mantel ticked loudly. The snow outside silently swirled, the only movement to be seen.

Gregor had his fingers buried in the palms of his hands, struggling mightily not to laugh.

Venetia sent him a fulminating glare, letting him know he was fooling no one, then turned back to Ravenscroft. "I have to ask you one thing."

He leaned forward eagerly. "Anything!"

"What was I supposed to be doing while you were working on this . . . this roman à clef?"

"Doing? I suppose I thought you would be keeping the cottage nice and clean, perhaps washing our clothes in a pail and hanging them on a line in the sun." He smiled a dreamy smile. "Your hair has the faintest hint of red. It shows every time you are in the sunlight."

Gregor almost choked. Red? Where had Ravenscroft gotten that from? Although . . . the light from the fire did indeed cast some reddish glints in Venetia's brown hair. Odd, he'd never noticed that before.

Venetia leaned forward, her face level with Ravenscroft's. "You thought I would *enjoy* washing my clothes by hand, hanging them on a clothesline?"

His smile slid a bit. "I thought you would not mind helping while I wrote my book."

"By hanging up your laundry?"

"And yours. And our children's."

She closed her eyes.

"I know just how you feel!" he said eagerly. "You are overwhelmed. I was the same way myself when it dawned on me what we were to do. We'll go to Italy, leave civilization behind, and live a simpler life. A more pure one. And perhaps," he added naively, "when you've time, you could take in a few local children as students and teach music and English and such."

"Students?" Venetia repeated blankly. "You thought I would do all of that *and* become a governess?"

"Just a few students," he said hurriedly, his expression uncertain. "I wouldn't wish you to be overworked."

Gregor almost felt sorry for the man. "Venetia, you always said you enjoyed helping your fellow —"

"MacLean, do not say another word." She did not look at him, but her frigid voice said it all.

Gregor settled deeper into his chair, placing his hands behind his head and leaning back. "Ravenscroft, I can see that I underestimated you. I am surprised at the amount of thought you put into this concept, and I apologize for assuming you were impetuously running into things."

The younger man brightened. "I'm certain it sounded like a harebrained idea to begin with. It did to me! But after a short reflection —"

"No doubt, over a few glasses of port," Gregor guessed.

"Why, yes! Four, to be exact —"

Venetia pressed her fingers to her forehead.

"— I realized that Italy was the place for us. Once there, I know the muse will visit me, and my idea for a novel will come to fruition."

"Do you have any of this novel written?" Gregor asked, curiosity strong in his tone.

Venetia yearned to hurl one of her boots at Gregor. The ass was begging for a setdown, and poor Ravenscroft was too dimwitted to do more than cheerfully answer.

"No, I haven't written any of it yet," he said now. "But I have some notes." Ravenscroft reached into his jacket pocket and pulled out a crumpled piece of paper. He smoothed it out and said, "I've named two of my characters and have decided to use my travels in Italy as the basis."

"An educational book, then. One about the history of the state. Very good."

"What? Oh, no! It's to be a mystery. A murder of some sort has occurred — I haven't decided who or how — and a young man is accused of the crime. Of course, he is innocent, but he must prove it, or else he will end up in jail for all time."

Gregor quirked a brow. "Let me guess . . . this young man, he is your age?"

"Why, yes."

"And about your height? And hair color?"

"Yes! How did you know?"

"A fortunate guess," Gregor said, smiling broadly.

"Indeed! I've been thinking of writing this novel for three years now. I am certain I could do it, if I but had the time."

"Which the lovely Miss Venetia will give you, once she begins her life as a cleaning maid."

Ravenscroft looked horrified. "I would *never* think of Venetia as a cleaning maid!"

"I am glad to hear it," Venetia said dryly. "I and my dishpan hands will thank you."

Ravenscroft captured one of those hands now. He lifted it to his cheek, his gaze fixed on Venetia's face. "Venetia, you are the most beautiful woman in the world, inside and out. I hope you know I would never do anything to disrespect you."

Until now, Gregor had been enjoying every utterance that slipped from the pup's lips. But the unconcealed admiration that shone in Ravenscroft's eyes as he held Venetia's hand to his cheek sent an unfamiliar — and devilishly sharp — pang through Gregor.

It was the oddest feeling, and it wiped away his amusement in a flash. Venetia should have been offended by such familiarity. She should have been outraged by the suggestions this fool had made.

Instead, she sighed, her lips curling into a reluctant smile as she turned her hand and patted the insolent pup's cheek. "Oh, Ravenscroft, you are so young. I keep forgetting that, don't I?"

It was hardly a compliment, but it only encouraged the fool. Ravenscroft had the temerity — the *audacity,* by God — to cup her fingers to his lips and press a kiss to her bare palm.

Something inside Gregor snapped. *"Venetia."*

Venetia blinked at Gregor's black expression. Dark as a thundercloud, he now stared down at her, his gaze flickering between her and her hand.

She followed his gaze to her hand, where Ravenscroft clasped it almost reverently. It was improper, although there was so much about this entire situation that was improper that holding hands with Ravenscroft seemed a minor infraction indeed.

Ravenscroft smiled up at Gregor, unaware of the danger he was in. "Isn't she an *angel?*"

Venetia's cheeks heated, and she freed her hand from Ravenscroft's rather tight grasp. "Yes, well, now that everything has been said that needs to be said, we must find a way out of this mess."

"At least," Gregor said in a sharp tone, "you finally admit this *is* a mess."

She cut him a sharp glance. "I admit nothing except that circumstances are not as I'd wish them to be."

"I will marry you," Ravenscroft said simply. "That will solve one issue, at least."

"No," she said firmly. "That is not an option."

"But, Miss Oglivie, I love you. With all my heart!"

"Ravenscroft." Gregor's voice chilled the air.

The young lord sent a harried glance

at Gregor.

What happened next, Venetia would never be able to explain. One moment, Ravenscroft was standing there, imploring and earnest. The next, he was backing up toward the door, stumbling a bit in his haste.

"I-I-I just remembered — important meeting!" He tugged on his neckcloth.

"Here? At this inn?" Venetia didn't know when she'd heard a more ridiculous assertion. Well, other than the thought that she might support the poor youth in his quest for fame as a novelist. "How on earth could you possibly have a meeting here?"

But she spoke to empty air. She heard the thuds of Ravenscroft's well-shod feet as he hurried out the front door, closing it behind him. Seconds later, he could be seen through the window, buttoning his coat as he made his way through the wind to the stables.

Venetia watched him. "That is most odd!"

Gregor shrugged, coming to stand beside her. "He is a fool."

Venetia glanced up at Gregor. "What did you do?"

"He was getting out of hand. I merely stopped it."

She frowned at him, suspicion clear in her gaze.

The light from the snow softened the line of her brow and cheek. He regarded her critically, trying to see her as Ravenscroft evidently did.

Venetia was not an ordinarily beautiful woman. Her figure was rounded and pleasing and a bit heavier than was fashionable. Her arms were lovely and round, her breasts full and lush, as were her hips. She was not a small woman, which was a good thing. A frailer body could not have contained such a passionate soul. Gregor had to admit, there was something taking about her. Her face held an amazing mixture of intelligence, humor, and liveliness.

"What's wrong?" she asked now, her brows lowering. "Why are you looking at me like that?"

"I am just wondering what Ravenscroft is so enamored of."

Her cheeks heated. "Don't strain your eyes."

"Oh, stop being missish. I see plenty to admire."

She regarded him suspiciously, and he laughed. Her eyes were by far her best feature, a light, silvery gray framed by thick black lashes. Her skin was fresh and smooth, though not particularly fair. She tanned easily, and even now he could detect the hint of a few freckles on her rather ordinary nose. Her lips were plump and remarkably pert, her teeth white and even. Her dark brown hair was unremarkable except for its tendency to wave and curl at the faintest hint of moisture.

He smiled a bit, remembering how many times he'd heard her complain about that trait, one he found rather attractive, truth be told. Now that he thought about it, Venetia actually was an attractive female. He supposed his prolonged acquaintance with her had inured him to that fact, which was probably a good thing for them both. He treasured their friendship and had no wish to give it up, especially for a fleeting attraction, as all such affairs were. Still, there was something damnably taking about her in this light, something that drew him to her. To her plump lips. Her soft shoulders. Her full breasts. Heat flooded him, and he found himself walking toward her.

Venetia's eyes widened, her skin flushed a rich pink. "Gregor, what —"

What indeed? Gregor stopped, amazed at himself. *Bloody hell, what am I doing?* First he came charging to the rescue, which he rarely did, and now he was looking lustfully at the one woman he knew not to touch.

Gregor turned on his heel and gathered

his coat. "I'm sorry. I was just thinking about this situation." He pulled on his multi-caped coat, careful not to meet Venetia's gaze. "I'll join Ravenscroft in the barn and see how the horses are faring."

She nodded, hesitation in her eyes. His gaze lingered on her face, on her darkened eyes and her flushed skin, on the way her full breasts pressed against the thin material of her gown, and —

"I'll return shortly," he snapped, angry for some reason as much with her as with himself for the odd direction of his thoughts. "Request dinner. Ravenscroft and I will be starving by the time it is served."

He left, stepping into the frigid air with a sense of profound relief.

CHAPTER 4

They say the MacLeans once't tried to use their curse fer good, bringin' rain t' the lowlands durin' a horrible drought. But it rained fer twenty-nine days and washed away ever'thin' the drought hadn't yet stolen. Such is the nature of a curse: it ne'er gives but that it also takes away.

Old Woman Nora from Loch Lomond
to her three wee granddaughters
one cold evening

Mrs. Treadwell pulled a large key from her apron and unlocked the first door at the top of the stairs. "Here ye are, Miss West! The second-best room in the inn." She opened the door with a grand sweep and stood aside.

Venetia entered, carrying the bandbox she'd brought from London. The bedchamber was smallish, with a lopsided bed beside a large window that overlooked the innyard.

Blue curtains matched the homespun bed hangings and the large pillow that graced the bed. A lone chair took up residence beside a washstand containing an old-looking pitcher and bowl, both painted with yellow and blue flowers.

All told, it was nicer than Venetia had hoped. The bed might look lumpy, and a faint draft of air came from the window when the door was ajar, but she was certain it would be warm, and that was all that mattered. Venetia set down her baggage. "This is lovely," she said.

Mrs. Treadwell beamed. "I decorated it meself to look jus' like a picture I saw in *Ladies Grace* magazine." She looked about critically. "O' course, I couldn't exactly get the shade of blue fer the hangin's, and the bed isn't as grand as the one in the picture, but it's close enough."

"Are all the rooms this nicely turned out?"

"Oh, the large chamber is the nicest! Mrs. Bloom and her companion are in there. They came in late last night and desired a bit of a nap today, else ye'd have seen them when ye arrived. I daresay ye'll meet them at dinner, fer Mrs. Bloom isn't one to skimp on her meals, if ye know what I mean." Mrs. Treadwell puffed out her cheeks in a meaningful way.

Venetia smiled. "What of the other room we bespoke?"

"Now, that one's a bit small, especially fer two gents. But I thought it best to put ye in here, as 'tis the cozier chamber, being right over the common room. If ye touch that stone right there, it'll toast yer fingers, it's that warm." Mrs. Treadwell sent Venetia a sly glance. "If'n ye don't mind me askin', how did Lord MacLean come to get such a scar?" She added hurriedly, "Not that it makes a mite o' difference in his looks, fer he's still as handsome as one of them knights I once seen in a picture book."

"He had an accident when he was fourteen. He and his brothers were forever staging mock battles, and one day, when using a new set of fencing foils, one of the buttons came off the tip. Gregor's brother didn't realize the button had fallen off, and —" Venetia shrugged.

Mrs. Treadwell clicked her tongue. "Highspirited, were they?"

"They still are, all but one," Venetia said. "Callum, Lord MacLean's youngest brother, was killed a year and a half ago." Gregor still grew quiet whenever Callum was mentioned.

Mrs. Treadwell clucked again. "That's difficult, losin' a brother. I daresay ye know that, seein' as how yer own brother could have come to harm today. Daresay that set ye back a bit."

"Ah, of course. He seems indestructible to me."

"I feel the same way about me own brother, Cyril. He rides half-broke horses, races carts, and does all sorts of dangerous things and never comes to the least of harm." She shook her head.

"Yes, Mr. West is just the same. Never uses the least common sense, and yet he's cocksure he will never pay for his own foolishness, which is very annoying." A low grumble in her stomach made her realize that in the excitement of the accident, she hadn't had lunch. "Thank you for your kindness, Mrs. Treadwell. May I ask when dinner will be ready?"

"Very soon. Mr. Treadwell got us a girl to help in the kitchen. Her name's Elsie, and a better cook ye'll not meet. Ye'll not go hungry here, miss! The Blue Rooster's known fer her hospitality, and I'd not have it any other way."

"I'm certain everyone here would agree with you."

Mrs. Treadwell beamed. "Thank you, miss! Now, if ye'll excuse me, I'll go and see if Elsie needs any help. I can't cook, but I can stir a pot, if'n need be." With a quick smile, she left, closing the door behind her.

Venetia walked to the bed and fell across it, hands clasped beneath her chin.

She couldn't believe Ravenscroft's ill-conceived plans had landed her in such a mess. Even more surprising had been Gregor's expression right before he'd left the common room. There'd been a moment, a mere second, really, when he'd looked at Venetia as if he'd *desired* her.

Her heart thrummed a bit. In all the years she'd known Gregor, he'd never looked at her like that. Actually, now that she thought about it, he had never *really* looked at her at all. He never seemed to notice if she'd cut her hair or had a new pelisse or anything, really.

She had certainly noticed *him,* though, and who could blame her? He was dangerously, devastatingly handsome. Worse than that, he knew it.

She grabbed a pillow and hugged it, the worn linen soft as silk under her chin. Fortunately for her heart, although Gregor was almost perfect in appearance, he had plenty of character flaws. He was arrogant, easily irritated, and frequently standoffish with his fellow man. His worst flaw was that he regarded all acts of charity as signs of weakness. If there was one thing Venetia believed in, it was the benefits of being involved with one's fellow man.

Gregor's better traits made their friendship worthwhile. He was intelligent, witty, and very close to his family, and he possessed an old-fashioned sense of chivalry, though it would kill him to admit it. Best of all, he was an excellent friend, listening to her woes and celebrating her triumphs without the least reserve. If she fell from her horse, he was the first to help her back on and never utter a criticism. If she took a superior jump, he was the first to congratulate her unreservedly — a rare trait in men, she'd found.

She rolled to her side and looked up at the ceiling, absently noting a crack in the heavy white plaster shaped like a question mark. She and Gregor had done well in maintaining their friendship, which wasn't easy given Gregor's natural — what would she call it? — sensuality.

She thought of the look he'd given her in the common room and nodded to herself. Oh, yes. She would definitely call it sensuality. Now that she'd experienced that look, Venetia knew why so many of the young women in London had made fools of themselves over him. She had felt attractive, seductive, lightheaded, almost punch-drunk. All from one little look.

Gregor had the ability to intrigue and captivate without even trying. He was a pied piper, drawing women after him with the invisible strains of a mysterious melody so potent that one might well fall over a cliff before she even knew she was in danger. Venetia had seen it happen again and again, each time shaking her head at their foolishness. Now, however, she thought perhaps she understood a little bit more.

Outside, she heard a shout, then the creak of the bolt being thrown open on the barn door. She got up and went to the window, pushing the heavy curtain aside. Cold air seeped from the loose panes of glass and she shivered. She leaned one hand on the windowsill and used her other arm to rub the glass free of fog. Ravenscroft's groom was just arriving, riding one carriage horse and leading the other.

The hostler and Gregor's groom, Chambers, came out to help with the horses. Gregor stood by the huge barn door, ready to close it as soon as the others entered, the snow landing in his black hair before melting away. She wondered what it would be like to be a snowflake and to land in his soft hair, right at that tantalizing spot where his warm skin disappeared beneath his collar.

A faint shiver traced through her. *Stop that,* she told herself firmly. *It is just Gregor.*

But "just Gregor" was something to behold. He was still wearing his greatcoat, though it was unbuttoned as though he'd just shrugged it back on. Beneath it, she could see his dark blue coat with silver buttons, his cravat as white as the snow, his red waistcoat with dark buttons fitting snugly against his broad chest. His black breeches outlined his muscular thighs before tucking down into a pair of shiny black boots.

The window fogged from Venetia's breath, and she had to use her sleeve to wipe it clean again. The movement caught Gregor's attention, and he turned to look up at the window.

Venetia froze, unable to move as their eyes met. Her heart quivered, her blood heating wildly. Despite the cold window, her skin burned, her body quickened as if heated.

His eyes darkened, his brows contracting a bit. Venetia forced herself to smile naturally, despite her heart thundering in her ears. *It's just Gregor. Only Gregor.*

The hostler said something to Gregor, and he turned to reply. The spell was broken, and Venetia slid to the side, deep in the curtains. She could still see outside but was out of sight from the barn, where Gregor stood.

She paused there, imagining him turning back to see if she was still at the window. Would he look disappointed? Perhaps he wished her to be there and —

What am I doing? I don't want him to wish to see me here, mooning over him like a fool! "Stupid carriage accident," she muttered. It had muddled her brains.

She took a steadying breath. She wasn't really mooning over him; she was just watching. That was totally different. She leaned forward a bit, catching a glimpse of Gregor as he held the horse Chambers had been leading. They were examining the horse's rear haunch.

Venetia frowned. Had the poor animal strained a muscle from the accident? She'd go and see to it herself, after dinner. Her gaze flickered back to Gregor. He was now standing beside the horse, one arm along its back, his head bent toward Chambers, who was talking rapidly, no doubt describing the accident in full detail.

Venetia sighed. It was rather annoying to see so much and hear so little.

She stared at the back of Gregor's head, noting how his damp hair was once again curling at the collar. Venetia scrunched up her nose and closed the curtains with a decided flick, hoping Gregor had noticed. Blast it, it was difficult being friends with a man whose hair always seemed to look better than hers.

A brisk knock sounded on the door, and Venetia went to answer it.

Mrs. Treadwell stood in the hallway, holding a pail of water that steamed invitingly. "Thought ye might want some warm water to wash with." She bustled past Venetia and went to fill the smaller basin on the washstand. "It's been an excitin' day, hasn't it?"

"Yes, it has. I don't suppose — no, never mind."

"Don't suppose what?"

"I was wondering if I might get a full bath at some point?" Venetia asked a little wistfully. She loved a hot bath almost as much as she loved hot scones covered with cream.

Mrs. Treadwell beamed, her plain face bright. "O' course ye can! I have a real copper tub, I do. Me own sister sent it to me from York. She has one just like it, and when I went to visit her, I says, 'Oh, how I'd love to have a tub like that!' and blame me if she didn't send one out the very next year!"

"How lovely of her! A bath would be perfect."

"I'll set Elsie to warming the water whilst

ye're supping. Supper's nigh on the table. William — that's her husband as works in the stables — can fetch the tub and water here. Ye'll have a nice, hot bath in no time."

"Thank you so much."

"Oh, 'tis nothin'. I want me visitors happy, I do. Mayhap then ye'll mention me to yer London town friends."

"I will be glad to," Venetia said, though she couldn't think of any who might be eloping any time soon. "I shall freshen quickly and join the company downstairs."

"Very good, miss." Mrs. Treadwell went to the door. "I'll take the rest of this water to Mrs. Bloom and her companion. Mrs. Bloom do seem to be a disagreeable sort, forever complaining about this and that. Reminds me a bit of Mr. Treadwell's mother, she do." Mrs. Treadwell's expression darkened. "Why, Mrs. Bloom has already had the temerity to tell me that the beds were damp! As if I'd allow a bed in my inn to dampen!"

"Perhaps she's had a trying day today, too."

"That don't give her reason to call my beds damp. Mr. Treadwell and I have never had anyone say such a thing in all the years we've owned the Blue Rooster!"

Venetia sent a cautious glance at the

doorway across the hall. She was certain whoever occupied it could hear every word. If Mrs. Bloom was out of sorts before, she'd be *very* out of sorts now, after hearing her landlady maligning her in the open hallway. "I'm sure the beds are fine, Mrs. Treadwell," Venetia said hastily. "Thank you again for the fresh water."

The woman nodded, her silver curls bobbing as she turned to the other door, straightening her shoulders as if preparing for battle. Venetia shut her door and turned to unpack her portmanteau.

She had just lifted the latch when she heard the door across the way opening and a woman's high, shrill voice complaining about the fact that the curtains didn't quite shut and demanding to know what could be done about it.

Mrs. Treadwell seemed to have described Mrs. Bloom accurately. The voices faded, and Venetia turned back to her portmanteau.

Every gown she'd brought was horridly wrinkled and, worse, wet from the baggage taking a tumble in the snow. She'd packed in haste, too, so nothing was as it should have been. She hadn't thought to bring more hairpins, and she'd lost quite a few when she fell. She hadn't imagined it would snow, either, and so except for the damp half-boots she had on her feet, the slippers she'd packed would be woefully inadequate. She'd brought her white round gown with the blue ribbons to wear in the morning but hadn't remembered to pack the matching ribbons to tie up her hair; she'd brought a lovely gray gown for visiting, but in her haste to leave she hadn't packed any white gloves; and while she'd remembered to bring her embroidery hoop and her latest efforts, the packet of thread was gone, probably lost in the snow.

It was frustrating, though her rumbling stomach didn't allow her to linger on it. She spread out the damp clothes as well as she could, changed into the only gown that was halfway presentable — a deep green with a split front skirt over a striped tan underskirt, long sleeves, and a high, rounded neck. Though wrinkled, it was in better shape than her others. Venetia washed her hands and face with the deliciously warm water, found her silver comb (though not the mirror), and repinned her hair with the few pins she had left. As she slid her feet into her brown silk slippers, she realized with a sense of relief that not once in the last ten minutes had she thought of Gregor, not even a little.

The thought made her smile, and it was with a lighter heart that she made her way downstairs. She entered the common room just in time to see Ravenscroft throw himself into a chair by the fireplace, his face lined with exhaustion, his clothing rumpled.

Gregor was dressed as if ready to be accepted at any house in London. He was bowing over the hand of a large woman in a puce-colored gown, her white hair ridiculously adorned with a thick mass of ostrich feathers.

His gaze immediately flickered to Venetia and ran down her from head to toe, leaving the oddest trail of prickly heat and a delicious tickle. Her cheeks suddenly hot, Venetia looked away and found herself facing a rather plain, thin woman wearing a drab gray dress and lackluster pearls.

The woman immediately dropped into a deep curtsey. "Good evening," she said in a rather breathless voice. "I am Miss Platt."

Venetia curtsied in return. "How do you do? I am Miss Venetia O—"

"Miss West!" Gregor's deep voice came from across the room.

Venetia forced a smile and managed a nod to Gregor, though her heart was still galloping like a shied horse at her near blunder. "Lord MacLean."

He bowed. "Miss West, I am sorry to interrupt you, but your brother and I were just making the acquaintance of Mrs. Bloom and her companion, Miss Pl—"

"Miss West," Mrs. Bloom said in a loud voice that boomed like artillery fire. "Your guardian just informed me that you live in London. Might I ask what part?"

A rather superior smirk crossed the woman's heavy jowls. "I know most of the town, as I've lived there for more than twenty years now. I believe I know about everyone, don't I, Miss Platt?"

The companion nodded immediately, her gaze darting nervously toward her employer, then away. "Oh, yes," the lady said in a breathy voice, "Mrs. Bloom knows absolutely *everyone* in town! I am forever saying that dear Mrs. Bloom is related to half of London and on the guest list of the other half!"

Venetia's heart sank. If the woman was indeed an accepted member of society, which was vaguely possible, then they could run into each other at some later time, and the game would be up.

She sent a cautious glance at Gregor, to see if he recognized the dangers as well, but his urbane smile did nothing to alleviate her fears. He was completely impervious to the situation and the possible outcome. Heart heavy, she mustered a smile and kept her head high. *Good God, I shall be ruined after all.*

CHAPTER 5

It takes a patient woman to handle an impatient man. Unfortunately, there's naught that can handle an impatient woman.

> Old Woman Nora from Loch Lomond
> to her three wee granddaughters
> one cold evening

Ravenscroft cleared his throat, sending Venetia an apologetic glance. "I'm sorry, Mrs. Bloom, but my sister and I spend more time in, ah, Yorkshire than elsewhere. I doubt you would have seen us in London."

"Which is entirely my fault," Gregor said in a serious tone. "I do not approve of the frivolity associated with London. I prefer that my charges spend their time in a more worthy manner, such as reading devotionals or studying Greek."

Mrs. Bloom waved a hand. "I am sure that is wise." She sent a significant glance at

Miss Platt. "Like your brother, my dear. There are many as would be led astray in a place like London, if they are not cautious."

Miss Platt turned a bright red. "My brother Bertrand was not led astray; he was taken advantage of. That is quite a different thing!"

Suddenly, Gregor, who had been staring at a far wall, visibly started.

Everyone turned to look at him.

He pointed to a painting by the window. "Mrs. Bloom, pray look at that painting and tell me if you think it might be a Vreeland. I daresay with your London experience, you are more familiar with the arts than anyone else here."

Venetia frowned. Here she was, on the verge of ruin, and Gregor was discussing *art?*

Mrs. Bloom swelled with importance. "Like the prince, I adore the Dutch masters. My late husband, God rest his soul, bought a lovely picture from the king's own collection just two years ago. It's hanging in my library even now."

Gregor nodded. "You must be an expert, then." At Mrs. Bloom's tittered agreement, he added, "Would you be so kind as to examine that picture and give me your opinion if it is a Vreeland?"

"Of course." She turned and squinted toward the wall. "But, ah . . . what picture?"

Venetia blinked. The picture was as large as a platter. If Mrs. Bloom couldn't see it, she must be as blind as a bat. Relief flooded Venetia; even if she ran into Mrs. Bloom again, there was a very good chance the older woman wouldn't recognize her. *That* was why Gregor had not been upset.

Mrs. Bloom squinted until her eyes were almost closed as she walked toward the wall. About three feet from it, she straightened. "Ah! *That* picture! It could indeed be a copy of a Vreeland. He has a light touch."

Breathing easier, Venetia sent Gregor a thankful look that caused him to smile slightly and shrug.

"It's a lovely pasture scene," Mrs. Bloom said, returning to their group by the fire. "As peaceful as it looks, I, for one, cannot imagine why anyone would like to live in the country when London has so much more to offer. I spend at *least* seven months of each year in town, for I cannot abide the countryside more than that."

"Oh, I love the countryside," Venetia said brightly. "Miss Platt, which do you pref—"

"I only like the Lake Country," Mrs. Bloom said, not even sparing a glance for her companion.

As Miss Platt sent Venetia an apologetic smile, Venetia seethed at the older woman's rudeness. Mrs. Bloom seemed determined to cut poor Miss Platt at every corner. Well, she wouldn't put up with such nonsense.

She smiled gently upon Miss Platt. "I do hope you'll sit by me at dinner, for I'd enjoy speaking with someone who has the same love for country life."

Mrs. Bloom gave a rather heavy laugh. "Really, Miss West. There is no need to encourage Miss Platt. She is a town dweller and has frequently said she cannot stand being locked away in the country, either."

If Venetia was simmering before, she was boiling now. "Mrs. Bloom, you are the most —"

"Ah! I hear someone in the passage outside," Gregor said, placing a hand under Venetia's elbow and literally strong-arming her away from Mrs. Bloom and toward the table. "Dinner must be coming."

Venetia glared at him, but before she could answer, the door opened, and Mrs. Treadwell entered carrying a large tray, followed closely by a large-boned girl with a ruddy, freckled face, an upturned nose, and flaxen curls. " 'Tis dinner!" the landlady called, setting the platter on the table set for five.

The girl placed a large soup tureen near the head of the table and grinned broadly. "They's thick-sliced ham hock, a dish of pickled eggs, a small platter of quail breasts, kippers, some candied pears, and a basket of warm bread. Oh, and there's soup, too. Parsnip soup, which me mam told me was good fer keepin' the digestion."

Mrs. Bloom peered at the tureen. "I have never heard of parsnip soup."

Mrs. Treadwell's smile faded, a wary look in her eyes. "Elsie made it. Mr. Treadwell says it's the best he ever ate."

Elsie beamed. "Me mam taught me how t' make it when I was but knee high to a flea!"

Venetia took her place at the table. "I am quite looking forward to the soup. Nothing could be better in this weather."

"Exactly!" Ravenscroft said, rallying to Venetia's aid.

She rewarded him with a bright smile, which made Ravenscroft beam at her. Gregor caught this exchange and his gaze narrowed. For a long moment he held Venetia's gaze, then deliberately turned away. He spoke very little for the rest of the meal and Venetia felt doubly alone. What was wrong with the man? As soon as the meal was over, she was going to find out.

Dinner was a horrid affair. Mrs. Bloom seemed determined to discover more about Mr. and Miss West, despite Venetia's best efforts to steer the conversation to safer topics. Though Ravenscroft tried to help, he was simply overwhelmed and far too tired to be of assistance, which left Venetia on her own.

As the hour progressed, Venetia's temper grew thinner, especially when Mrs. Bloom began to remind Miss Platt in an arch tone of "the sewing" that waited to be done in their room. Every time Mrs. Bloom mentioned the sewing, some of Miss Platt's glow faded. Venetia began to imagine baskets and baskets of neat work waiting for Miss Platt, who was forced to slave away by the light of a single candle late into the night.

When dinner was finally finished, Mrs. Bloom stood, announcing in a loud voice that she and Miss Platt would be retiring forthwith. Miss Platt did not look happy but obediently put down her fork and rose.

The moment the door closed behind them, Ravenscroft stretched his arms over his head and yawned. "Thank God they're gone! I've never met such a prosy bore in my life."

"Oh, I have," Gregor said, looking directly at Ravenscroft.

The youth didn't notice. "Lord, I was about to fall on the floor in a stupor!" He yawned again, even more mightily. "Excuse me, but the day has caught up with me. I should go to bed."

"An excellent idea," Gregor said. "I will be along in a few moments. I want to check on the horses one last time."

Ravenscroft turned to Venetia. He lifted her hand to his lips and placed a gentle kiss on her fingers, smiling at her rather shyly. "I dare not hope that you'll dream of me."

She pulled back her hand, thinking he looked absurdly youthful, far younger than his twenty-two years. Venetia's heart softened a bit. He *was* young and very naive. And he looked at her with such hope in his eyes that she couldn't help but be affected. She smiled. "I'm so tired that if I dream at all, it will be of sleeping."

His smile faded, and he added, "I am sorry about this morning. I should have told you what was occurring. I am afraid I didn't think things through as I should have."

She shrugged. "It's over now. There's nothing more to be said."

Ravenscroft's eyes darkened. He took an impetuous step toward her, catching her hand once more. "Venetia, I —"

"That's *Miss Oglivie* when the other guests

are not present." Gregor's voice chilled the room despite the fire blazing in the fireplace.

Ravenscroft turned a bright red, releasing her hand. He ignored Gregor to say in a stiff voice, "Miss Oglivie, I will speak to you of this later. Meanwhile, I bid you a good night." With a deep bow to Venetia, followed by a chilly nod in Gregor's direction, he turned on his heel and left.

Venetia sent a hard glance to Gregor, who now stood beside the fireplace, one arm resting across the mantel, one hand deep in his pocket. "There was no need for that."

He shrugged, his eyes hooded. "The puppy was mauling you."

"He was not." Venetia sighed. "You really should stop teasing Ravenscroft so."

"I treat him as he deserves to be treated." Gregor turned to the fireplace, grabbing the poker and stirring the fire. "Have you forgotten that just this morning he absconded with you?"

"He is aware that he made an error."

"In getting caught."

"In thinking I cared about him enough to agree to such a harebrained scheme. Italy indeed."

"That got your goat, I noticed."

"Especially the part about washing clothes. Oddly enough, I might not mind doing it, provided I wasn't *expected* to do it." She smiled tiredly. "If that makes any sense."

"I suppose it does." He replaced the poker. "You'd do it for love but not for duty."

She gave him a wondering look. "Exactly! I can't believe you understand that."

"Why? It's not so unusual a thought."

"Because in all the years I've known you, I've never once heard you mention love except to say you didn't believe in it."

"I believe in it. For other people."

She crossed to the fireplace and held out her hands to the warmth. "But not for you?"

He gave her a lopsided smile. "One day, perhaps. But I see no use for it now, while I'm young enough to wipe soup from my own chin."

She shook her head, laughing a little. "So, to you, love is for the infirm."

"And those who are too lazy to make their own happiness."

"I don't know that I agree with you." She shrugged. "But it won't be the first time we've disagreed."

His eyes crinkled with laughter. "And I hope it won't be the last."

"You enjoy arguing?"

"With you. You have more sense than

most." He crossed his arms over his chest and leaned back against the mantel. "Usually."

She smiled, and a warm, comfortable silence fell. The flames crackled merrily, the scent of woodsmoke mingled with the savory aroma of their dinner. It was delightful, standing there with Gregor. After that moment this afternoon of painful . . . should she call it awkwardness? Or awareness? Whatever it was, it was nice to have things return to normal.

"I wonder if Ravenscroft will ever write his book," Gregor said in a musing tone.

"I wonder if we'll be in it," she returned with a rueful grin. "I think I'd make a delightful heroine, but you . . ." She tilted her head and regarded him thoughtfully. "I'm not sure you have hero qualities."

His brows snapped down. "Why do you say that?"

"You're anything but a knight in shining armor. Of all the people I know, you're the last one to move yourself to do something for others."

His eyes sparkled, though he shrugged and said, "I rode hell-for-leather through some horrid weather to rescue you, didn't I?"

"Yes, but that's very unusual for you. For a real knight, rescuing maidens would be an everyday event."

Gregor bent down until his face was even with hers. The firelight cast a line along his jaw and traced his scar with silver, shadowing his green eyes until they appeared almost black. "Perhaps a true knight saves himself for the right maiden."

Venetia's heart skipped a bit. Why on earth had he said that? Could he mean — She shook herself mentally. *This is Gregor. He talks like that to every woman.*

The thoughts calmed her thundering pulse, and she turned away, saying in a breathless tone, "Do you think we'll be able to leave tomorrow? Or will we be stuck here for another day?"

Gregor's brows drew together. He hadn't meant to say such a thing, but Venetia had looked so appealing, the firelight dancing red across her hair, her face soft as she watched Ravenscroft leave. He didn't understand her fondness for that fool, but she made an appealing picture when she flashed that reluctant smile.

He'd never noticed the way she dipped her head a bit when she asked a question or how her lips quivered just before she laughed. In all honesty, he was beginning to notice a lot more about Venetia than he should. But was that such a bad thing? Why shouldn't he appreciate her unique beauty?

Perhaps it was because he'd known her since she'd been five and he eight. They'd been guests at a tedious birthday party held for a self-important son of an earl, a spoiled bully who Gregor had been ordered not to challenge to fisticuffs, though he longed to do just that. Miserable, Gregor had been sulking in a corner when he'd found himself standing beside Venetia.

At five, she was already precocious and just as mutinous as he at being ordered to behave. Her gray eyes had sparkled from beneath a mop of brown curls, her pretty white dress torn and muddied from a scrape she'd fallen into earlier. When the guest of honor had mocked her unruly hair, she'd calmly lifted her foot and kicked him squarely in the shins with such grace and accuracy that Gregor had been left speechless with admiration. The two fell instantly into a deep, lasting friendship that neither time nor the determined efforts of Venetia's parents had been able to dissuade.

Twenty-nine years later, Venetia was the same confidante and companion he'd always known, but now he caught a glimpse of the woman who seemed to have enthralled Ravenscroft. It was intriguing, to say the least.

Perhaps it was a result of discovering Venetia missing and thinking her in danger. That had certainly made him realize how much she meant to him. He smiled at her now, glad she was there and safe. "Are you so tired you must rush up to bed? Or are you awake enough to stay and talk a bit?"

She blinked as if surprised, a faint color touching her skin. "I suppose I could stay for a few more moments."

"Good." He reached out and lifted a loose curl that rested on her shoulder.

She grimaced. "No matter how many pins I use, it never stays where I put it."

Her hair slipped between his fingers, silky and soft. "It's too fine to be held by a mere pin." His elbow on her pillow, though, that might hold it in place. He had a sudden image of her nude, her hair rippling over her pillows. That would be a sight to enjoy indeed.

As if his errant thoughts had been spoken aloud, he found himself looking into Venetia's remarkable eyes. The air around them grew heavy and thick, the heat from the fire seeming to expand to fill the space between them.

Somehow, he was no longer standing a respectable arm's length from her. He wasn't sure who had moved closer, though he suspected it might have been him, drawn like a moth to a flame. She was bare inches from him, her skirts brushing his legs, her eyes wide, her lips parted as if she knew the banked fire that simmered within him.

Venetia didn't know what had changed, but something had. She found herself looking up at Gregor, at his mesmerizing green eyes, his firmly carved lips. It would be heavenly to kiss him — heavenly, tantalizing, and forbidden. Yet her body seemed to have silenced her brain and was now leaning precariously toward the rocky cliff that was Gregor.

One single, slim thought held her back. If she crossed this line, she could very well lose him forever as a friend. She'd seen him go through too many women. He dallied, and the second he thought his current lover was beginning to care too much, he moved on.

No, she decided reluctantly, trying not to stare at the sensual line of his bottom lip. No matter how beguiling the thought might be, she would not be just another.

Her entire body suddenly ached, and the events of the day seemed to weigh her down. "I am more tired than I thought; I should go to bed," she said in a husky voice.

Gregor's gaze darkened. He placed a

finger beneath her chin and lifted her face. "Then I shall wish you good night, Venetia." He bent and kissed her cheek.

Venetia closed her eyes, her body trembling. She leaned toward him, savoring the warmth of his lips upon her skin, soaking in every sensual second. Slowly, without breathing, she pulled away and met his gaze.

His green eyes smoldering with intent, his mouth suddenly covered hers, and passion exploded. He lifted her from the ground, molding her against the hard length of his body.

He plundered her mouth, possessed it in a way no one ever had. No kiss had encouraged her to go beyond that point, none had tempted her to try more, and none had ever burned through her like a hot flame.

Gregor moaned low in his throat, a possessive growl that made Venetia's knees weaken even more. His mouth was hot and demanding, his tongue sliding between her lips, taking more and yet more.

Venetia couldn't think, could only *feel,* and, oh, what she felt! Her skin tingled, her lips burned, her heart thundered, and her toes curled.

It was a branding, and Venetia feared she might explode with the heat that burned through her. Just as she thought she might faint from the overwhelming feelings, Gregor broke the kiss, slid her to her feet, and released her.

As quickly as it had begun, it was over. They stood, breathing heavily, stunned amazement on both of their faces.

Gregor raked a hand through his hair. "Venetia, I —"

"*No.*" She turned and almost stumbled toward the door.

She heard him take a step after her, and she ran as if the hounds of hell were nipping at her heels, slamming the door behind her and taking the stairs in a blur of motion. She needed to be alone, to release the confused feelings that tore through her.

She had stumbled to her door and reached for the knob when the door across from hers opened, and Miss Platt came out onto the landing, still dressed in the gown she'd worn to dinner. The woman jumped a little at the unexpected sight of Venetia, and then frowned. "Why, Miss West!" Miss Platt said in a pseudo-whisper. "Are you ill? You look flushed."

Venetia whispered, "I'm just tired, that's all."

Miss Platt gave her a comforting pat on the shoulder. "I daresay you are; it has been a busy day."

The kind words, combined with the comforting pat on the shoulder, almost broke Venetia's tenuous control. With an effort, she managed a smile and said, "Miss Platt, I would like to speak with you tomorrow." She glanced at the closed door behind Miss Platt. "In private."

"Very well. Perhaps in the morning? I am an early riser." She tittered nervously and whispered, "Mrs. Bloom is forever telling me to be quiet in the mornings so I will not wake her."

"Excellent. I shall look forward to —"

"Miss Platt!" called Mrs. Bloom, her voice booming through the quiet inn.

Miss Platt started. "Oh, dear! I must fetch some water! Excuse me, Miss West." She dashed down the stairs, her skirts flying behind her.

Shaking her head, Venetia slipped tiredly into her own room and undressed. Though she wished to think more about Gregor's startling kiss, she could not keep her eyes open. Within seconds of slipping between the sheets, she fell into a deep, deep sleep, where she dreamed of knights in shining armor with dark green eyes and wicked smiles.

CHAPTER 6

We all do things fer which we're woeful
and sorry. Indeed, ye'd not be human if ye
didn't err a wee bit now and ag'in!
    Old Woman Nora from Loch Lomond
            to her three wee granddaughters
                        one cold evening

Venetia awoke slowly, pulling the covers
higher and snuggling deeper into the cocoon
of warmth. Then the painfully clear memory
of Gregor's kiss shocked the last few vestiges
of sleep from her mind.

Her lips tingled as if longing for another.

She scrubbed them with the back of her
hand. It had really happened, then. Gregor
had really kissed her. Which meant . . . what?

Nothing, she told herself. She said it again,
aloud. "It means nothing. Gregor kisses
women all the time. It was merely the strain
of the day's events."

When they met today, they would pretend

the kiss had never happened. Though things might be awkward at first, she was certain they'd quickly settle back into their normal pattern.

She climbed out of bed, shivering when her feet hit the wood floor. Where on earth was her robe? She glanced around, finally seeing the edge of it peeking out from under the bed. She snatched it up and bundled into it, wishing it possessed less lace and more material, then made her way to the window and flicked back the edge of the curtain.

Sunlight streamed into the innyard below, blindingly bright and sparkling on the snow. For the first time in two days, there was nary a cloud in the sky. Better yet, there was a line around the barn where large fat icicles dripped away, slowly melting.

Venetia smiled with relief and dropped the curtain back into place. Perhaps they wouldn't be stuck here very long — which was a good thing, considering how things between her and Gregor had gone awry so quickly.

Unwilling to examine the events of last night without her breakfast, she crossed to the washstand, picked up her silver comb, and began to tame her long hair.

Venetia tugged through the last tangle,

wishing she'd brought her handheld mirror. The one over the washstand was so spotted and cloudy she could hardly make out her face, much less tell anything about her hair.

Sighing, she began the laborious task of pinning up her long locks. She was just sliding the last pin into place when she heard the door across the hall open.

Miss Platt's voice drifted into the room. "Yes, ma'am! I will go at once and see why no one brought hot water."

Mrs. Bloom's shrill voice complained at length.

When she finally paused, Miss Platt said in her breathless voice, "Oh, yes, my dear Mrs. Bloom! It's most disgraceful. I'll go at once, and I will not return until I find some water."

Venetia went to the door and cracked it open. Miss Platt was just closing the door to Mrs. Bloom's room, a harried expression on her face.

"Miss Platt!" Venetia whispered.

Miss Platt paused, glancing back over her shoulder. She was dressed in gray again, with no ornamentation to alleviate the drabness of her attire. "Miss We—"

"Shhhh!" Venetia opened her door wider and whispered, "Do you have some time to speak? It will take only a moment."

Miss Platt glanced nervously at Mrs. Bloom's door. "I don't know if I —"

"Please."

The thin woman managed a nervous smile and entered Venetia's room.

Once there, Venetia took Miss Platt's hands and led her to the only chair. "Pray have a seat. I am sorry I don't have more comforts here, but we have to make do."

Miss Platt shook her head. "Oh, I couldn't possibly take the only chair!"

Venetia rather wished Miss Platt could. The woman was far taller than she and it was a bit of a strain to look up into her angular face. The light from the window was not very kind to Miss Platt. Her skin was sallow, her lips very thin, and her eyelashes nonexistent. Her only claim to attractiveness was the unusual light blue color of her eyes.

Of course, the exterior was a poor indicator of the soul, as Venetia knew after countless lectures from her father. It had often been proven that a plain exterior harbored a pure soul.

Looking up into Miss Platt's plain features, it was easy to imagine that they shone with an especially angelic goodness. "Miss Platt, I hope you don't think I'm being forward, but Mrs. Bloom seems — that is to say, she's not always — how *did* you come to be in her employ?"

Miss Platt flushed a rich hue that showed her to even more disadvantage. "That's a very complicated story."

Venetia had expected as much. "I didn't wish to bring it up at dinner last night, because there were so many people present, but I couldn't help but wonder."

Miss Platt wrung her hands, glancing nervously at the door. "Mrs. Bloom does not like me to tell."

"Because it might show her in an ill light?"

"Oh, no! It's not a bad story, but Mrs. Bloom feels that some people might take her part wrong."

Indignation warmed Venetia's heart. Her instincts had been right once again; Miss Platt was in sore need of a champion. "Pray tell me what happened! At least, do so if you wish."

"It's not much of a story. It — it has to do with my brother, Bertrand." As she said the name, Miss Platt's thin lips curved into a shy smile, her face softening. "My brother is a wonderful man, quite handsome and debonair, though a bit —" She hesitated, clearly unable or unwilling to say anything bad about him.

"Naive?" Venetia offered helpfully.

"Yes!" Miss Platt looked relieved. "Bertrand is several years younger than I. Through an odd set of circumstances, he found himself in London." She leaned forward and said in an awed whisper, "With more than a *thousand pounds!*"

"That's quite a sum of money."

"He inherited it from my uncle. My brother and I were raised in the wilds of Dover, and nothing would do but that Bertrand must go to London with his funds. I fear he was a bit out of his element there. He is quite impulsive." Miss Platt's voice came in a rush, her hands tightly clenched before her, a trace of color on her thin cheeks. "It's a family trait, I am afraid. My father suffered from just such an affliction."

Venetia placed a hand on Miss Platt's shoulder and squeezed sympathetically. "I think I know what happened. Someone took advantage of your brother and encouraged his weakness?"

"Oh, *yes!*" Miss Platt grasped one of Venetia's hands between hers, a beseeching look in her eyes. "Miss West, you cannot know the agonies of being so far away from one's only blood relative!"

"Your brother is the last of your family?"

"Oh, yes. Except for Mrs. Bloom."

"You are related to her?"

"She married my mother's brother, which makes her my aunt by marriage. My uncle, Mr. Bloom, was a very wealthy man. He and Mrs. Bloom took care of Bertrand and me until he died, some years ago. He left the two of us some funds."

"That's where Bertrand got his thousand pounds."

"Yes." Miss Platt's expression darkened. "I've always thought Mrs. Bloom resented that."

Venetia patted Miss Platt's hand. "Where is Bertrand now?"

"In London." Miss Platt's lips quivered. "In debtor's prison."

"Oh, no!"

"Yes! Mrs. Bloom and I are on our way to save him."

Venetia's mouth opened. "Mrs. Bloom is going to pay his debts?"

Miss Platt flushed awkwardly. "Yes, but —" She closed her lips for a moment before speaking again. "I am not to speak of that. Mrs. Bloom doesn't wish me to say more on the matter."

Suddenly, Venetia saw it all. Miss Platt was serving as Mrs. Bloom's companion to repay the clutch-fisted old bat for getting poor Bertrand released from gaol. Of all the mean, uncharitable behavior! Mrs. Bloom had completely taken advantage of poor Miss Platt.

Venetia's father always said that charity was an act not counted in gold, but Venetia was certain Mrs. Bloom was doing just that. She probably thought she was doing Miss Platt and poor Bertrand a great favor, congratulating herself on her grand charity and reminding poor Miss Platt a thousand times a day of how much she "owed" her benefactress.

Venetia squeezed Miss Platt's hand. "I don't wish to say anything untoward, but there are other ways to find funds than selling yourself into servitude."

Miss Platt blinked. "What other ways?"

"Well . . . there is . . . I mean, surely you could . . ." Venetia bit her lip. "I don't know right now, but I am certain I will think of something." At Miss Platt's fallen expression, Venetia said earnestly, "You must have hope. Surely you don't see yourself serving as a companion for Mrs. Bloom all of your days."

"Well, no — I suppose not. I hadn't really thought of it. Except, of course, in my dreams. But that is another matter altogether."

"Your dreams?" Venetia smiled a little at that. "What do you dream?"

Miss Platt couldn't turn any redder. She waved an agitated hand. "Nothing, really. I — I just sometimes daydream. Mrs. Bloom says I'm perfectly useless when I do so, though I can't help but wonder . . . never mind."

"No, no! What were you going to say?"

"I shouldn't be so silly. Mrs. Bloom says one must face realities, but sometimes it is so lovely to dream."

"I don't care what Mrs. Bloom says! Tell me about your dreams! *Please?*"

"I — I suppose it won't hurt." Miss Platt said in a low voice, "One day, I would like to get married."

Venetia nodded encouragingly. "And?"

Miss Platt blinked. "And . . . that's all. I would just like to get married."

"Oh."

Miss Platt blushed. "It's a silly dream, isn't it? And not very likely to happen."

"I wouldn't say that," Venetia said bracingly.

"No. For me, it's a dream and nothing else. I'm not like you, Miss West. I don't have a beau like Lord MacLean."

"MacLean? He's not my beau!" He was a thorn in her side, a pain in her —

"But you two seem so familiar with each other."

"We are. I've known Gregor MacLean since I was five."

"Oh! So you are more like brother and sister!"

"We are just friends. Nothing more."

"I thought he told Mrs. Bloom he was your guardian."

"He's my guardian and friend. But that is all." Venetia could see the woman's brow furrow as she considered something. "Miss Platt, what is it?"

"I was just thinking. Miss West, do you think —" She winced, then shook her head. "I'm sorry. I'm just being silly."

"Silly? Why do you think that?"

"My father always said that one should know one's place in life and not live above, for there was naught but heartache on that path."

"Of all the horrid things to say!"

Miss Platt blinked. "It was?"

"Absolutely. There is no telling where you might find yourself, if you will only take a few chances. Stop letting life and other people dictate who you are, and tell them instead!"

"Chances?" Miss Platt looked positively amazed. "You think it's good to take chances?"

"Of course! I take them all the time, and

they *always* work out." Venetia thought for a moment. "Well, most of the time."

Miss Platt stood, eyes wide, blinking slowly. Then, in an awed voice, she said, "I *love* taking chances. And I used to, but Mrs. Bloom always says —"

"Forget about Mrs. Bloom! What about you? What chances do you wish to take?"

"Oh, Miss West, there are so many! I should like to learn how to flirt and how to attract a gentleman. A real gentleman like Lord MacLean!"

Venetia's smile faded, an odd sense of alarm pressing against her. "You wish to learn to flirt? With Gregor?"

"Or someone else. I'd like to learn to flirt and then marry. It's the only way I might catch a man." Miss Platt pressed her hands to her cheeks, a sublime look upon her thin face. "I should like to marry a gentleman with a title and money, and he would have to be handsome, too, of course! *And* have a lovely house. And horses. Servants. At least one carriage, maybe two." Miss Platt giggled, her face alight. "In fact, you are right. I *should* like to marry someone like Lord MacLean."

"But . . ." Venetia said blankly.

Miss Platt clasped her hands beneath her chin and closed her eyes. "He is the handsomest man I've ever met."

And the most arrogant.

Miss Platt dropped her clasped hands to her lap, her bright blue gaze on Venetia's face. "Miss West, do you think that a gentleman like Lord MacLean might be interested in someone like *me?*"

Venetia looked at Miss Platt, with her flat chest and too-large feet and hunched shoulders, at the lank, mousy brown hair and the hooked nose over the too-thin lips. Venetia then thought of Gregor, with his savage male beauty that was defined by the rapier-thin scar down his face. The scar began above his eyebrow, skipped his eye, and continued in a pale slash down his cheek. But his disfigurement hadn't dampened the enthusiasm of the women of London. It seemed to enflame them all the more, adding an element of exotic danger to an already heart-stirringly handsome man.

Venetia had seen woman after woman throw herself at Gregor, which was why her heart sank at Miss Platt's hopeful tone.

As she opened her mouth to reply, Mrs. Bloom's shrill voice rang out. *"Miss Platt!"*

Miss Platt started. "Oh, dear! I must go!" She gave an awkward curtsey, and scurried to the door. "I don't know why they didn't bring hot water this morning, but Mrs.

Bloom won't rest until she gets it." She paused at the door, smiling shyly. "Thank you for speaking with me, Miss West. I don't know if I can ever do what you suggest, but —"

"Of course you can!" Venetia said, banishing her uneasy thoughts. "And you should be aware that there are far better men than Gregor MacLean."

Miss Platt shook her head. "I can't imagine!"

Venetia gave Miss Platt a bracing smile. "Just wait until you reach London and spend a little time amongst civilized society. There are many men far more charming."

Miss Platt tittered. "La, Miss West! How you do talk! You are very kind, though, and I appreciate —"

The door across the hallway could be heard to open, and Mrs. Bloom's shrill voice snapped, "Miss Platt! Pray come at once!"

The door slammed closed.

Miss Platt winced. "I had better go. Thank you for your advice." With a wiggle of her fingers over one shoulder, she was out the door.

Venetia followed Miss Platt to the landing and watched her rush down the steps and disappear around the corner. Who would have thought poor Miss Platt's one dream was to flirt? Obviously, there was a lot more work to do in raising Miss Platt's sense of value. If Miss Platt did not develop a sense of purpose for her own life, other people would run right over her. People like Mrs. Bloom.

Venetia looked at Mrs. Bloom's closed door and sniffed. Overbearing harridans who thought themselves better than their fellows had a serious lesson to learn. But before Venetia could address that wrong, Miss Platt's unflattering opinion of herself had to be improved. Yet how?

It was too bad Venetia couldn't enlist Gregor's assistance. If he would just pay the slightest bit of attention to the lady, it would do wonders for her sorely missing sense of self-worth and might give her the confidence to face down Mrs. Bloom's bullying.

The memory of the kiss burned through Venetia, and she gulped back a maelstrom of emotions. Perhaps Gregor was too intoxicating a force for Miss Platt.

Gregor was too much, but Ravenscroft . . . Venetia nodded thoughtfully. That might work. If Ravenscroft could be prevailed upon to pay a bit of attention to Miss Platt, it might drive up her sagging sense of worth.

The problem was Gregor; he wasn't acting with his usual reserve. Indeed, he'd become oddly possessive since his arrival, as if rescuing her had given him some sort of rights over her actions.

Of course, that had been yesterday, when emotions had been running high. Today things should be back to normal — though she wasn't completely certain that Gregor would sit idly by while she attempted to assist Miss Platt. Gregor never appreciated the gratification of helping a fellow man. Even now, it astounded Venetia to think that he'd ridden to her rescue — though she supposed it had been more a matter of pride for him than anything else. He certainly hadn't seemed suffused with the milk of human kindness since his arrival. All he'd done thus far was mock her every effort. Which was why she had to keep Gregor from interfering in her plans.

She could almost pity him for his misconceptions. If he didn't suffer from such a superior attitude, she might have worked up a bit of sympathy rather than irritation.

There had to be a way. Fortunately, she knew from dealing with life's many challenges that she only needed to be patient and the answer would occur to her. It always did.

And woe betide Gregor then!

CHAPTER 7

'Tis an odd fact o' life that some marriages
are part pure love and part pure frustration. Sometimes the very thing that drives
a man and wife apart also glues them
together.
                Old Woman Nora from Loch Lomond
                        to her three wee granddaughters
                                            one cold evening

Before going down to breakfast, Venetia
spent some time going through her limited
wardrobe. To prove to Gregor that she was
unaffected by their accidental kiss, she
needed to sail into the common room
laughing and talking, completely unaffected
by his presence. Which meant she would
definitely need to wear her best gown.

With this thought in mind, Venetia dressed
in a blue round gown of a deep color, which
was fortunate, as her only petticoat had
ripped in the accident. Elsie had promised

to mend it, but it would be the next day before it was ready.

The gown was beautifully made, decorated at the hem and on each sleeve with tiny pink rosettes backed with tiny green leaves. A bright green ribbon tied directly beneath her breasts, while a delicate lace collar adorned the modest neckline. Though she'd forgotten to bring the matching blue shoes and the green ribbon for her hair, she hoped she appeared at her best.

Gathering her courage, she marched to the common room, reaching it at the same time as Ravenscroft. He was dressed in a coat of blue superfine with a deep wine-colored waistcoat, his collar so high that he couldn't turn his chin to either side. Gregor never adopted extravagant fashions, scoffing at anything he considered either uncomfortable or excessive. For that reason alone, Venetia was willing to look upon Ravenscroft's dandified clothing with a kinder eye than usual.

She smiled at him. "Goodness! How did you get your shirt points so high?"

He beamed. "Mrs. Treadwell's girl is quite handy with an iron. Who would have thought it, in the middle of nowhere?"

"Fortunately for us, Elsie is also good with a cooking pot. How are you feeling this morning? Are you much bruised from our accident?"

"My head is still a bit tender." He touched a spot over one temple. "Other than that, I'm fit as can be."

"Excellent," Venetia said.

He hesitated a moment, then said in a rushed voice, "Venetia, I must apologize for my behavior in bringing you to this wretched place. I never thought — that is, I shouldn't have — although I didn't expect — I had no way of knowing that —"

"I know," Venetia said, laughing a little. She patted Ravenscroft's arm. "You were very wrong for what you did, but I must admit, your intention was quite romantic."

"Yes, it was! Venetia, I love —"

"Don't begin that again!" she interrupted hurriedly, removing her hand from his arm. Seeing his expression, she softened her tone. "You know I am not in love with you. I am sorry, but that is the way things are. And I will not discuss it again."

He flushed, his shoulders sagging. "Very well. I will try not to say anything more. But if you change your mind, or if you think of something you need done, or wish to have, I hope you'll tell me." He regarded her with burning eyes. "I'd do anything for you, and it's not just because

137

of your dowry."

"Dowry? What dowry?"

"Why — your father said — not that I paid him any heed, of course — but he mentioned that if you married, he wished to give you a large sum for your dowry."

Venetia chuckled. "He said he *wished* to give me a dowry, because that's all he could do — just wish. I hope you didn't believe he was actually going to settle funds on me."

A definite flash of disappointment settled on his face. "Oh. No. Of course I didn't believe him. I just mention it because, ah, well, he did say it, though I assure you that had nothing to do with why I wished to marry you."

Venetia raised her brows. "Indeed?"

"Indeed," he said somewhat testily.

Her lips quivered. "Poor Ravenscroft."

"Venetia, I love you. Even if you cannot return my feelings, I would do anything for you. Just say the word, and I'll prove it."

She'd already turned to enter the door when his words halted her. She paused. "There *is* one thing I need."

Ravenscroft grasped one of her hands and pressed it to his heart. "Please! Allow me to be of some service to you."

Venetia eyed the young man for a moment. He wasn't dangerously handsome like Gregor, with his intriguing scar and bold manner. Nor could Ravenscroft make a woman feel shivery with just one look. Still, she was fairly certain Miss Platt would think Ravenscroft's dandified dress quite the thing.

The woman deserved a chance, and if Venetia did not do *something,* the opportunity might pass. "Very well, Ravenscroft. You may do me a favor, but I warn you, it might be quite difficult."

He leaned forward, every line of his body eager.

Leaving her hand within his grip, Venetia explained her plan.

Despite his promise to do anything she wished, Ravenscroft put up surprising resistance. But eventually, armed with both his promise and the happy knowledge that he was performing a great service for the good of mankind — or *woman*kind — Ravenscroft finally capitulated.

Venetia entered the common room with a satisfied smile on her face.

Gregor didn't realize until the moment Venetia entered the room how tense he'd been, waiting for her, but the second he saw her, his body fired awake.

Damn it all, this was not what he'd hoped.

Last night, after their impetuous kiss, he'd most unusually found himself unable to sleep. Never had he allowed an incident with a woman to rob him of his God-given right to rest.

But somehow, every time he'd closed his eyes, he'd found himself thinking of Venetia, of the surprising flare of passion that had flamed between them, of the incredible softness of her lips beneath his. Over and over, he'd relived the moment, thinking of all the implications.

Though she was no young girl, Venetia was an innocent in many ways. He was certain she would feel embarrassed at her reaction to their embrace. He'd imagined she would be subdued and pale this morning. He would, of course, ignore that she was ill at ease and reassure her by acting as if nothing had happened. He had some experience with such things and it would take her some time to realize that he was not about to betray her.

So it was something of a shock when Venetia finally arrived in the morning room, wearing gay colors, laughing at something Ravenscroft must have said. Her gaze didn't so much as flicker toward Gregor. Without pause, she merrily answered a comment made by Mrs. Treadwell, teased Ravenscroft about being famished and remembered to call him "brother" in a particularly beguiling tone, gave an enthusiastic greeting to Miss Platt, inquired after Mrs. Bloom's health, and even managed to assume an interested look during the older lady's lengthy answer.

Upon meeting Gregor's gaze for a fleeting second, she blithely turned away and went to peer out the window at the melting snow, commenting to Miss Platt that they would soon all be on their way, and what a delight that would be.

Inwardly, Gregor seethed. He wasn't the only one who'd noticed her cool reaction to him, either. Mrs. Bloom was looking from Venetia to him and back, obviously bursting to know what had happened between them. As soon as she could, she made her way to his side. "Well?" She eyed him as if he were a particularly tasty morsel. "What have you done to Miss West that she is ignoring you?"

What had *he* done? Hah! He'd done nothing that any other red-blooded male wouldn't have done. To halt Mrs. Bloom's rampant curiosity in its tracks, he shrugged. "I'm not sure what you are talking about. Miss West is simply seeing about the weather. I think the snow *has* come to an end, don't you?"

That sent Mrs. Bloom off in a scurry of speculation about the weather, just as he wanted. All the lady required in the way of conversation was someone to nod occasionally and murmur "Quite so!" every now and again.

Meanwhile, he was free to slip a look past her to where Venetia stood by the window. The second he did, he wished he hadn't.

It was blazingly bright outside, the sun reflecting off the snow. The light poured in, Venetia to one side of the window, partially in the shadow, though the light touched the crown of her head, shimmering on her hair until it appeared burnished with gold.

It was odd, but in London he'd never really had the opportunity to see Venetia just so. When they were there, they rode together in the park and occasionally danced with each other at some amusement. She frequently met him at Lady B's Chocolate House on Bond Street, where she'd sip a cup of hot chocolate while they talked and laughed and discussed horses, people, and books, their most common interests.

An oddly wistful pang shot through him. Were those days gone? Would they ever be back to the easy friendship they'd once shared?

As he wondered, Venetia moved slightly to

her left, the window's bright light now shining directly on her . . . and through her skirts.

He started. Bloody hell! Why wasn't she wearing a petticoat? Her gently curved legs were plainly visible, the fullness of her calf, the delicate line of her ankle.

Gregor's body flared to life, his heart thudding hard as pure, primal lust jolted through him.

"Lord MacLean?" Mrs. Bloom's demanding voice cut through his thoughts.

He blinked down at her, suddenly remembering he'd been listening to her diatribe about the weather. "Quite so," he said, hoping that answered her question.

Her prim mouth folded in disapproval, her eyes flashing. "Lord MacLean, I asked you twice if you thought a good rain might melt this snow, and you have yet to answer!"

Gregor struggled to understand her words, his mind still on the vision by the window. Venetia should take more caution when in public. Any man might look at the window and see — good God, where was Ravenscroft?

Gregor turned to find the younger man in conversation with Miss Platt. Just then, Ravenscroft sent a harried look toward Venetia and then froze in place. His mouth fell open, and his eyes bulged.

Damn it all!

"Mrs. Bloom, that is an excellent question. Allow me to ask Miss West for her opinion. She knows all about thunderstorms." Gregor crossed the room, captured Venetia's elbow, and yanked her out of the light.

She stumbled, her warm body soft against his chest before she pulled away. "What are you doing?" she hissed, her face bright.

He turned her firmly toward Mrs. Bloom and modesty. "I am keeping you from making a spectacle of yourself," he said under his breath.

She planted her feet, bringing them both to a halt. Her silver eyes flashed up at him. "I beg your pardon?"

Gregor leaned down. "You were standing in front of the light from the window."

"So?"

"I could see right through your gown, as could Ravenscroft and everyone else."

Her cheeks burst into color. "Oh! I didn't know — that is, I never thought — my undergown was torn, and Elsie hasn't yet finished mending it."

Gregor suppressed a strong desire to trace his fingers over her heated cheeks. "You won't get a coherent word out of Ravenscroft for the rest of the day," he said curtly.

Her color heightened, even as her lips quivered into a smile. She peeped up at him to say mischievously, "I'm not sure that will impede his normal speech pattern all that much."

Despite his irritation, Gregor had to laugh. "The lad is not a wordsmith, is he?"

"No, though his heart is good." She glanced past Gregor to Ravenscroft, who was back in conversation with Miss Platt, though he kept sending red-faced glances at Venetia. "I find very little fault with him except a sad propensity for being romantic at the most importune times."

She sounded fond of Ravenscroft. Gregor's smile faded, though he supposed it should not have been surprising. Venetia had a tendency to adopt any stray that came her way. Still, was that all she felt? What if, in making such a grand though misguided gesture as eloping with Venetia, Ravenscroft had accomplished what Venetia's father had at first hoped for and ignited a spark of something more than fondness?

Venetia was even now watching Ravenscroft with Miss Platt. Whatever she saw there did not please her, for she frowned mightily and then, to Gregor's surprise, made a subtle "go forward" gesture with her hand.

He glanced over to see Ravenscroft straighten his shoulders and say something to Miss Platt that made that lady turn pink.

Gregor stole a look back at Venetia and caught a satisfied gleam in her eyes. *Hmmm.* What was the minx up to now? Her smile was particularly smug, but Ravenscroft's eyes were wild, his posture lacking his usual boyish bounce, and his smile nearly maniacal. Though he stood beside Miss Platt, his eyes were everywhere but on her, as if he were afraid to meet her gaze.

Gregor's brows rose when Venetia gave Ravenscroft a very encouraging nod. Gulping noisily, the young man lifted his chin as if preparing to march to his death, then asked Miss Platt in a stuttering voice if she didn't think it a particularly fine day, and could they perhaps go for a walk at a later time.

Miss Platt flushed, spiraling down into a mad mangle of incoherent speech. Venetia, meanwhile, beamed upon the two.

Bloody hell, she was at it again! Despite their precarious predicament, Venetia was up to her neck in some scheme.

He leaned forward and said in a low voice, "I don't know what you are doing with Ravenscroft and Miss Platt, but you'd best have a care."

Some of Venetia's glow faded. "I don't need you to tell me how to run my life. I've been doing it myself for the last decade, and I am quite capable of making my own decisions."

"So one would think," he retorted. "Yet you continue to make bad choice after bad choice."

She stiffened. "What do you mean by that?"

"Only that we are not yet out of the woods, and getting embroiled in the lives of our fellow travelers is the last thing we should be doing."

"I am not 'getting embroiled' in anything. I am merely assisting Miss Platt in developing a bit of confidence."

"You are encouraging Ravenscroft to make a fool of himself," Gregor returned in a low voice, his eyes sparkling dangerously, his hand coming to rest on her wrist.

The second he touched her, a flare of heat raced up her arm, causing her skin to tingle, her breasts to tighten in a most nerve-rattling way. She pulled away, rubbing her wrist where he'd touched her.

Gregor's brows lowered, his eyes flint hard. "Stop meddling in Miss Platt's life."

Venetia's lips thinned. "Gregor, it has

been a pleasure speaking with you, as usual. Good day." She spun on her heel and went to stand with Mrs. Bloom by the fireplace.

Gregor was not a man who expected flattery wherever he went. But he *was* used to a certain amount of respect, so Venetia's refusal even to listen to his opinion resulted in an immediate swell of indignation.

He followed Venetia to the fireplace and placed his hand under her elbow. "Excuse us, Mrs. Bloom. My charge and I have something to discuss."

Venetia frowned. "I am not discussing anything else with you."

"Miss West," Mrs. Bloom said in her heavy voice, "Lord MacLean is your guardian. One should always pay service to the proprieties. Besides, I think I shall go ahead and take a seat at the table. From the sounds in the hall, breakfast is about to be served." She nodded regally and left.

Venetia pulled her elbow free, her eyes snapping angrily. "What do you want now?"

He crossed his arms over his chest. "I want to know what scheme you are hatching with Ravenscroft and Miss Platt."

Venetia shrugged airly. "Why must you always think I am scheming?"

"Because in all the years I've known you, you've done nothing else *but.* You've always gotten involved in things beyond you."

"Oh! That is not true! Give one example."

"The time you assisted that French émigré with his search for his supposed family," he said promptly.

Her face fell. "I was afraid you'd remember that one."

"If I remember correctly, you later discovered that 'Pierre' was an art thief; not even French but Corsican; and he thanked you for your hospitality by stealing two of your father's favorite paintings."

Venetia pursed her lips, then shrugged. "That was just one. Name another."

"There was the woman from the lending library who told you she was a relative of the duke of Devonshire, and you believed her —"

"She had the look of the Devonshires," Venetia said hastily. "Even you admitted that!"

"Yes, but *I* did not hire her to serve in my house as a maid, where she caused a ruckus at one of your father's dinner parties by throwing herself at the duke's feet and declaring herself his love child from a washwoman at his estate!"

Venetia bit her lip, a gleam of humor in her eyes. "That was a bit embarrassing, wasn't it? Not for me, of course, but for the duke. It's a wonder he still speaks to me."

"It's a wonder anyone still speaks to you," Gregor said, fighting the inane urge to grin. It *had* been rather humorous, especially when it was later proven that the woman in question had mistaken her "dooks" and meant to accost the Duke of Claridge.

The entire room had been in chaos, people shouting and calling for a footman to eject the woman, when Venetia had calmly assisted the poor woman to her feet, suggested perhaps she would like to speak to the duke in private, and escorted her away. As Venetia had passed Gregor, she'd tossed him an irrepressible grin and a wink, which had made him laugh all the more.

He twinkled at her a bit now. "There are other instances of your madness, you know. There was the time you brought some homeless urchin into your father's house —"

"*That* was not my fault. He was supposedly a chimney sweep. He had burn scars on his legs, so I believed him."

"But he wasn't a chimney sweep, was he?"

"He might have been at one time," she said loftily.

"He was a bona fide pickpocket. I know, because I lost not one but *two* watches to that scoundrel before you found out what he was doing."

"At least *you* didn't lose your mother's locket. We never recovered that, either."

"You see where I am getting with this, don't you?"

She sighed. "Yes, yes. You think I am too trusting and that I ought not get involved in other people's lives. We've had this discussion repeatedly, and I thought we'd agreed to disagree."

"So we did. Until now."

Venetia's silver eyes met his. "What is so different about now?"

"You tell me."

Their gazes locked. Color rose on her cheeks. "I am sure I don't know," she said in a breathless voice, turning away. "I am not doing anything that could cause any problems; I merely wish to assist Miss Platt. Even you must concede that she is not an evil woman or a pickpocket or else. She hasn't asked me to do a single thing for her. If anything, she's indicated that she wishes the opposite."

"She sounds like a woman of good sense. I hope you are listening to her."

Venetia wrinkled her nose at him. "When did you become so stuffy?"

He stiffened. "I am not stuffy."

She shrugged, looking past him as if she'd

lost interest. "You seem so, but perhaps it's just me."

Gregor scowled. For years, he'd watched as Venetia had smoothed the path of life for her chaotic parents, taken up with unsuitable acquaintances with the intention of "assisting" them, and generally put herself to a great deal of trouble attempting to right all of the wrongs of the world. But the world didn't appreciate such efforts; no one ever really said thank you. Yet for some reason, she seemed to thrive on it.

Though this tendency of hers had always bothered him, he'd been able to accept it because it hadn't affected him. That had all changed once they'd become trapped here together. Now everything seemed different, and everything she did affected him in the most direct way.

Gregor did not like that at all.

He glanced at the window, noting with relief that the ice was melting faster in the warmth of the sun. Perhaps they would be able to leave soon, and things would once again grow comfortable. Venetia could accomplish her charity works without it interfering with the time she spent with Gregor. That was the way things were supposed to be.

He looked down and found her regarding

him with a critical air. Her eyes were a smoky gray this morning, a question lurking in their depths.

"What is it?" he asked.

She tilted her head to one side. "Does it ever bother you?"

"Does what bother me?"

"That you never get involved in life, but stand by and watch it pass by." She shook her head as if she pitied him. "One day you'll wake up and it will all be gone, and all you'll have done is *watched*."

He frowned, but the entrance of Mrs. Treadwell and Elsie with platters of food forestalled his answer.

"Come," she said, "we had best join the others."

Gregor had no choice but to follow. He almost choked when he overheard Ravenscroft solicit Miss Platt's opinion about the proper cultivation of azaleas.

It was too odd, as was the way Miss Platt was behaving — giggling like a ninny and turning every shade of pink whenever Ravenscroft managed to spurt out some compliment in an oddly arch manner, as if he were playacting on the stage. Through it all, Venetia watched with a pleased air.

It was enough to spoil Gregor's appetite. Did the pup think to make Venetia jealous?

The door from the hallway opened, and Gregor's groom, Chambers, stood in the opening. "I beg yer pardon, my lord, but there's another carriage two miles up the road as fell into a drift and overturned."

"Heavens!" Venetia said, standing. "Was anyone injured?"

"No, though 'tis feared one of the horses has a broken leg. Mr. Treadwell has gone to fetch the passengers, a gentleman and his daughter."

Mrs. Bloom's lips folded in disapproval. "They cannot come here. We've barely enough room, as it is."

Venetia's brows lifted delicately, telling Gregor that the battle flags were rising.

She said in a cool voice, "Mrs. Bloom, I am certain *none* of us will shrink from performing our duty as hosts, since *none* of us is ill mannered or unfeeling."

Mrs. Bloom's heavy cheeks stained an unbecoming red. "I wasn't suggesting we be uncharitable, but we must be realistic. There is only so much food and no more beds. Where would this man and his daughter sleep?"

"I shall share my bed with the young lady," Venetia said. "I'm not certain where we'll put the gentleman." She looked meaningfully at Gregor.

Gregor wisely kept silent, turning his attention back to his plate. He knew that Venetia believed he was proving her earlier point about his ungenerous nature, but it didn't matter: he'd be damned if he'd give up his bed for a man he'd never met. Hell, he wasn't certain he'd give up his bed for someone he *did* know. Had it been one of his brothers, he might have tossed the ass a blanket, but no more. Such was the way of men.

Besides, what benefit would there be to make himself uncomfortable in this case? The other person might be more at ease, but wouldn't Gregor's discomfort count, too, and demand a remedy itself?

He suddenly became aware of Venetia's and Mrs. Bloom's stern gazes upon him. He merely raised his brows and stared back. He was already sharing his room with Ravenscroft, who snored. Surely that was enough sacrifice to expect of one human being.

Venetia's brows rose a bit more, her eyes flashing. "Well?"

Gregor put down his fork and knife. "You are right."

Her smile was blinding, and he almost, but not quite, regretted what he said next. "Something must be done, and right away."

He flicked a glance at Ravenscroft. "Well?"

The younger man blinked. "Well what?"

"Are you willing to share your accommodations, as Miss West suggests?"

Ravenscroft caught Venetia's glance and colored. "Yes, yes! Of course I am!"

"There you have it," Gregor said smoothly. "Ravenscroft will give up his trundle bed for the worthy gentleman. I only hope he doesn't snore."

"But," Ravenscroft said, "where will — what will I —"

Gregor reached over to clap the young man on the shoulder. "We will throw a pallet on the floor for you. Don't give it another thought."

Ravenscroft sighed. "I suppose so."

"Good man!" Gregor said bracingly. He drew in a deep breath. "Ah, there is nothing as invigorating as doing a good turn for one's fellow man!"

Venetia regarded him with a flat look. "That was a dirty trick, MacLean."

"All's fair in love and charity, my dear." Gregor reached for the platter of eggs and added some to his plate.

"Gregor, what are you doing?"

"I think it's rather obvious. I'm eating."

"But this man and his daughter —"

"Are being taken care of by Mr. Treadwell. If he needs more assistance, he will inform us. Am I correct, Chambers?" He flicked a glance at his groom.

"Yes, my lord. Mr. Treadwell told me to notify the women so they might be ready to assist the young lady, should she be upset at the event."

"I shall order some hot tea immediately," Venetia said. She sniffed in Gregor's direction. "I do not mind assisting my fellow man." With that, she swept from the room.

"Oh, my," Miss Platt said. "I shall, um, perhaps I should —" She cast a wild glance at her employer.

Mrs. Bloom didn't hesitate. "Go to my room, and fetch my hartshorn. It is in the small vial by the bed."

Miss Platt rushed off to do as she was bid.

Gregor managed to finish his breakfast at his leisure.

Sometime later Venetia returned to the common room just as their new companions entered. The man was older, with a round face that matched his girth. Dressed in quality clothing that lacked fashion, as typified a landed country squire, he introduced himself. "Good day. I am Squire Higganbotham."

Entering the room behind him was a lady wrapped in a wet cloak, the hood over her head. Behind her stood what was plainly a maid, her broad face agleam from the cold, dressed in a serviceable cloak and thick, country boots.

The squire gestured to the hooded lady. "This is m'daughter, Miss Elizabeth Higganbotham."

All present introduced themselves as well.

The squire beamed at them. "Nice to meet you! I must say that it's good to be out of the cold. We were beginning to believe we'd be stuck in that demmed drift forever, weren't we, Elizabeth?"

His daughter nodded and reached up to push the hood from her head.

Ravenscroft gasped, catching the attention of everyone in the room. Amused, Gregor followed Ravenscroft's wide gaze to the squire's daughter.

Mussed golden curls framed a heart-shaped face that was bright pink with cold. Large china blue eyes surrounded by a thick smudge of dark lashes gazed fiercely at them all over a perfectly tiny nose and rosebud lips. Not more than seventeen, she was pretty enough to take London by storm.

She favored them all with a quick, almost desperate glance, then lifted her chin proudly and turned away as if refuting her father's claim. The whole effect was somewhat ruined by the fact that her teeth were chattering uncontrollably.

Venetia noted that everyone was admiring Miss Higganbotham except Gregor. He was looking at the squire, his brows drawn as if puzzling something.

Venetia swept forward to grasp Miss Higganbotham's trembling hands. Even through the fine kid gloves, they were freezing cold. "You poor dear, look how you are shivering!" She drew the girl toward the fire. "Ravenscroft, let the poor child have your seat."

"Ravenscroft?" Miss Platt asked, blinking. "Why do you call Mr. West that?"

"Oh. Well. It's — it's a nickname. When we were children, he, ah, enjoyed making raven noises, so we called him Ravenscroft."

Miss Platt nodded, looking vastly interested.

Ravenscroft seemed frozen by besotted shock, staring at Miss Higganbotham as if entranced.

Smiling to himself, Gregor supposed he could see where Ravenscroft might be captivated. Personally, Gregor liked a woman with a bit more curve to her, not to mention some maturity and intelligence. None of that was evident in Miss Higganbotham's wide-eyed gaze or in her immature and slightly hostile expression.

A young woman like Miss Higganbotham bored Gregor senseless. But for a man like Ravenscroft . . . Gregor's brows went up. Perhaps this would open Venetia's eyes to the sort of man Ravenscroft really was.

The thought held possibilities. His gaze flickered back to the squire, and an odd feeling sifted through him yet again. There was something familiar about the man. Almost as if —

"Lord MacLean!" the squire said, stepping forward eagerly. "I didn't expect to see you here!"

Gregor bowed politely, though inwardly he grimaced. "I'm sorry, but I'm afraid I can't quite place you."

"No, no! We've never met. Saw you in White's, and someone mentioned your name. Don't think we've ever spoken, but I know one of your brothers. The one who wears the French clothes."

"Ah, Dougal. He's become quite the dandy. My other brothers and I can barely countenance him."

The squire chuckled. "I am certain it's just a phase. I spoke to your brother about investing in a property with me." The squire puffed up his chest, sticking his thumbs through the buttonholes of his fine woolen coat. "I'm a bit of a hand at turning a profit. It's a cold day indeed when Ned Higganbotham don't come out on top! I shouldn't mention this, but I turned well more than twenty thousand pounds last year, and that was only on two ventures!"

"Ah," Gregor said smoothly. "That explains why you were speaking with Dougal. He can smell a good investment a hundred miles away."

"He's right sharp, I'll grant you that. My godfather, the Duke of Richmond, says he knows his funds are in a good place when he releases some to me. I've made him a tidy profit in the last decade, I can tell you that."

Mrs. Bloom came forward, her eyes agleam at the mention of a real live duke. "How do you do? I am Mrs. Bloom. I'm on my way to visit my friend, the Countess of Cumberland. Did I hear you say you are a member of White's?"

"Aye. I've been a member since I was seventeen, as was m'father and m'father's father."

Venetia, who was rubbing Miss Higganbotham's icy cold hands between her own, caught sight of Gregor's expression. A frown rested between his eyes, the tight lines down each side of his mouth indicating displeasure about something. Venetia frowned. The squire had said nothing untoward; why would Gregor look so stern? It was almost as if he disapproved of their new company.

She glanced at the squire. He was rather rotund, with a protuberant nose and reddish skin. His features were broad and common, but his eyes shone with good humor, and though he was a bit coarse in his speech and dress, he seemed nice enough. It was a pity Gregor was holding the squire in dislike for nothing more than a rough manner.

Mrs. Treadwell brought in a tray holding a steaming pot of tea and an assortment of cups and saucers. She set it down beside Miss Higganbotham and poured a cup. "Here ye are, miss! This'll warm ye up!"

She placed the cup and saucer in Miss Higganbotham's hands, but the girl was shaking so much that half the tea sloshed into the saucer before her maid leapt forward and rescued it. The girl set the brew back on the table. "She's done frozen through 'n' through. The carriage fell into a drift, and we was tossed into a puddle, the both o' us!" The maid turned to show the back of her cloak completely wet. "Miss Higganbotham's is the same, 'tis just that I'm more used to the cold than she is."

"La!" Mrs. Treadwell took Miss Higganbotham's hands between her own and rubbed them briskly. "We'd best get ye out of those wet clothes before ye take ill!"

Venetia turned to the squire. "Miss Higganbotham may stay with me in my room and —"

Gregor interrupted. "No."

Silence met this.

Venetia's cheeks heated. "Gregor, what do you mean?"

"I'm certain the squire would rather not stay."

Venetia's brows rose, while the squire flushed a deep red. "Now, see here," he began, but Gregor cut him short.

"It will be grossly inconvenient for all involved; there's hardly space for the five of us as it is. I'm certain that Miss Higganbotham merely needs a few moments to compose herself, and you'll be able to leave. I will even see to it that your injured horse is replaced." He met the squire's gaze evenly. "Besides, I daresay you were in a hurry to reach London, or you wouldn't have been traveling in such weather to begin with."

The squire sent his daughter a hard look before saying in an abrupt tone, "That's true; we were in a hurry. I had thought to reach my brother's house before nightfall, but the roads are far worse than I'd imagined."

"It's daylight still. You should be able to reach Eddington in less than an hour. There is a lovely inn there." Gregor turned to Mr. Treadwell. "Isn't there?"

Mr. Treadwell blinked. "Aye, but 'tis four miles, and the roads —"

"I am certain they're passable," Gregor said curtly. "With the snow melting —"

Miss Higganbotham sneezed.

The squire's expression darkened.

Venetia took the poor young lady's hand and pulled her to her feet. "Enough of this. I won't hear another word about anyone going back out in that weather. The snow may be melting, but it's still piled high, and travel would be dangerous."

"Aye, and making a muck where it has already melted," the squire said briskly. "There's drifts as high as my head and muddy spots as could swallow a carriage.

"There you go, m'dear," the squire told his daughter bluffly as Venetia led her from the room. "Thank you, Miss — ah? I'm afraid I didn't catch your name."

Venetia had started to reply when something about Gregor made her shoot him a look. He returned her regard grimly, his eyes shimmering with anger. The look took her aback, and she had to compose herself before she replied. "I am Miss West, and this" — she gestured to Ravenscroft, who'd leapt up to hold the door — "is my brother, Mr. West."

"Nice to know you," the squire said, bowing briefly. "Thank you for taking care of my daughter. Elizabeth, you go with the nice lady, and none of your shenanigans, do you hear?"

Miss Higganbotham sent her parent a glare from her fine blue eyes and chattered out, "I w-w-will st-st-stay here, but only until I f-f-feel better. Then I w-w-will leave!"

The squire's bushy brows lowered. "Stop being dramatic. Now, off to bed with you, and not another word!"

Miss Higganbotham lifted her chin, which still quivered piteously. "D-d-do as you wish, Father. M-m-my happiness has already been d-d-destroyed."

Venetia raised her brows. "Heavens! I wouldn't say that. The inn's nice and warm, and your tremors are already receding."

"It's not the cold, it's my circumstances," the young woman said. "I am n-n-not here willingly; I am b-b-being abducted!"

Miss Platt's mouth dropped open.

Mrs. Bloom uttered, "Well! I never!"

Ravenscroft's fists clenched as if he yearned to fight whoever had perpetrated the evil deed.

Gregor glanced at Venetia to see if she'd witnessed her paramour's reaction but found her slipping a sympathetic arm around the girl. "Oh, my dear! Who abducted you?"

"H-h-he has!" Miss Higganbotham proclaimed, pointing a trembling finger at the squire.

Venetia's brows rose. "Your own father?"

"Yes. I told him I will not g-g-go to London, e-e-even if I have to kill myself!"

CHAPTER 8

I dinna think 'tis romantic when a man says he's willin' t' give his life fer the woman he loves. Give me instead a man who'd fight to keep us both alive and kickin'! There's naught romantic about a dead man, beau or no.

Old Woman Nora from Loch Lomond
to her three wee granddaughters
one cold evening

Venetia made the squire's daughter comfortable in her room, helping the poor girl to bed while her maid hovered nearby and Miss Platt clucked her concern.

"There, there," Miss Platt said, holding Miss Higganbotham's hand. "You'll be warmed soon."

"I hope so!" the girl said. "Though it w-would serve my father right if I d-d-died!"

"What a horrid thing to say!" Venetia said

cheerfully, hanging Miss Higganbotham's cloak over the chair to dry.

"Yes," Miss Platt agreed. "Mrs. Bloom always says one should look for the positive."

Venetia turned a look toward Miss Platt. The homily didn't sound like the Mrs. Bloom they all knew and avoided.

"What p-positive?" Miss Higganbotham asked, her lips quivering.

The door opened then, and Mrs. Treadwell entered.

"Look!" Miss Platt said, smiling. "Mrs. Treadwell has brought an extra blanket and a warmed brick. That's two things to be thankful for!"

Mrs. Treadwell set the brick on the windowsill with the tongs nearby. "The brick's too hot for now, but the blanket can be used right away."

Venetia took the blanket and spread it over Miss Higganbotham. "There. While you're warming, you can tell us all about your travails."

Miss Higganbotham needed no more invitation to pour out her troubles. She explained how her father had wished her to go to London and be "sold upon the marriage mart" to bring a title into the family. She had originally agreed, for who wouldn't wish to go to London for a season or two? But then she had met Henry, the son of the vicar. It was love at first sight, and a secret courtship had begun. Elizabeth knew her father had his sights set higher than Henry. She'd pressed her beau to elope, but Henry refused. He believed he could win the squire over if he talked to the old man and explained things.

Elizabeth refused to agree to this, fearful that her father would whisk her away where Henry would never find her. Before she and Henry could find a solution to their dilemma, the squire had happened upon one of the servants delivering a secret missive from the insistent Henry. The squire had exploded in fury and done exactly as Elizabeth had feared. Despite the raging snowstorm, he had packed up his daughter and headed for London, far away from Henry.

"Miss West," Miss Higganbotham said, reaching for Venetia's hand, "Father has indeed abducted me. He says I am to go to London, but I would rather die!"

"Aye," said Miss Higganbotham's maid, who hadn't stopped smiling once. "Miss Elizabeth is determined, she is. She'll not marry other than her Henry."

"How old are you, Miss Higganbotham?" Venetia asked.

Miss Higganbotham wiped her tears. "Sixteen."

That explained a good deal. Venetia helped Mrs. Treadwell place the wrapped brick under the covers near the girl's feet, then tucked the blanket back in place. "It sounds as if you have had a difficult time of it. For now, let's get you warmed up, and then, after you've rested, we'll see what's to be done."

"Yes," Miss Platt said, patting Miss Higganbotham's hand. "Miss West is a godsend. If anyone can help you, she can."

Venetia wasn't sure whether she should be flattered or worried by such unalloyed praise.

Mrs. Treadwell nodded. "Put your feet against that warm brick, my dear. I wrapped it in cloth so it won't burn, but oh, how toasty it will be!"

Miss Higganbotham's chattering stopped almost immediately. She sighed, snuggling beneath the covers, her eyes sliding shut. "Oh, how nice!" She forced her eyes open to smile at Venetia. "Thank you for making Father stay here, Miss West. I could not have gone another foot. Tomorrow, perhaps, you can find a way to assist my poor Henry and me." With that, her eyes slid shut, and she was asleep in a trice.

"I thought as much," Mrs. Treadwell said, picking up the tongs she'd used to carry the hot brick. " 'Tis nerves, is all."

The maid nodded brightly. "She has plenty of those, she do!"

"So we see," Mrs. Treadwell replied. "She'll be better for a nap. Do ye need anything, Miss West?"

"No, indeed. As usual, you have taken care of everything."

The innkeeper's wife beamed. "Oh, 'twas nothing. I may warm another brick and take it up to Elsie's room. She's had a bit of a headache, ye know, and asked to lie down a bit. Could be the very thing to set her to rights."

"I am certain it will," Venetia said.

"Let me know if ye need anything else." With a brisk nod, Mrs. Treadwell left, softly closing the door behind her.

Miss Platt hung the girl's wet clothes over the back of the chair. "I hope those will dry before she wakes."

"From the look of that thick wool and the amount of trim on her cloak, I don't believe Miss Higganbotham suffers from a lack of wardrobe," Venetia replied.

The maid nodded. "Oh, la! She has *four* trunks full, as the squire got her the best of everything. 'Tis why young Henry refused

171

to run off with Miss Higganbotham. He said she was used to having nice things, and he'd be hanged if she'd ever go without because of him."

Venetia thought young Henry sounded like quite a gentleman. "Would you mind finding Miss Higganbotham's trunks and fetching some dry clothing?"

The maid bobbed a curtsey and went to the door, saying over her shoulder as she left, "I'll bring up enough for the week. With this weather, she might need it."

A week! Venetia hoped not.

Miss Platt ran a hand over Miss Higganbotham's fine cloak. "It's a beautiful cloak, isn't it?"

Venetia nodded. "The squire appears to have done well in life. Unfortunately, he seems overly aware of that fact."

"He was a bit full of himself, wasn't he?"

"Very. I daresay that is why he decided that his daughter was marrying to disoblige him. I almost feel sorry for the man she has fixed upon."

"I daresay her beau is a fine gentleman in spite of what the squire thinks," Miss Pratt said, her chin jutting out. "I don't usually take people into dislike, but he was so pompous! It quite makes me feel for poor Miss Higganbotham."

172

Venetia thought so, too. The poor child, dragged away from the man she loved, only to be subjected to a terrifying accident and left bruised and freezing cold. Worse, when she and her father had finally found shelter, Gregor had received them with all the warmth of the snow bank that had caused the accident.

She scowled. She could not believe Gregor would be so uncharitable.

"Miss West?"

Venetia turned to find Miss Platt standing beside her. "Yes?"

The thin woman clasped her hands, a glowing look in her eyes. "I *must* thank you!"

"Whatever for?"

"For suggesting that perhaps there were other avenues open to me. After poor Bertrand's situation, I had given up hope. But today, at breakfast, Mr. West —" Miss Platt broke off, a round spot of color on each cheek. "I never would have noticed him except for what you said to me before breakfast. I want to thank you for helping me see that there is more to life than fetching things for Mrs. Bloom."

Venetia hugged her. "I am just glad to see you smile."

"Thank you. I wish I could stay and help here, but I need to attend Mrs. Bloom, as there's a bit of sewing to be done this morning."

Venetia wondered how many stitches Miss Platt would have to make before Mrs. Bloom considered their debt canceled.

Miss Platt patted Venetia's shoulder, then left, her head held high, a smile in her eyes.

Miss Higganbotham stirred at the sound of the door closing, turning to one side. As she did so, her mouth opened, and she emitted a huge snore. Venetia held her breath and waited, but the snoring did not abate.

She grimaced. Though the girl looked angelic with her golden curls and long lashes, she snored like an old bull — which didn't augur well for peaceful sleep tonight.

Imagining Gregor's expression if he heard the delicate Miss Higganbotham's snores, Venetia had to grin. Gregor had the same appreciation for the ridiculous as she did; it was one of the many things they shared.

It was good to remember that, she thought. Lately, she and Gregor had been at such loggerheads.

She sighed a bit at the thought. A deep restlessness stirred her, and she realized that she hadn't been outside all day. No wonder she was feeling out of sorts.

Glancing at the snoring girl in her bed, Venetia changed from her slippers to her half-boots, collected her pelisse, and left, closing the door softly behind her.

Downstairs, she heard the squire and Ravenscroft speaking in the common room. She felt sorry that Ravenscroft was forced to listen to the squire's pedantry, but not enough to become a victim herself. She buttoned her pelisse to her throat, pulling the collar up about her ears, then stepped outside.

The snow sparkled fresh and clean, and the air was still frosty, though not as cold as the day they'd arrived. She lifted her skirts to clear the top of the snow and made her way to the stables on the snow-packed path, smiling in the crisp air.

The stables were housed in a large barn that held ten stalls and a decent tack room in the back, all heated with a surprisingly efficient woodstove that was tucked safely away from the stores of hay. Gregor's man, Chambers, was there, as was Mr. Treadwell's groom. Venetia visited each animal, Chambers narrating its ills and treatments. He'd already cleaned most of the injuries and applied an effective poultice to those in need.

After making certain the grooms had the supplies they needed to continue their work, she stepped back outside. Smiling a little, she lifted her face to the bright sunlight and closed her eyes, letting the quiet fill her with peace.

"Don't stand there."

Her peace fled. She opened her eyes and found Gregor standing before her. He was dressed in his multicaped coat, a red muffler around his neck, his hat casting a shadow over his eyes.

"Why shouldn't I stand here?"

He took her hand and pulled her forward, his lips curved into a smile. "Look down."

In a line under the deep eaves around the stables was a graveyard of icicles, each one stabbed deep into the snow, a line of wetness connecting them. "Oh."

"They've been falling off all morning." He glanced up. "There aren't many left, but I wouldn't stand beneath the overhang for long."

"I shall pay more attention," she said lightly, noting how the bright sun made his green eyes lighter. He truly had beautiful eyes, with long lashes that hid his expression even as they emphasized it.

Just before he'd kissed her last night, his eyes had darkened in color. A shiver traced through her, and suddenly, every moment of the kiss flashed through her mind, including the way her body had heated and —

Goodness! What was wrong with her? She curled her gloved fingers into the palms of her hands to force the thoughts away.

A puzzled look crossed Gregor's face. "What is it?"

She shook her head. "I was merely thinking about the dangerous icicles and glad you were here to warn me."

He half smiled. "I have come to the belated conclusion that the only danger you need to be warned about is yourself." He glanced past her to the stables. "How are the horses?"

"Better than I had hoped. Your man, Chambers, is excellent."

"He ought to be, for what I pay him."

"Oh? How much do you pay him?"

Gregor raised his brows. "Thinking of stealing him?"

"Perhaps," she said mischievously. It was an old joke of theirs, to be forever threatening to steal each other's servants. Venetia had never managed to lure any of Gregor's capable grooms or footmen away, but she'd tried, more to tease him than anything else.

His gaze lingered on her lips. "I am glad to see you're getting back to normal."

"I was never gone," she retorted sharply.

Something flickered behind his gaze, and he turned to glance at the barn. "I didn't think you'd be able to stay away from the horses for long."

"I yearn to ride," she said wistfully. The snow-covered woods around the inn seemed to beckon.

"Why don't we?"

She sighed. "I didn't pack my habit. I thought Mother was ill, and I didn't expect to have time to ride."

Gregor reached for her arm, tucking it into the crook of his. "Come, Venetia. Walk with me a bit. You weren't made to be locked inside for days on end."

She had to admit that it was beautiful outside. Plus her fur-lined pelisse and boots were keeping her snugly warm. "Very well, but not for long. Miss Higganbotham is likely to awaken in an hour or so." Venetia planned on having a talk with the young woman to discover what she could about that Henry fellow.

Gregor led her around the stables to a winding trail path that disappeared into the woods. "This goes to the river and then back to the main road. It's a picturesque path."

"You've already been here?"

"I took one of the horses out this morning to see how the roads look." Gregor stopped walking, his expression suddenly serious. "Venetia, you do realize what the arrival of the squire and his daughter means for us?"

"I shall definitely get less sleep. Miss Higganbotham snores even worse than Ravenscroft."

He choked back a laugh. "That little thing snores?"

"Terribly. Whoever marries her is in for a horrid surprise."

"I daresay." Gregor pushed a branch out of the way and stepped back, allowing Venetia to precede him. "Walk carefully," he ordered. "Some places are slick."

Venetia wondered if Gregor had always been so peremptory in his manner and she simply had not noticed, or if it was something new. It was entirely possible that he'd always been so and she'd ignored it. Perhaps it was time she paid more attention.

When a large drift of snow fell from a tree and landed on the path before them, Gregor took her elbow and helped her step over the mound. "If it continues to warm like this, we may be able to leave soon."

"Providing, of course, that you don't lose your temper again."

He gave her a mock scowl. "If you would stop crossing me, I wouldn't lose anything, much less my temper."

"I haven't crossed you."

"Oh? What about an hour ago?" At her blank look, he added, "In the common room, with the squire."

"Oh, that. You made me quite angry."

"*I* made *you* angry?" Gregor appeared astonished.

The trees overhead drooped heavily, the snow outlining each limb. "You were so ungracious. I could hardly turn that poor girl away; she was almost frozen to death!"

He sighed. "I was trying to protect you. Squire Higganbotham is the godson of the Duke of Richmond."

"I met the duchess once. She struck me as a horrid scandalmonger."

"The worst, and the squire is not the sort of man to understand the word *discretion*. I spoke with him this morning, and he plans on going straight to London. It is entirely possible you will meet him at some future function."

Venetia moaned. "Where he will discover that I am not Miss West and that Ravenscroft is not my brother."

Gregor's expression was grim.

Her heart sank. "There will be no explaining it away."

"No," Gregor said shortly. "Now you see why I attempted to turn them away. I thought if they only saw you a moment, we could dismiss any future recognition."

He was right. She fiddled with a button on the front of her pelisse, knowing she should say something apologetic but unable to find the words.

"I was not being coldhearted."

She kept her head down. "I didn't say that."

"You thought it. I saw it in your eyes."

She peeked up at him. She *had* thought it. And loudly, from the dour expression on Gregor's face. Blast it, what had happened to their comfortable friendship? They had been at loggerheads since his arrival and she wasn't certain why.

Of course, he was mainly at fault; he'd been quite rude in his treatment of Ravenscroft, which had sparked her protective nature. She rather glumly wished she hadn't reacted quite so strongly and championed Ravenscroft; she was sure that had galled Gregor. But really, what else could she do when he'd practically called her a fool and worse?

She sighed. "Gregor, I don't know what's happened to us since we arrived here, but we seem out of step in some way."

His expression softened. "Perhaps we are just experiencing each other under different

181

circumstances."

"What do you mean?"

"In the past, we've used each other's company to alleviate our boredom with life. Now, we must accomplish something together — namely, saving your reputation. That is very different from enjoying a simple canter in the park."

"That doesn't explain why you suddenly believe I've lost my common sense."

He gave her a lopsided smile. "I don't think you've lost *all* of your common sense, just a portion of it."

She couldn't smile back. Something else had changed, too. It had changed with the kiss neither of them was willing to mention aloud. They'd been friends since childhood; she'd seen him fall from his horse and knock loose a tooth when he was nine, and he'd seen her covered in mud at age seven after she'd climbed out of a window in a disastrous attempt to avoid a dreaded dancing lesson. These events and hundreds of others had given them a protection from any sort of romantic involvement.

Venetia grimaced to think of her parents' noisy, emotional relationship. She would never make a fool of herself over something as silly as "grand passion," if it even existed — especially not with Gregor.

She'd seen how he reacted to the heartsick women in London who'd succumbed to his devastating smile and brilliant green eyes, and she was not about to see him wince whenever she was present. She'd protected her heart by keeping a litany of his faults foremost in her mind and by chastising herself if her imagination should wander. But now, with one kiss, her layer of protection seemed to be tearing as easily as a gauze curtain.

She straightened her shoulders, pushing away her unease. This was nothing. When they returned to London, things would return to normal and they could go back to their lovely, easy relationship. All she had to do was keep this tension between them at bay until they were in better circumstances. She glanced at him through her lashes.

Unfortunately, she was still excruciatingly aware of him, and couldn't help but notice the way his cravat was simply knotted to fill the opening at his neck, his strong throat rising from there. Despite her best intentions, she found herself imagining what it would be like to trace the line of his throat with her fingertips or, even better, her lips.

The thought sent a cascade of shivers through her.

"Venetia?" His voice was warm, concerned. He leaned closer, his gaze dark as he captured one of her hands in his. "Are you cold? Perhaps we should go inside —"

"No, no! I am fine. I was just thinking about this mess." Venetia looked down at his gloved hand, which was large and well shaped. She had placed numerous cups of tea in his hands and had grasped them getting in and out of carriages without ever noticing them.

Yet suddenly they seemed so . . . virile. So seductive. The heat of his skin through the gloves tugged at her, and her blood leapt at the feel of that hand clasped between her own. Would their kiss feel as powerful now, when she wasn't so tired, so drained? Surely, her powerful reaction last night was merely due to —

"Venetia?"

His voice seemed richer, deeper than she'd ever heard it; the soft timbre made her skin prickle in the most annoying way. She looked into his eyes. She had to think of something to say to break the spell, to stop herself from leaning toward him, from seeking yet another kiss like the one she'd had before, wondering if it would taste as good, if her body would leap in response the same way.

Her hands were shaking, her knees weak,

all from wondering about that embrace. Goodness, she *couldn't* keep thinking like this! Yet it was a lost cause. She *wanted* him to kiss her again, she *wanted* to taste him, to have him touch her, mold her to him, take her —

His gaze darkened. "Damn it, don't look at me like that."

She tried to swallow. "What do you mean?" But she knew exactly what he meant; she could hide neither her excitement nor her curiosity.

His brows snapped down, and an almost savage look crossed his face. "Don't, Venetia. I am not used to resisting temptation, much less from you."

Heart pounding, Venetia ripped her gaze from his and stared down at the tips of her boots. It was madness to tempt him, to tempt this feeling, whatever it was. She'd stand there until her heart ceased pounding against her throat and her body stopped feeling as if she stood before a blazing fire.

A small voice whispered, But what if she *did* look up at him? What if she threw her arms around him and kissed him the way they'd kissed last night? What if it not only felt as good but even *better?*

Venetia fisted her hands, fighting the urge to look up and step forward . . . right into his arms. But that would be reckless and imprudent. Her relationship with Gregor was worth more than a mere kiss. She was in charge of herself and her feelings, and she would be utterly foolish to put their friendship at risk.

But somehow, in thinking about why she shouldn't look at Gregor, Venetia did just that.

The second their eyes met, Gregor made a sound that was a cross between a laugh and a groan and swept her into his arms, pulling her hard against his chest. Instantly, warmth enveloped her. "I warned you," he murmured against her ear, his breath hot and shivery. "Now, my love, you'll pay the price."

CHAPTER 9

Ah, me wee lassies, there's only a very few who will tell ye how things really are. Cherish those as tell ye the truth, whether or not ye wish t' hear it.
Old Woman Nora from Loch Lomond
to her three wee granddaughters
one cold evening

Her pulse thundering, Venetia stopped thinking and gave herself up to the kiss.

Passion roared through her, exhilarating her like the wild dawn rides through the park she and Gregor loved. The feel of his hot mouth over hers and the pressure of his strong hands as they molded her to him spurred her to want more. Her desire flamed higher, grew wilder.

She moaned against his mouth, her body on fire. She pressed against him, restless and hot, her tongue teasing his.

She savored the way he was holding her,

his hands cupping her intimately, lifting her from her feet as he held her against him. Her hands slid down his back, over his hips, grasping him and —

Gregor set her on her feet, grasped her wrists, and pushed her away.

They stood panting heavily, their breaths puffing in the cold air as they regarded each other with a mixture of amazement and uncertainty.

Gregor shook his head. "We are mad, the two of us."

Venetia's cheeks flushed; her heart thundered in her ears. *Mad* didn't begin to describe it. What had she been thinking? This was *Gregor,* for heaven's sake! She knew the cost of such wanton behavior with him, knew the ultimate outcome.

Embarrassed, she tried to free her wrists, but Gregor held her tight.

"Be still," he admonished, his gaze burning into hers.

She wished with all her heart that she could run away or take back the last few moments and make them disappear.

But that was impossibile. What had happened between them would be there forever.

"Gregor," she whispered, "what are we going to do?"

The question hung between them.

Gregor couldn't look away from Venetia any more than he could release her. She stood before him, fully covered from neck to toe, her hair mussed and barely held in a loose bun, a straw from the stables sticking out of the back. Her nose was shiny and sprinkled with freckles, her lips swollen from his kiss, their plush slopes glistening with moisture.

He was fascinated with everything about her. It was all both endearingly familiar, exquisitely new, and completely wrong. He slowly released her wrists, sliding his hands to hers and lacing their fingers. He didn't wish to release her yet.

Her lashes trembled against her cheeks before she looked up at him, her cheeks becomingly flushed. She was amazingly sensual, something he'd somehow missed all these years.

More than anything in the world, Gregor wanted to take her right there — push her to the ground, lift her skirts, and answer the passion he'd felt in her embrace, seen in her eyes. But he couldn't. This was no ordinary woman but Venetia. He could never do something that might hurt her, even a little. Though he knew without question she would enjoy their lovemaking, afterward . . . He frowned. Therein lay the problem.

A woman like Venetia deserved more than his usual "afterward." He wasn't a philanderer, but he'd had a healthy number of relationships, most of which ended amicably within a few months, as all good relationships should. All began with passion — though looking at Venetia now, at her pink nose and sparkling eyes, he had to admit that none of those relationships had offered the promise of this one. There was something about her now, here at this inn, in the snow, that fired his senses and stirred his imagination. He yearned to pursue it, to pursue her, but . . .

He shook his head, slowly releasing her hands.

Venetia turned away, her gloved fingertips resting on her lips a moment before she dropped her hand with a self-conscious blush.

"Don't," he said gruffly, wishing he could ease the awkwardness of the moment.

"I'm sorry, Gregor. This —" She gestured lamely at the space between them. "It never should have happened."

"No, it shouldn't have, but it did." He met her gaze. "And I can't say that I'm sorry for it."

She managed a creditable smile. "I don't suppose I am, either. But it would be stupid to allow it to continue."

She was right, though that didn't make it any easier. Bloody hell, how had things gotten so out of hand? He *never* lost control.

He caught Venetia's eyes, a question lurking in their gray depths, and he heard himself say in a harsh voice, "You're right. It won't happen again. Ever. We must keep our relationship as friends and nothing more."

Something flickered in her eyes. Disappointment? That was certainly what he felt, as heavily as if a stone had been placed on his chest.

Suddenly, it all seemed unfair. It was unfair that Ravenscroft had caused such disruption in their lives, unfair that they'd gotten stuck there by Gregor's own damnable temper, and damned unfair that others had been snowbound with them and were cutting up their peace. Every irritation he'd had to deal with since discovering Venetia's disappearance grew into a huge mass of palpable fury. "We must return to London as quickly as possible."

"Yes. Of course. Will we be able to leave today?"

"No. But if the weather keeps on warming, we might make it tomorrow." He sent her a level look, then added, "Venetia, when we return, things may be different for you."

"I know," she said evenly. "I know Papa was worried about me, and since he wears his emotions on his sleeve, he may well have said something to the wrong people."

"I asked Dougal to make certain he didn't say anything, but —" He shrugged. "That may not matter once Higganbotham arrives in town, for he will certainly recognize you. Unlike Mrs. Bloom's, the squire's eyesight is excellent." He raked a hand through his hair. "Venetia, you must limit your time with the other guests until we can leave. The less you speak to them, the better." He smiled grimly. "You have a tendency to make yourself memorable."

She eyed him incredulously. "I can't promise that."

"You must. Your reputation is at stake."

"Balderdash," she snapped, her eyes flashing. "It's too late now; the squire will recognize me already. Besides, there are things that I must do in order to —" She caught Gregor's gaze and closed her mouth.

"In order to do what?"

Venetia shrugged, her chin tilted to a challenging level.

"Venetia, you must stop meddling in the lives of others. Leave Ravenscroft alone and cease encouraging him to make a cake of himself with Miss Platt."

"He is helping to give her confidence."

"He is making a fool of himself, and nothing more. Just as he did when he abducted you, spouting all that nonsense about wanting to run away and live in a cottage. Ridiculous."

She tilted her head to one side and regarded him somberly, her gaze narrowed as if judging his every word. "Gregor, have you *ever* been in love?"

"No, I've never been that foolish."

"Perhaps that's what's wrong with you, then," she said with asperity. "You've been so undisturbed by pesky emotion that you have no sympathy for those around you who are."

Gregor's mouth tightened. "If I have too little emotion, then you, my dear, have too much."

"There's no such thing."

Her words raked across him like the screech of a rusty nail. Fanned by her obstinacy and his own frustrated lust, his irritation burst into full-fledged anger. "Let's stop this right here, shall we? I know you're scheming something with Ravenscroft and Miss Platt, and I will not stand for it."

"Gregor, our relationship is one of friendship. Therefore, you have no claim over me or my actions."

He scowled. "Because of the difficult situation we are in, I have a claim whether you like it or not."

Her mouth tightened and she plopped her fists on her hips. "I don't like your tone of voice."

"You don't have to like it," he said baldly. "Your right to like things ended when you were so foolish as to climb into that carriage with Ravenscroft."

Her chin tilted up. "I thought the note he'd written was from my father and — oh, blast, I've explained all of this to you already!"

"And it's still not sufficient," he retorted, his temper and lust both bubbling to the surface. "I used to think you a woman of good sense, but since yesterday, I have decided that what you really need is a keeper."

"*Oh!* How can you say that? I've done nothing but attempt to help, first with Mama, and then with Miss Platt —" She met his gaze boldly. "Never mind. I don't have to explain myself to you. You, Gregor, are the most demanding, arrogant, selfish person I've ever known."

Gregor's eyes seemed unusually bright. "At least I am not a meddlesome brat who tries to run the lives of those around me, and thinks my opinion more important than that of those directly involved. You, my dear, have a certain amount of conceit when you think you know everything."

"Do not say another word," she said through clenched teeth.

"I can and will. If you wish to return to London with your reputation intact, you will not get involved with Miss Platt and her perceived problems."

Too furious to answer, Venetia rammed her fists into the pockets of her pelisse, shivering as a cold breeze stirred the branches overhead and knocked snow to the ground around them with soft plops.

Gregor raked a hand through his hair, eyeing her furiously. "This entire situation has been nothing but a bother and a mess since the beginning. *This* is what happens when you try to help someone; everything goes awry."

The bitterness in Gregor's voice hurt Venetia. Did he mean she was a bother and a mess, too?

Gregor eyed her in a way that answered her question all too well. "If you wish to return home and enjoy your life as it was, then you'll do as I say. *No more meddling.*"

She stiffened. "I am not one of your

servants, so you can stop barking orders at me right now."

"No, you are not one of my servants; they are far more cooperative."

"And neither am I one of your — your — *ladybirds*" — the word dripped distastefully from her lips — "who are always panting after you, willing to do anything to garner your favor. I don't care what you think about my 'schemes,' as you put it. I am a grown woman and know what I'm about, so keep your opinions and your overbearing attitude in your own pocket."

Gregor's lips thinned.

A ripple of thunder rolled in the distance.

Venetia frowned up at the sky, realizing with chagrin that as they'd talked, clouds had moved in and had almost obscured the sun. "Blast it, Gregor! Keep your temper. I'd like to leave this inn sometime before next year."

His mouth whitened, and thunder cracked overhead, a brilliant fork of white fire crossing the sky.

She jumped at the sound, her hand pressed to her heart. "Stop that!"

"You know I can't control it after it comes. That's why it's called a curse," he snapped.

"You had better *find* a way to control it." She eyed the sky overhead, pulling her pelisse closer to ward off the suddenly cold air. "Perhaps if you stop now, it will not collect as before."

"I can keep my temper just fine, providing *you* don't try it. I want your promise to stay out of the other guests' business."

She turned, presenting him a profile of her raised chin. "I have no obligations to you. If I think something needs to be done, I will do it, will you, nil you."

Thunder cracked overhead, shaking the ground, the sky darker still. Small snowflakes began to sift down.

Venetia pointed to the sky. "Look what you've done now! We'll never leave."

Gregor leaned down, his nose level with hers. "I came a damned long way in this miserable snow just to save your precious hide. The least you can do is stay out of trouble."

Her skin flushed a delicate pink, her lips quivering slightly, her bottom lip glistening. Painful awareness tore through him, igniting something hotter than anger, something deep in his veins.

He wanted to reach out and yank her back into his arms, to press her lush curves against his chest and kiss her until she couldn't breathe.

He tightened his jaw, fighting off the

tantalizing image. Women like Venetia did not flirt. They loved, and they married. That was it. There was nothing in the middle for her — nothing for a man like him.

Gregor thrust his hands into the deep pockets of his overcoat. "We had better return to the inn before anyone notices we are missing." He gestured toward the path, but she didn't move, merely stared at him with blazing eyes.

"Fine, then." He turned on his heel, saying over his shoulder, "Be careful when you return; it is slippery in spots."

With that calm, impersonal good-bye, Gregor left. He walked down the path, his boots crunching in the snow, lifting his face to the cooling fall of new flakes. God only knew how much snow they'd get this time. Damn it all, how Venetia got under his skin!

What was it about her here, away from London, that made him notice things he'd never noticed before? Whatever it was, he hoped it would go away soon. Being so close to Venetia, stuck at that small inn with so many people around, was torture. Something odd was happening between them. Something unforeseen and growing in power. What could it —

The sound of crunching snow made him stop and turn. Venetia was approaching, her dark hair dusted with snow, her posture stiff, as if she were weighing her words. Perhaps she'd come to apologize.

She marched past him to the beginning of the trail, where she stopped and waited for him to catch up, hands behind her back.

Ah. She wished to speak to him with the inn in plain sight. Considering their propensity to fall into each other's arms when alone, that was a wise decision.

He strode toward her, glancing down to avoid a slick rock. Thank goodness she'd come to her senses. She'd apologize for her recalcitrant behavior and cease her machinations concerning Miss Platt and Ravenscroft. He'd accept her apology, of course, so they could go back to their easy relationship and —

Thwack! A snowball hit Gregor on the side of his head. He stood there, unable to believe what had happened. The icy mass took the opportunity to slide into his collar, freezing his skin as it went.

He roared and raced forward, icy tree roots be damned, but it was too late. Venetia was gone in a swirl of hiked skirts and fleet booted feet. Before he even reached the yard, the inn door slammed closed.

Gregor stood stock-still, the cold wind blowing through his clothing, his collar wet and cold, the heavy rumble of snow thunder echoing through the wind's moan.

Damn Venetia Oglivie! Damn her impetuous, intractable nature, and most of all, damn her for looking so damnably *touchable!*

Gregor turned his face to the sky and cursed loud and long, the snow pelting down.

CHAPTER 10

There's only one thing worse than losin' a beau, and that's ne'er havin' one t' begin with.

Old Woman Nora from Loch Lomond
to her three wee granddaughters
one cold evening

"Don't you agree, Miss West?" Miss Platt asked loudly.

Venetia blinked, realizing she hadn't been paying attention — again. "Um. Yes. Of course, I agree."

Miss Platt cocked her head to one side, a considering gaze in her light blue eyes. "Is something wrong?"

Venetia's face heated. "Oh, no. I was just . . . thinking." About Gregor. Ever since yesterday morning, when he'd kissed her again — or, rather, she'd kissed him — she'd been unable to do anything *but* think about him.

It had been bad enough during the day as the inn had seemed too small for them both, but last night, she hadn't slept a wink. Miss Higganbotham's snoring hadn't been as much of a problem as the hot thoughts that filled Venetia's mind — memories of the kiss and imaginings of far more intimate contact.

And when she managed to sleep, her unruly mind roamed even more freely. In her dreams, she desired him passionately and insatiably, every touch igniting the desire for another.

Since that kiss, Venetia had avoided being alone with Gregor, which hadn't been difficult thanks to Miss Platt and Miss Higganbotham. They had attached themselves to her so thoroughly that she scarcely had a moment alone. Ravenscroft had continued his attentions to Miss Platt, which had caused Gregor to glower and eventually order the younger man to visit the horses with him after dinner. Ravenscroft hadn't realized he was being manipulated and had eagerly agreed. Gregor had sent Venetia a triumphant smirk as he led Ravenscroft off.

Venetia sniffed. He was being unbearable lately, ordering everyone around as if they were his lackeys. She wasn't the least bit sorry about yesterday; Gregor had *deserved* to be smacked in the head with a fat snowball even if it had made the snow fall for another two hours.

"This weather is horrid," Miss Platt said. "We've had another foot of snow since yesterday."

Which was all Gregor's fault, blast him. He might wish to blame her, but *he* was the one who'd been so arrogant and high-handed.

Miss Platt retrieved her sewing from a basket she'd brought into the room with her. "The weather is so very odd for April, and the way it trapped us all here — I wonder if it wasn't meant to be."

"Do you believe in fate?"

"I am beginning to," Miss Platt said in an earnest tone as she deftly threaded a needle. "I wonder if I was brought to this place at the same time as Mr. West because —" She colored. "Oh, dear, I shouldn't have said anything to you, since Mr. West is your brother, but I was just thinking — oh, never mind!"

Venetia blinked.

Surely Miss Platt wasn't developing real feelings for Ravenscroft in such a short period of time? It had been only two days, and Ravenscroft didn't possess the sort of address that could sweep a woman off her feet. Of course, Miss Platt wasn't an ordinary woman, but still.

"I know what you're thinking," Miss Platt said, stabbing her needle into the cloth. "We haven't known each other very long."

"Well, yes, and —"

"But I knew as soon as I met Mr. West that this was true love."

Venetia lifted her brows. "But . . . at first, you were attracted to Lord MacLean."

"Was I?" Miss Platt made a small line of neat stitches. "I don't remember."

"Miss Platt, I hate to be a naysayer, but Ra— I mean, Mr. West is still quite young and a notoriously unstable character. He simply is not yet capable of the level of emotion necessary for a prolonged relationship." Which was the sad truth. "After he's matured, it is possible he might be able to love someone, but not now."

Miss Platt laughed. "Oh, Miss Venetia! Spoken like a true sister. I suppose it's difficult for you to see your brother in a manly light. I am the same with poor Bertrand. But trust me on this, Mr. West is fully capable of deep emotions." She dropped her sewing in her lap, clasped her hands to her heart, and sighed. "I have seen his soul in his eyes."

Venetia rubbed her temple, where an ache was beginning to form. This would never do; she'd have to speak with Ravenscroft as soon as possible. What would he say to the idea that Miss Platt might be growing fond of him? It was probably best not to think too much about that now. Yet somewhere in the back of her mind, she could hear Gregor's deep voice warning her of the dangers of getting involved in other people's lives. She resolutely squelched the voice. She'd rather be trussed up in a sack and tossed into the Thames in the dead of winter than become as hard-hearted and unfeeling as Gregor.

"Miss West." Miss Platt's soft voice brought Venetia back to her surroundings. "A woman as lovely as you must have had plenty of beaus."

"I wouldn't say plenty." She could count them on only one hand, since most of the men she met seemed lacking in some way, as if they didn't measure up to some invisible standard.

Miss Platt shook her head. "I daresay you've had *hundreds* of admirers. Perhaps even *thousands*."

Venetia had to laugh. "I have had a few, but I fear I am far from the type of woman the ton admires." She looked down at her plump form. "Try as I might, I cannot give up pastries. I am not willowy enough for current fashion."

"I must disagree," Miss Platt said devoutly.

"That is very kind of you, but I am not complaining. If I were unhealthy or could not be active, I would be tempted to change. As it is, this is who and what I am and how I seem to be the happiest."

Miss Platt looked at Venetia dubiously, then down at her own body. "I wish I had some of your curves. No one ever notices me, because I'm so flat in the chest."

"A fact easily hidden by the right gown," Venetia said. "In fact —"

The door opened, and Miss Higganbotham stood in the doorway, her golden locks held on top of her head by sapphire pins, her morning gown adorned with French lace.

She paused dramatically, shading her eyes as if the light was too strong.

Venetia had the distinct urge to roll her eyes, aware that her mother would have applauded such an entrance.

But Miss Platt cried, "Miss Higganbotham! Whatever is wrong? Have you something in your eye?"

The younger girl dropped her arm and looked around the room. "Oh. It's just you two. I thought my father and Lord Mac-

Lean were still here."

"Lord MacLean?" Miss Platt's eyes brightened with curiosity. "Why would you wish to see *him,* I wonder?"

Miss Higganbotham shrugged, though she couldn't seem to contain a small smile. "I am quite devoted to my Henry, of course, but . . ." Her smile deepened.

Miss Platt tittered. "Oh, my dear Miss Higganbotham, I know *exactly* what you mean. If it wasn't for dear Mr. West, I do believe I'd be in love with Lord MacLean myself!"

Miss Higganbotham raised her soulful eyes and sighed deeply. "He is almost beautiful, even with that scar." She shivered deliciously. "I plan on asking him about it before dinner tonight. I wonder if he was involved in a duel? That would be quite dashing of him, if it was true."

A strange emotion stirred Venetia's heart. What did this *child* have to do with *Gregor?* He would never take the slightest interest in someone like her, and the sooner the little minx realized it, the better it would be!

Venetia forcibly shook off her uncharitable thoughts. Really, she was going mad. First, she'd allowed Gregor to kiss her and had enjoyed it, and now she was allowing a feeling almost like jealousy to raise its ugly head. Next, she'd be writing "Lady Mac-Lean" on all of the scrap paper and making faux wedding invitations on the backs of old dress patterns!

Unaware of the turmoil she'd stirred in Venetia's breast, Miss Higganbotham closed the door and leaned against it as if barring it against an unspeakable evil. "I am so glad to see the two of you! Do you know where my father might be?"

"He is in the stables," Venetia said. "Your groom believes that the lead carriage horse did not break his leg as feared but has merely sprained it."

"Why does he care for the horse when his own daughter is here, declining away?" She came to sit across from Venetia and Miss Platt.

Miss Platt reached over to pat the girl's hand. "You don't appear to be declining. In fact, Mrs. Treadwell said you'd eaten every tray she's taken to your room and even asked for more."

"What does she know of pain and suffering? Or anyone here, other than me, I ask!"

A lovely pink suffused Miss Platt. "I'm sure I don't know, for *my* love life has been nothing but delightful of late."

"Miss Platt!" Miss Higganbotham said in a soulful voice. She grasped one of the older woman's hands. "Perhaps I have wronged you. Have you also felt the transports of pure love?"

Rather than breaking into giggles at such extravagant talk, Miss Platt beamed. "Oh, yes, I know all about true love. I was just speaking to Miss West of that very topic when you arrived."

Good God, Miss Platt needed to be warned about wearing her heart on her sleeve. It was true Ravenscroft had been nicer to Miss Platt than she was used to, but only in public and only under the watchful eye of Mrs. Bloom and Venetia. Never had he gone over the line of the acceptable.

Miss Higganbotham smoothed her delicate skirts, then looked at Venetia and Miss Platt. "Did I disturb your private conversation?"

"Oh, no," Miss Platt said immediately. "Miss Venetia and I were just discussing men."

"I think all men are difficult," Miss Higganbotham announced. "I would not be in this mess if my beloved Henry had listened to me. I told him how it would be once Father found out, but Henry refused to elope. And now, here I am, torn from his arms!"

Though Miss Platt seemed impressed, Venetia wasn't. "Miss Higganbotham —"

"Call me Elizabeth, please. Everyone does."

"Very well. You may call me Venetia."

Miss Platt leaned forward. "And I am Delilah."

Elizabeth and Venetia looked at Miss Platt, who blushed. "My mother felt Delilah was unfairly treated. Everyone thought she was so horrid, cutting Samson's hair and stealing his strength, but perhaps she was *forced* to cut Samson's hair!"

Elizabeth nodded. "I never thought of that, but I daresay you are right. Men always wish to blame women for their travails."

Venetia's headache was now very real.

"I know all about men," Elizabeth added loftily. "I have been engaged three times."

"Three?" Miss Platt blinked. "You could not be!"

"They were all secret engagements, of course, for Father is very strict. But they were engagements nonetheless. Henry even gave me a ring."

"Elizabeth," Venetia said. "Didn't you tell me you are only sixteen?"

"Some people say I look a lot older."

"How old were you for your first secret engagement?"

"Fourteen. I probably shouldn't count that one, as it was only to the underfootman. It didn't last more than a fortnight, but still, it shows that I understand men."

"Only a man can understand a man," Venetia said shortly.

"Ask me a question about men," Elizabeth said. "I'll show you."

Miss Platt clapped her hands. "Oh, excellent! I know just the question. Suppose a man, a young man with considerable address —"

Surely Miss Platt didn't think Ravenscroft had considerable address? Why, he could barely eke out a complete sentence.

"A man," Miss Platt continued, "who has shown one particular attentions. How long before you can assume his interest is something more than flirtation?"

Elizabeth pursed her rosy lips. After a moment's thought, she said with a great deal of authority, "A week."

Miss Platt's face fell. "A whole week?"

"Nonsense!" Venetia said. "You cannot fall in love in a mere week."

Elizabeth shrugged. "I did. And so did Henry."

"Are you certain it is love?" Miss Platt asked.

"You can't be absolutely certain how a

man feels until he gives you that *look*."

"What look?" Miss Platt said eagerly.

"Like this." Elizabeth looked very intently at Miss Platt.

Venetia had never seen such a silly thing in all her life.

Miss Platt squinted back. "I hope you will forgive me, Elizabeth, but I am not certain how to tell that look from a normal one."

"Look closer." Elizabeth put her hands on Miss Platt's shoulders and leaned closer, their noses almost touching. "See? See how my eyes are gazing directly into yours?"

"Oh, yes!" Miss Platt said, her eyes wide.

Elizabeth leaned back in her seat. "There! You can see how powerful the *look* is."

"I see it now. Oh, if Mr. We——" She glanced at Venetia and blushed. "I mean, I hope someday a man will look at me in such a way."

Venetia sighed, suddenly wishing for some solitude. "If you decide that every man who simply looks at you is in love, none will dare raise his eyes from the floor."

"Not all men are such hardened cases. Some men enjoy engaging a woman's interest," Elizabeth said, tossing her hair. "It makes them feel manly."

Miss Platt nodded quickly. "As you are engaged to be wed now and have been engaged twice before, I daresay you know all about that."

"Yes," Elizabeth said naively. "I have *vast* experience, which is a great pity, for it is quite difficult to be romantic when one is so disillusioned."

"Poor thing!" Miss Platt murmured, patting Elizabeth's knee.

Venetia could not stand another moment. She quickly made her excuses, then left the two women talking cozily by the fire. She'd better warn Ravenscroft to stop paying attention to Miss Platt; he might be in grave danger if he even looked at her!

Venetia went up to her room, grimacing when she saw the mess left by Elizabeth. It looked as if an entire trunk had exploded, clothes laid across every surface, the scent of lavender strong in the air.

Venetia cleared off the chair, piling Elizabeth's clothes on the bed. She was not the neatest of roommates, even with a maid to clean up after her. Boots and slippers were strewn across the floor. Three hairbrushes had fallen beside the washstand. A tangled knot of hair ribbons had been tossed over the back of the chair, two pelisses and an opera cloak with them.

Venetia wasn't certain she could keep a civil tongue in her head if she had to spend many more days living with such slovenly housekeeping, or nights filled with more snores and snorts. The entire inn seemed several rooms too small, and tensions were beginning to build.

Crossing to the window, she tied back the curtains to allow welcome light into the room. Fortunately, the weather had cleared. She opened the window a little and let the light breeze in. Snow-fresh air seeped into the room, dissipating the cloying scent of lavender.

Leaning against the sill, Venetia breathed in the cool air, gazing absently about the innyard. The snow was definitely melting. It was so thin along the edge of the stables that the grass was almost visible, and in a few places, the packed dirt from the innyard had mixed with the snow to make a muddy mess.

Please let us leave soon.

The stable door opened, and Venetia heard Gregor speaking with the squire about the horses. She leaned forward, watching the two men walk toward the inn as they discussed the merits of various mounts.

The squire said something to Gregor about the fallibility of hired cattle, and Gregor laughed. The breeze teased his dark hair, ruffling it around his brow.

When the two men reached the inn door, Gregor opened it. As he stepped aside for the squire, he glanced up and met Venetia's gaze.

For a long moment, neither moved. Then Gregor's expression softened into a smile. He lifted his hand and gave her a quick wink. It was so much like the old Gregor that Venetia smiled back, her heart leaping. Perhaps nothing was changed after all. It was then that she realized how much she'd been worried about ruining the friendship she held so dear.

Venetia listened to Gregor's footsteps as he joined the others in the common room. No doubt Miss Platt was even now wondering if Gregor's welcoming glance meant anything. Venetia shook her head. Miss Elizabeth Higganbotham was a wealth of misinformation, although Venetia would wager her best shoes that the flighty Elizabeth wouldn't have avoided Gregor after a mere kiss. No, she would have enjoyed the embrace, discussed it with all of her friends, and boldly gone back for more.

A wave of determination warmed Venetia, and she closed the window, then left the room and ran down the stairs, her boots clacking on each step.

"There you are."

Gregor leaned against the wall at the bottom of the steps, his arms crossed over his chest. It wasn't fair how good he looked.

He appeared perfectly groomed, his cravat straight, his coat smooth and well fitting.

He pushed away from the wall and came to the bottom of the steps. "Venetia, we must talk."

He saw her hesitate, a shadow crossing her face. Then she straightened her shoulders and came down the last few steps. "Yes," she said, "we do have things to speak about." She looked up at him, her gaze clear and direct.

He smiled reluctantly. No woman ever looked him in the eye the way she did, without flirting or prevaricating. After her snowball attack, he'd imagined that she'd be contrite and would prettily beg his forgiveness, concerned about his good opinion and worried about his feelings toward her. Instead, she met his gaze without the slightest hint of apology.

His chest warmed a bit; her frosty attitude this last day had affected him more than he'd wanted to admit. He'd come to rely on Venetia in some ways, and being in her bad graces was not a position he enjoyed. She knew him better than anyone else, even his own family. She knew his likes, his dislikes, his family woes and successes, and about the family curse. And like a true friend, she accepted him, lumps and all. As he accepted her, appreciating her uniqueness.

Which was why last night, unable to sleep yet again, he'd decided that he couldn't just walk away from the sparks that flared between them. He couldn't.

She wet her lips nervously and said in a rushed voice, "Gregor, we need to forget what happened yesterday and go back to the way things were." She peeped up at him through her lashes as she spoke. "Surely you agree?"

"I agree that would be the best course of action . . . if it could be done."

Her shoulders sagged. "We can't go back?"

"Venetia, I don't think you understand how these things work."

"What things?"

"Desire. Passion. Lust."

"Oh," she said in a small voice, "those things."

"I cannot become unaware of you simply because you wish it or because it would be more convenient for us. We can ignore it, perhaps, though I'm not even certain of that."

His gaze flickered to her hair, and he

smiled. Every day seemed to find her with fewer pins until her usual neat hairstyle had softened, silky tendrils clinging to her ears, curling along the delicate line of her throat.

Gregor's body tightened. *This* was what had changed. Now he saw Venetia as she actually was, not as he expected her to be. In London, she was the same little girl he'd met all those years ago, rebelling against her parents and laughing all the way. Over the years, she'd changed, but he'd been blind to it all.

Now he couldn't look at her enough. Last night, tossing and turning in the small, lumpy bed, the squire's deep snores punctuated by Ravenscroft's sleep murmurs, Gregor had been haunted with thoughts of Venetia. He'd told himself over and over that she was not for him, that the attraction would fade once they reached London — but some part of him whispered that it would be a waste to let that happen. That they should explore the tempting madness for their mutual benefit, if nothing more.

He'd tried to reason away that thought, to tell himself that Venetia was not a woman to enjoy trifling. But he could not deny the passion in her kiss, the way her lips had trembled beneath his, and how she'd unconsciously clutched him closer.

By morning, he'd been determined to speak to her. The only way to truly exorcise this madness was to embrace it, to follow it to its logical conclusion, whatever that was. Denying it only made it grow stronger, and God help them both if that happened.

He took her hands in his and said in a soft voice, "Venetia, though we can't go back to what we had before, we can move forward." He lifted his hand and slid it over her cheek.

Venetia shivered, her eyes closing for a moment, her lashes resting on the crests of her cheeks.

"Do you feel that?" he asked in a low voice. "Do you feel how the touch of my fingers makes your body react?"

She nodded, biting her lip in a way that made him ache.

"Venetia, we can still be friends, but we can also —"

"No."

"At least listen to —"

"Gregor, we *can't* let this attraction mean anything."

He leaned forward so that his legs were pressed against her, his breath tracing over her cheek as he said into her ear, "At this very moment, I am raging with the desire to touch, to taste you. How am I to stop that?

Are you certain you want me to?"

A shiver raced through her.

Gregor placed his hand on her shoulder, sliding it slowly down her arm. "I want to release your hair and watch it stream over your bare shoulders. But I can't. Not here." He dropped his hand and moved away. "But in London . . . when no one is about . . ." He let the words linger, filling the intimate space between them.

For the barest moment, she swayed as if she'd follow him, then caught herself and crossed her arms in a protective move.

Gregor watched her with a sense of satisfaction. Desire had darkened her eyes and flushed her skin. She couldn't stop it, either, no matter what she said.

"Venetia, we would be foolish to let this opportunity slip away."

Her lips tightened at his words. "Gregor, whether it was the snow, or being too close together, or just pure irritation boiling over into . . . whatever it was, I don't *want* to know more about it, and I definitely do not wish to experience it again."

He knew that with one touch, he could prove her wrong.

When her eyes met his, he realized that she knew it, too. Knew it and was fighting against it for all she was worth.

He took a step toward her, his blood simmering, his body tight with desire, but she whirled away, almost running to the common room. She sent him one last glance over her shoulder before she slipped into the room, then closed the door firmly behind her. Gregor started to follow, but the chorus of welcoming female voices from inside the room stopped him. She was not alone, damn it.

He stood for a long while, his gaze locked on the closed door, his body aching. Blast her for denying this physical attraction. It would never go away unless they dealt with it.

Never.

Gregor finally headed outside, the cool air welcome on his skin. Venetia might be safe from him now, but there would come a time when they'd be alone.

Things would be different then.

CHAPTER 11

The MacLeans are men of great, great passion, which can be a blessin' and a curse.

Old Woman Nora from Loch Lomond
to her three wee granddaughters
one cold evening

Gregor strode toward the barn. Damn it all, what did she expect from him? To ignore the passion that flared between them? That was a stupid way to handle the situation. They had to act on that passion, investigate it, find out what fueled it. Only then could they begin to control it. The only other remedy was to stop their friendship, and never again see one another, and he refused to do that.

Gregor paused outside the barn to let the sun warm his face. It was still too cold for the snow to melt, and he shivered a bit, wishing he'd stopped to get his greatcoat.

A noise from the stables caught his attention, and he saw the warm light that shone from the cracks in the doors. It would be warmer there than in the middle of the innyard.

As he headed to the barn, his boots crunched in the new snow, mocking him. What a horrid mess.

Gregor's breath puffed into the frosted air as he reached the barn doors. He paused there and glanced back at the large window of the common room, but no face showed between the curtains.

He turned away, disgusted at his disappointment. What had he expected? That Venetia might be peering out, remorse on her face? He snorted loudly, grabbed the barn door, and swung it open, then closed it quickly behind him. The barn appeared empty, but the murmur of voices and the glow of a lantern in the far stall told him otherwise.

Of course, Ravenscroft was there. The youth had left the inn after breakfast, probably to avoid the overly female presence inside — especially Miss Platt, who'd seemed to hang on his every word.

Gregor made his way toward the glow in the back of the barn, pausing to pat the noses of the horses, their heads hanging out of their stalls for attention.

A large, sturdy bay whickered when Gregor approached. Gregor rubbed the animal's nose and received a playful butt against his arm for his trouble. "Feeling your oats, hm?"

Ravenscroft's head appeared around the corner of the far stall. "Halloo there, Mac-Lean! Come and join us! Your man Chambers and I are enjoying a nice rum toddy!" Ravenscroft's voice was slurred with drink.

"A bit early for that, isn't it?" Gregor asked. The last stall door had been propped open, and a circle of barrels was placed around a small, glowing stove that Chambers was refilling with wood. A pot simmered on the stove, the pleasant scent of rum toddies sifting through the air.

Chambers closed the door of the stove and set the poker in a metal ash bucket. "Nothing like a good rum toddy to beat the cold weather from your bones." The groom looked shrewdly at Gregor. "Ravenscroft here has been saying there are a few too many petticoats in the inn fer his liking."

Gregor grunted in agreement.

The groom nodded. "I thought you might come out here sooner or later."

"Yesh," Ravenscroft interjected. "He tol' us all you would be here, and he made us leave you the best barrel!" Ravenscroft found his way back to his own barrel and gestured for Gregor to join him on a nearby empty seat. "Isn't thish the best parlor in the inn?" Ravenscroft's face brightened. "Has Mish Oglivie missed me yet?"

"No." Gregor made himself comfortable on the barrel. "Why is this barrel better than yours?"

Ravenscroft stood, turned, and bent over, displaying his rump to Gregor. "Splintersh."

Chambers bit back a laugh. "Lord Ravenscroft, Lord MacLean does not need to see your, ah, posterior."

Ravenscroft plopped himself back onto his barrel and winced. "It hurts like the dickensh, it does."

"Then why do you continue sitting there?"

"Because it's near the rum toddies." Ravenscroft found his cup, which had fallen to the ground. He picked it up, stared deeply into it, ran his finger around the inside, and licked it. He sighed. "It'sh all gone."

"So are you," Gregor said.

The groom sent Gregor a sharp glance. "Seems like the weather has settled a bit."

"Shnow!" Ravenscroft snorted. "In April! Whoever heard of such a thing?"

"Whoever indeed?" Chambers murmured.

He picked up an empty cup and used a small pewter ladle to fill it, then handed it to Gregor. "Here, my lord. To warm you a bit."

Gregor took the cup, the warmed metal sending feeling back into his numbed fingers.

"Where's your coat?" Ravenscroft asked, suddenly sitting straighter.

"I left it inside," Gregor said shortly.

Chambers quirked a brow. "On the run, are you?"

"What?" Ravenscroft said, outrage in his voice. "Did thoshe — thoshe *harridans* throw you out, too?"

"No one threw me out. I came of my own free will." Gregor took a sip of the toddy, the warmth spreading through him immediately.

"You are jusht trying to keep your pride. I undershtand."

"No, I'm not. I came here because I wished to —"

"Ha!" Ravenscroft lifted his fist toward a wall. "Damn all of you, you — you — you *women!*"

Chambers poured himself a toddy and eyed the younger lord with mild curiosity. "That's not the direction of the inn."

Ravenscroft stared at the wall. "It's not?"

"No. That's the direction of the road."

"Oh." Ravenscroft grabbed the sides of his barrel and turned in the opposite direction. Slowly, he rose to his feet and stood swaying, lifting his fist again. "Here! Thish — thish — whatever I said before!"

"Well done," Chambers said. "Perhaps you should sit down again."

"Yes," Gregor said, noting how the younger lord was swaying. "You might fall against the stove and I do not wish to hear you howl."

Ravenscroft sat, holding his empty cup.

As Gregor drank, he began to relax and feel more like himself. Some of it was the toddy, but a good bit was the distance between himself and Venetia.

He sighed. He'd handled his conversation with Venetia with the finesse of a fishmonger. She didn't understand desire. But how could she? In many ways, she was more innocent than the squire's painfully naive daughter.

Which was yet another reason her passion astounded Gregor. He took a fortifying drink, wishing Venetia had been willing at least to discuss the issue with him, but she'd rejected him before he'd even gotten the words out. In all of his years, no woman had ever been so adamantly set against him.

For a long moment, he simmered over that. Yet even as he did so, he realized he should have agreed to follow whatever course Venetia desired. Then at least he still would have had the easy contact with her that he'd always enjoyed. Now she would regard him with suspicion no matter what he did. If he ignored her, she'd think he was still angry, and if he paid attention to her, she'd think he was attempting to seduce her.

Good God, what a mess! Perhaps . . . perhaps if he just acted normally, things would go back to the way they had been. Perhaps when they returned to London, the usual bevy of beauties would dull the attraction that had sprung up between him and Venetia, and it would disappear.

He slowly sipped the toddy. Perhaps that was what it was: a lack of competition. If he'd been caught in this infernal storm with any woman, he would most likely see her in a different light.

Ravenscroft found his mug again and held it out to Chambers, who informed him the first batch was gone.

Ravenscroft fell into a fit of sullenness, mumbling about ill fate, uppity servants, and capricious women.

Sighing, Gregor stretched out his legs toward the stove. It was snug and warm inside the stall, the fire blazing merrily, the wood crackling and popping, the sweet smell of cloves and brandy from the toddies soothing.

Ravenscroft suddenly lifted his head. "Know what I think?"

Neither Chambers nor Gregor answered.

"I think that it's warm enough in here to melt one of those big icicles hanging on the barn door."

Chambers, mixing more toddies, looked disgusted. "Of course 'tis warm enough. We've a fire."

"I know that," Ravenscroft said indignantly. "I just think it would melt really *fast.*"

Chambers's thick brows rose. "Oh? How fast?"

"Very fast."

"Hmm. Suppose I bring one of those icicles inside, and we make a wager." Chambers shot a cautious glance at Gregor. "A small wager, of course."

Gregor shrugged. "Make it as big as you wish. Ravenscroft may sound like a child, but he is not."

Ravenscroft looked behind him. "*Who* is not a child?"

"You," Gregor said. "If you wish to throw your money away, you've no one to blame but yourself."

"Excellent!" Chambers rubbed his hands together, then left to fetch an icicle.

Moments later, the groom returned, pulled an empty barrel forward, and placed a large icicle in the center. "Well, Lord Ravenscroft? How long do you think it will take?"

The young lord bent to squint at the icicle, wavering as he did so. Finally, he said in a triumphant voice, "I give it twenty-two minutes!"

"Twenty-two minutes 'tis. I think it will take less time m'self." Chambers took his seat, pausing to refill his own and Gregor's mugs as he did so.

Gregor took a sip. "Chambers, you've outdone yourself. This is the best toddy I've —"

"Shhh!" Ravenscroft said, staring intently at the barrel. A few drops of water dripped from the icicle. He whispered in a dramatic voice, "If you talk, you will warm the air, and it will melt fashter!"

"I am not going to be silent because of a silly wager."

"This is not shilly," Ravenscroft said with great dignity, ruining the whole effect when he fell off his barrel.

Chambers set down his mug and helped

the lad back onto his seat. "Stop squirmin' about, or you'll fall forward and hit the stove next time."

Ravenscroft held on to the sides of his seat and resumed his dogged stare at the icicle.

Gregor flicked a glance at Chambers. "You've not named your stakes. What do you win if you're right?"

"The lad's coat."

Ravenscroft stiffened, his gaze jerked from the icicle. "*Thish* coat?"

"You have another?"

"Not with me."

"Then that one'll do."

"But . . . what if I win?"

The groom scratched his chin. "I'll give you my rum toddy recipe."

Ravenscroft frowned. "That'sh not much of a win."

"You can lord it over all your friends when you make it fer them in your apartments," Chambers said with a faint grin. "They'll come from miles around to try it."

Ravenscroft's expression expanded into a blissful grin. "I will be in much demand."

"Everyone will want to be invited to your lodgings," Chambers assured him. The groom smiled then and looked at the heavy, wool, multicaped coat that adorned Ravenscroft's narrow shoulders.

"It's not going to fit you," Gregor said.

"I'm not goin' to wear it meself. With this weather, I should be able to sell it back to the lad at a handsome profit." The groom grinned. "That icicle ain't going to make it. It's almost half gone now."

Ravenscroft hunched a sulky shoulder at Gregor. "That's because you two started talking."

Gregor set aside his mug and held his hands toward the fire. "Ravenscroft, you'd do well never to bet against Chambers."

Ravenscroft eyed the groom with a suspicious glare. "Does he cheat?"

"Lud, no!" Gregor said, grinning. "But he never wagers unless it is a sure thing."

"There are no sure things in this world," Ravenscroft said loftily.

Chambers looked up at that. "Yes, there are, and a good hot toddy is one of them."

Ravenscroft looked wistfully at his mug. "That was heavenly. But other than a hot toddy, there is nothing else."

"Oh, I can think of other sure things," Chambers said. "The sun comes up every morning, don't it?"

"It's not up right now."

"Yes, it is. It's just hidden by clouds."

"Oh." Ravenscroft leaned on his knee and plopped his chin in his hand. "Perhaps."

"And then there's women," Chambers added in a thoughtful tone. "They never change."

Ravenscroft gave a short, bitter laugh. "Women are never predictable! Just look at Mish Venetia. Not two weeks ago, she was flirting madly with me —"

"Flirting?" Gregor said, looking up from where he'd been contemplating the tips of his boots. "Venetia doesn't flirt."

"She told me I wrote wonderful poetry, better than that Byron fellow."

"That's not flirting. Even *I* could write poetry better than that Byron fellow. More likely, Venetia took pity on you and made you one of her projects."

Ravenscroft's eyes widened. "Like Miss Platt!"

"Exactly. I'm not sure why Venetia has been pushing that little game, but she has a plan of some sort."

"I'll tell you what it is," Ravenscroft said miserably. "Venetia asked me to pay attention to that Long Meg because she thought it might strengthen Miss Platt's sense of self-worth and give her the courage to speak out for herself with Mrs. Bloom."

"So that is it. Miss Platt certainly seems to enjoy having you about."

"That's just it," Ravenscroft said gloomily.

"This afternoon, Venetia warned me that Miss Higganbotham told Miss Platt that if a man looked at her a certain way, then he wanted to marry her."

"Looked?"

"Yes. Can you imagine how dreadful if at dinner you happened to catch a woman's eye, and she began to tell everyone in town that you fancied her, when you were just looking for the salt?"

"A pity," Gregor said in a brutal tone. "But that's what you get for listening to one of Venetia's schemes."

"But . . . she asked me to do it. How could I tell her no?"

"Like this: 'No, I will not become involved in your mad schemes.' You might want to practice before you see her again."

"I couldn't tell her no!"

"How on earth did you find the sand to abduct her, then? You make no sense."

"I didn't think of it as an abduction; I thought she loved me!"

"Had you truly thought she was interested in you, you wouldn't have had to lie to get her in the carriage."

Ravenscroft considered this. "Do you think if I'd asked her to marry me in a more romantic way, she would have agreed? Perhaps if I'd given her flowers and gotten down on one knee? Women like that, you know. Especially women like Venetia."

"Baldercock!"

Chambers paused in stirring the toddies and sent him a curious glance.

Gregor swallowed a knot of irritation. "I need more to drink."

Chambers refilled Gregor's cup at once.

The liquid burned Gregor's mouth, but the harshness of it crystallized his thoughts. "You are foolish if you believe Venetia is affected by romantic drivel. She is not like other women. She never has been."

"She is different, I'll grant you. But that doesn't mean she doesn't like the niceties. Women are very susceptible to such things as flowers and poems and —"

"Not every woman sets such a ridiculous store by such things."

"Yes, they do," Ravenscroft insisted. "Ask Chambers."

Gregor turned to his groom to find the man nodding.

"I'm sorry, my lord, but the lad has a point. Women find such things of vast importance — far more than you'd think."

Gregor scowled. "Some women. But not Venetia."

Ravenscroft tilted his head to one side, holding on to the barrel as if afraid it might tilt with him. "Why wouldn't she like those things if other women like them? What makes her so different?"

"Many things," Gregor said. "You don't know Venetia the way I do."

In the back of Gregor's mind, a little voice whispered that *he* didn't know Venetia as well as he'd thought, either. Her reaction that morning was evidence.

His chest grew unaccountably heavy at the thought, and he finished off the rest of his toddy in an effort to wash away the bitter aftertaste.

But there was a damnably knowing light in Ravenscroft's eyes. What if . . . what if Ravenscroft was right? What if Venetia *did* like such drivel as poems and flowers? Could he have misjudged her so much?

It was unthinkable.

Chambers scratched his nose. "I suppose 'tis possible that Miss Oglivie is a mite different from other women. She's a bruising rider and I've never seen her fall into a crying spell or seem upset the way other women do. Although her mother —" Chambers shuddered.

"Exactly," Gregor said. "Venetia has seen the price of such excesses and is immune to them." He lifted the poker and used it to open the woodstove door, then tossed a thick hunk of wood into the fire.

He turned to find Ravenscroft staring at him, outrage in every line of his face. "What do you think you're doing?" the young lord demanded in a tight voice.

"I added wood to the fire. It was dying."

"You are making it *hotter*." He turned to Chambers. "This is unfair. I demand a new wager! He just made it hotter in here!"

Chambers added some cloves to the toddy pot, where it gently simmered. "Aye. He did. And a good thing, too, fer I was growin' cold."

"But the icicle will melt faster now!"

"Perhaps."

"Then I demand a new wager!"

"No."

"Why not?"

"When Lord MacLean came in, he had to open the door, and that cooled it down some. So it makes things even if he warms it up a bit."

"Oh." Ravenscroft squinted as if trying to visualize this. "I see what you mean." He caught Gregor's gaze and said, "I suppose I am not mad at you after all. Well, except for what you said about Venetia."

"All I said was that she was different."

"I used to believe that, too, but now . . ." Ravenscroft frowned. "Lately, it has begun to dawn on me that perhaps she only seems different because she doesn't know she's not."

Gregor stared at Ravenscroft. "What in the hell does that mean?"

The younger lord flushed. "It means that she, like every other woman, wishes to be swept off her feet. She just doesn't realize it yet."

"Where do you come up with such nonsense?"

"It's not nonsense! No woman is immune to a man who would bring her flowers, whisper compliments in her ear, and tell her she is lovely."

Chambers rubbed his chin. "You know, my lord, the lad has something there."

Gregor didn't know which irritated him more, that his own groom was naysaying him or that Ravenscroft thought he knew Venetia better than he did. How to get Ravenscroft to see the error of his thinking?

Gregor's gaze fell on the barrel where the icicle lay melting, and a rumbling chuckle burst from him. "Ravenscroft, I will wager you a hundred pounds that Venetia is immune to such frippery as gifts and flowers."

Ravenscroft sat up straight. "Did you say a hundred pounds?"

"Yes."

"Careful there," Chambers murmured. "The lad cannot say nay to a wager."

Gregor ignored him. "Well? Will you take the wager?"

Ravenscroft nodded. "I will! Only . . . where will you get flowers and poetry and such?"

That was a problem. "I might not be able to find flowers, but I can find a gift for her."

"Such as?"

Good God, did he have to think of everything himself? "I can give her my pocket watch."

"There's nothing romantic about that," Ravenscroft scoffed.

Chambers cleared his throat. "I happen to have a gold neck chain I was takin' to me sweetheart. I could let you have it, my lord. Fer a price, of course."

"Done," Gregor said.

Chambers rose immediately to fetch a small packet from his bags and handed a velvet sack to Gregor in exchange for some coins.

Gregor pocketed the sack. "What else?"

"Poetry," Ravenscroft said. "I have a book." He fumbled in his pockets, then came out with a small leather-bound volume. "Here."

Gregor winced. "It's that Shelley fellow,

who writes such horrible drivel."

"Women love his horrible drivel, I promise you."

"Do you have anything else?"

"No. It's Shelley or nothing. I marked some passages, though. You can read any of those, and she'll swoon for it."

Gregor slid it into his pocket. "Very well. I am now armed with poetry and a gift. I will go begin this silliness and then report back to —"

"Waaaait a minute," Ravenscroft said, eyeing Gregor narrowly. "You can't just *say* you read poetry to Miss Oglivie and give her a gift. We have to *see* you do it."

"I am not going to read love poetry in front of you two fools."

"Of course not," Ravenscroft said in a lofty tone. "We will watch from outside the window."

Gregor scowled. Perhaps it would have been simpler to just challenge Ravenscroft to a duel and be done with it. "I am going to feel like an idiot."

"You're going to look like one, too," Chambers said. At Gregor's dark look, the groom added hastily, "But you'll be the richer by a hundred pounds. That'll take some of the sting out of it."

Being right would take a lot of the sting

out of everything.

"Well?" Ravenscroft asked. "Are we agreed?"

"Hell, yes." Gregor straightened his cravat and ran his fingers through his hair. "I will prove to you both that Venetia Oglivie is not like other women. And when I'm done, pup, prepare to pay."

CHAPTER 12

Oft times, love comes t' visit whilst ye are
sleepin'. It creeps in on wee fairy feet and
nestles in the quiet of yer heart. Ye might
not even know 'tis there 'til someone
wakes ye.

> Old Woman Nora from Loch Lomond
> to her three wee granddaughters
> one cold evening

Venetia was blissfully alone in the common
room. Mrs. Bloom had whisked Miss Platt
off to work on some sewing, while Elizabeth
had decided to go upstairs to read a novel.

Venetia stayed downstairs with her own
book, an improving work detailing the fall
of the Roman Empire. With a sense of
purpose, she settled into a chair and opened
her tome.

She hadn't seen Gregor since he'd left in
such high dudgeon, and Ravenscroft had
been conspicuously absent since breakfast.

She wasn't certain where the squire was, though she could hear his voice in the distance; perhaps he was in the wine cellars with Mr. Treadwell. The squire had commented several times on the quality of brandy kept at the inn.

Venetia turned a page and found a print of two women beside a marble pool. The rather supercilious matron reclining on a sofa reminded Venetia of Mrs. Bloom, which made Venetia frown. Just this morning, on hearing Miss Higganbotham complain yet again of the cold, the older woman had gone to her room and retrieved for Elizabeth a sumptuous cloak trimmed in fur. The girl had squealed in delight and impulsively hugged Mrs. Bloom, who had looked quite uncomfortable at being thanked. Venetia had been shocked at the older woman's generosity, though surprisingly Miss Platt took it in stride, commenting that it was Mrs. Bloom's way.

Venetia stretched out her feet toward the fire, letting the welcome heat soak into her gown and slippers. She found herself wondering where Gregor might be, then resolutely pulled her mind from that tantalizing question.

It was a pity she didn't care for Ravenscroft. Though he wasn't the ideal man, one always knew how he felt. He wore his emotions on his sleeve for the entire world to see, which was a refreshing change from some men she could name.

Gregor was a man of secrets, capable of great emotion yet never showing the slightest hint. Oh, he got angry, though never so much as he had this past week.

Venetia frowned. Would they ever smile at each other again without wondering if that smile meant something else?

Her hands tightened on her book. How could he suggest they explore their passion, as if it were a meaningless experiment of some sort? The thought made her blood boil. It was a good thing she didn't cause the weather to gather when she lost her temper, or it would be storming like mad now.

She glanced out the window. The skies were clearing, with large, fluffy clouds breaking apart to reveal snow-washed blue skies, and a faint breeze stirred the trees. It made her think of their walk in the woods, of the kiss that still made her lips tingle. One moment, they had been snarling at each other, and the next, they were in a passionate embrace. It had been heavenly. And confusing, too.

Venetia took a calming breath and shut

and opened her eyes, the book forgotten. She had to maintain her sanity, despite the feelings that burned through her every time he was near. The thought of her wanton response in the woods made her press her hands to her face. Her body ached with an odd restlessness. Blast it, everything was different now! She couldn't just —

"Venetia." A voice as deep as the sea, flavored with a smoky Scottish accent, ran over her like two warm hands.

She stood and whirled, her skirts flaring, her heart in her throat.

Gregor filled the doorway, one hand in his pocket, a small book in the other. His black hair, slightly damp from the melted snow, curled around his neck, and a sensual smile rested on his lips.

Venetia sucked in a breath, aware that something about him was different.

Whatever it was, it didn't make him any less appealing. She had to press her fingers into her palms against the desire to touch those errant curls.

I have to keep my wits about me, and — oh, heavens, have his eyes always been such a deep green?

Venetia forced a polite smile. "Good afternoon, Gregor." She cast about desperately for something to say, her gaze lighting on the book he held in his hands. "What do you have there?"

Gregor looked at the small book, an expression of distaste in his gaze. "Shelley."

She blinked. "The poet?"

"Is there another?" he asked in a scoffing tone, a bit put out at her disbelieving tone. "I do read, you know."

"Yes, but . . . Shelley?"

Gregor straightened from where he leaned against the doorframe. For an instant, the room tilted to one side, making him suddenly aware of how much rum he'd had. Until he'd entered the warmth of the inn, he hadn't realized he'd finished most of that blasted mixture by himself.

If he didn't have the doorframe within easy reach, he might actually stumble, which would be deadly to his wager. And this was an important wager, a true wager of honor, his hundred pounds to prove that Venetia was not an ordinary woman but an extraordinary one.

He glanced past Venetia to the window. The curtains weren't open all the way; someone in the innyard would be able to see only the front of the room. He'd have to throw the curtains wide, or Ravenscroft and Chambers wouldn't witness how wrong they were about Venetia.

It would take a master's touch to reach the window without giving away his condition, though. Venetia would not appreciate his coming to visit her while bosky.

No, that was what *other* women might do. Venetia would just laugh at him and then make jokes about it the next two thousand times she saw him, which was far, far worse than being scolded or condemned. Venetia really knew how to hurt a man.

Gregor looked down at the book in his hand, wondering dimly what he was supposed to do with it. Oh, yes. That fool Ravenscroft thought Venetia would swoon at this drivel.

Let the games begin! Gregor grinned, looking up at Venetia, wanting to share his thoughts, but as she crossed before the fire, her lack of a petticoat again became painfully obvious. For one instant, Gregor had a clear view of Venetia's legs and hips through her skirts, the light outlining each dimpled knee, each smooth thigh, each rounded hip.

Then she was on the other side, the skirt once again demure. Gregor opened his mouth but could not find a single word. All he could do was look at her, his body taut with desire.

"Gregor?"

He realized he'd been staring silently,

gawking like a lad of twelve.

Damn it, this was not the way to win his wager! He cleared his throat. "I brought you something. Are you busy?"

She shook her head, planting one hand on her hip and resting the other on the back of a chair. The gesture had the unfortunate effect of thrusting her breasts forward.

Gregor couldn't breathe, following the shadow under each full curve. He'd always known Venetia was pleasantly rounded, but somehow he hadn't realized how magnificent her breasts were. Not the calm, cool magnificence of a painting but the warm, fleshy magnificence of a real woman.

God, how had he missed those breasts? So full, larger than his hand could hold, and so beautifully rounded?

Gregor forced himself to yank his gaze away from those seductive breasts to Venetia's face. "I — I need air," he rasped out.

She frowned. "Air? Why? Are you ill?"

"No, no. It's just" — he waved a hand — "stuffy in here." He pushed himself from the doorframe and strode to the window, lust firming his wobbly steps. He threw open the curtains and let white light bathe the room.

There. Now he could face Venetia without worrying that she'd expose herself to him

248

even more than she unknowingly had. He smoothed his coat, taking a deep breath to calm his thundering lust, and turned.

Damn.

The light from the window now high-lighted the tops of Venetia's breasts, tracing the full curves with a swoosh of creamy color.

Gregor scowled.

Venetia's eyes widened, and she nervously crossed her arms.

Unfortunately, that pressed her breasts upward until they were clearly outlined against the thin fabric of her gown, the nipples puckered and eager. Gregor could make out every ribbon on her chemise, every nuance of her mouthwatering bosom.

A slow flush climbed through him. *Damn that rum toddy.*

Of course, he hadn't been drinking rum when he'd kissed her yesterday. That had been all him. And her.

He'd enjoyed a wide range of women in his life, yet he had never felt such an intense pull.

Familiarity should have been a protection. He'd seen her with tangled hair as a child, with spots when she'd been a lass, and woe-fully flat-chested until her fifteenth sum-mer. He'd watched her moon over men, though never with enough intensity to be of concern. He knew her skin turned a mottled red when she cried and a pale white when she was startled.

He should have been immune, damn it. Yet somehow, in racing off to rescue her and then seeing Ravenscroft's obvious admiration, Gregor actually *saw* Venetia for what she was now rather than what she'd been while growing up.

He now saw Venetia as a woman. And not just any woman but an intelligent, sensual woman, one he trusted more than . . . well, anyone. Perhaps even his own family.

Outside, something moved. He glanced over and saw Chambers and Ravenscroft standing in the snow-filled innyard, bundled to the ears as they tried to look innocuous, as if having a casual conversation in the middle of the snow.

Gregor looked down at the book in his hand. If he wanted those two to leave him be, he'd best get on with it. He shoved his hand into his pocket, retrieved the velvet sack containing the necklace, and held it out. "Venetia, I brought you something."

She eyed the sack obviously unimpressed. "What is it?"

"It's a present."

"For . . . me?"

"Yes, it's for you," he said impatiently, shaking the bag at her imperiously. "It's a necklace."

She didn't answer. Didn't move. Just stared at him as if he had two heads, a deep flush coloring her cheeks.

Gregor fought a smile of satisfaction. She *was* different from other women! Other women he knew would fawn all over him, laugh with delight, and flirt madly when presented with a gift.

He glanced out the window to where Chambers and Ravenscroft were openly staring. Heh! That would teach them to think he didn't know her.

Of course, she hadn't actually taken the present yet. Since he'd paid for it and didn't want it to go to waste, he grasped her wrist and set the sack in her hand.

She blinked at it.

"Well, don't just stand there," he chided. "Open it!"

Slowly, she undid the sack and poured the necklace into her palm. It gleamed softly in the light, a ribbon of gold stretched over her delicate fingers. A flicker of pleasure warmed Gregor. Chambers had excellent taste; the groom deserved a bonus.

Venetia didn't seem able to look away from the gleaming necklace.

"Do you like it?"

"I — I —" Her fingers closed over the gold chain, and she held it to her. "What's it for?"

Gregor frowned. Good Lord, he hadn't expected her to ask that. "It's for — for —" Hell and damnation, how was he to answer that? He glanced outside to see Ravenscroft and Chambers staring back.

Venetia turned to follow his gaze, and Gregor pulled her around to face him, away from the window.

She gasped, then frowned down at his hand encircling her wrist.

He'd never realized how delicate her wrists were; his fingers overlapped around the smooth warmth of her skin.

Damn, but she looked delicious. The flickering light from the fire kissed every inch of her peach-tinted skin.

Would she taste like the blush of a peach? Or the cream and sugar that she loved in her tea? Or the faint hint of smoky desire sweetened with passion?

It all sounded good, and he decided that he had to taste her. He sent a scowling glance to where Chambers and Ravenscroft now skulked behind a thin bush. If not for them, he might be discovering her intriguing flavors this very moment.

He pressed a kiss to her wrist, letting his breath brush over her skin.

Her lips parted; her eyes widened. "Gregor!" she breathed. "What are you — you shouldn't — I don't —"

She turned pink and yanked her hand from his grasp. "Gregor, I won't be made an experiment."

Experiment? He blinked, confused before his memory returned. "Ah! What I said in the hallway. It was a very poor choice of words. I don't know what I meant to say, but that wasn't it. Will you forgive me?"

She opened her mouth, then closed it, obviously deflated.

He smiled a bit. Venetia used anger like a shield. Take it away, and she was bared before him.

He liked that thought! Now, what had they been doing? Oh, yes, he'd given her the gift. Next came the poetry. As soon as Venetia was through laughing uproariously at that, he would excuse himself and collect his funds.

Feeling rather pleased with the way things were progressing, he flipped the book open to a page Ravenscroft had marked.

Gregor lifted the book and read, " 'When I rose and saw the dawn/I sigh'd for thee —' "

Venetia looked astounded. The poor girl must be hard pressed not to burst into whoops of laughter; best to get it over with and put her out of her misery. Gregor cleared his throat and continued, adding a bit of whimsy by placing his hand over his chest, " 'When light rode high, and the dew was gone/And noon lay heavy on flower and tree —' "

How could noon lie on anything, much less heavily? He'd once read a poem about a mighty ship that sank in a great storm. Now *that* was a good poem!

"Gregor?" Venetia's voice quivered the slightest bit.

He flashed her a wink. "Let me finish. 'And the weary Day turned to his rest, Lingering like an unloved guest/I sigh'd for thee.' "

He snapped the book closed, unable to stand another word. "There. Poetry. For you. What do you think?"

Venetia could not breathe. She looked at the necklace that glittered in her palm. Then she looked at the book of poems that Gregor held.

This could not be happening.

Gregor could not be there, armed with gifts and poetry, reading to her as if — as if —

Dared she think it?

Venetia clutched the necklace, the metal warm in her hand. Perhaps . . . perhaps he cared.

Her heart lifted and expanded. She could not help it. The words he'd spoken swelled about her — *I sigh'd for thee* — sending prickles across her skin, down her back, and lower. "I sigh'd for thee," she repeated wonderingly, and something inside her broke free. She stepped forward and threw herself against his broad chest, lifted her face to his, and pulled his mouth to hers.

For a stunned second, he stood stock-still. Venetia let the swell of passion sweep through her. She ran her tongue across his lips, her breasts flattened against his chest, her hands clutching at his lapels as she tried to pull him closer.

A *thunk* sounded as Gregor dropped the book, his large hands sliding down her back, cupping her to him, holding her closer, nearer. His mouth opened, and suddenly he wasn't kissing her but possessing her, bending her back, pressing against her —

He stopped, his eyes opening. Then he lifted his head and looked out the window.

Venetia followed his gaze. Outside, Ravenscroft and Gregor's groom stood in the snowy innyard, wearing identical expressions of shock and awe.

Gregor gave a muffled curse. He went to the window, threw it open, fished something out of his pocket, and tossed it into the snow. Then he yanked the curtains closed.

"Gregor, I —"

He went to the door and kicked it shut.

Venetia's heart raced; her hands grew warm; her heart beat against her throat. "Gregor?"

He stalked back to her. "Venetia, I want to kiss you and I will not be denied."

She opened her mouth, then closed it, unable to say a word.

Gregor slid an arm around her waist and pulled her flush against him.

"It — it's snow madness," she said breathlessly.

His body warmed hers through their clothes. "Yes," he growled. His lips grazed her cheek.

"It's also because we're in close proximity," she said breathlessly.

His lips caressed the sensitive skin on the side of her neck. "Mmmm."

Venetia tilted her chin, giving him more access. She clutched him closer, her breath coming in shorter and shorter gasps. "This . . . doesn't . . . mean . . . a . . . thing."

"As you wish," he murmured against her

ear, his tongue flicking across it and making her moan.

Venetia threw her arms around his neck and pulled his mouth back to hers. Within seconds, he was kissing her with all the passion he'd sworn to withhold. The kiss in the forest had been but a prelude to this encounter. Venetia's passion exploded to the fore, her body reacting so swiftly, so thoroughly, that all thought was suspended.

Gregor, too, was mad with lust, with wanting. She tasted of fresh snow and cream, of secret smiles and pure passion. He tasted her, devoured her, unable to think, unable to do anything but experience her delicious artlessness.

She slipped her hands beneath his waistcoat and clutched at his shirt. She undulated against him as she tried to get closer, her mouth as frantically seeking his as his was seeking hers.

Her passion and physicality practically begged to be touched, tasted, tempted. He trailed his lips along her cheek to her ear. "This is madness," he whispered, his heart thundering in his chest.

"Snow madness," she whispered back, her lips grazing his chin.

A shiver traced over him at her touch. God, she was as seductive as any woman he'd ever known. Her hands smoothed over his chest, down his arms, lingering as if memorizing every line, every muscle.

"Venetia, I want you."

Her gaze met his, shadowed and intriguing. "I know."

"You . . . you agree?"

Her eyes never left his. "Oh, yes. Ever so much."

Yes, his body demanded. *No,* his mind tried to shout. To his shock, Venetia slid her hands to his waist and, with a simple twist, undid the top button of his breeches.

Her eyes darkened, her cheeks flushed, even as she briskly undid the next button. This one was a bit harder, and she had to struggle, the backs of her hands brushing against him in an agonizing manner.

"Good God," he muttered.

She paused, looking at him in surprise, then withdrew her hands. "Did I hurt you?"

"No!" he exploded, grabbing her hands and returning them to his buttons, pressing them against the fullness of his manhood.

Her eyes widened, and he moaned. He should stop. He knew it, and yet he was powerless to do so. He felt like an adolescent faced with his first encounter. She was so seductive, so alluring — perhaps because she was forbidden, the one woman he should never touch, never kiss. But his body was tempted beyond thought.

"We shouldn't," she said, yet her fingers were busy with the third button.

"We could regret this," he managed, his hands caressing the curve of her back and lower.

"I'm certain we will." Her hands moved to his waistcoat, and in a remarkably short time, she was pushing it from his shoulders. She tossed it behind her, then went to work on his shirt, pulling it free from his waistband.

Never could he remember a woman who had been so determined. She was now seducing him, while he enjoyed every minute of it.

She *wanted* this, wanted *him*.

Pure passion ripped through his veins, and he slid his hands into her hair and kissed her deeply, giving up the last vestige of control.

There was no going back.

CHAPTER 13

'Twas a hot summer's day when I first met yer grandfather. I was comin' in from helpin' me pa in the fields, me hair tied up in a kerchief, me gown sticky from sweat, me feet jammed into boots twice't too big fer me feet. On days like that, I burned fer a better life. Yer grandfather was new, come t' town to see his aunt. He took one look at me, mussed and all, and said, "This is the woman I'm t' marry! Where have ye been all me life, me love?" And without a blink, I replied, "Don't start with me, ye scoundrel! If ye come with an empty purse, ye can leave now, fer I'd rather be unwed than unfed!"

> Old Woman Nora from Loch Lomond
> to her three wee granddaughters
> one cold evening

Venetia's mother liked to say that she'd swooned the first time Mr. Oglivie had embraced her. Venetia had thought that merely Mother's propensity to dramatize things, but now, caught in Gregor's heated embrace, she felt the same fainting, head-pounding, knee-weakening rush of emotion.

Her resolve never to breech propriety, never to allow her virtue to be thrown away on an impulse, weakened, folded, then disappeared, blown away like wisps of smoke before a strong wind.

She couldn't help but kiss him back, her hands unfastening his clothing. His coat and waistcoat dropped to the floor with satisfying quickness. Some small part of her realized that if she continued, there would be a cost. But right now, any cost seemed reasonable.

Her life until now had been so staid, so predictable. She deserved some unrepentant wildness. One moment, she'd been calm and in charge of herself, and then, because of a certain touch or the way he looked at her before turning to the window —

The image cut through the desire encircling Venetia. Gregor had thrown something into the snow. It had flashed like a coin of some sort. Why had he thrown that —

His lips trailed down her neck, and Venetia lost her train of thought, as well as her ability to stand. Her knees sagged, and he caught her to him; every line of his muscled body burned against hers.

His mouth was hot and possessive, his hands molding her to him, his body hard against her softer curves. He was passion and heat, danger and desire, and for this one instant, he was all hers.

His hands tightened on her shoulders, and he suddenly lifted his head and looked into her eyes. His mouth — his wonderfully carved, deliciously firm mouth — was open, his breath harsh between his lips. His skin was flushed; she smelled the faint scent of his cologne and the barest hint of rum.

Her body cried out at the fact that his lips were no longer on hers. She met his gaze, saw the return of reason, a flash of regret. Her heart ached that their mad, passionate moment was about to be over.

Desperate to prolong it, she sank her hands into his shirt and pressed her hips forward, brushing against him.

An expression almost of pain passed across his face, a moan breaking from his lips. "Venetia," he gasped. "Don't do that."

"Do what? This?" She rubbed her hips against his again, tossing dignity to the wind.

He groaned and yanked her to him, his arms wrapping tightly around her.

Against her hip, she felt a hard ridge. It

wasn't his hip, for that was to one side, and this was directly center, pressing against her in a most insistent way.

Venetia had been around horses far more than the average young lady; she knew the basic facts of life and what was pressing against her. She couldn't help but close her eyes and press back, gently rocking back and forth.

Gregor moaned deeper this time, his expression a cross between agony and ecstasy, closing his eyes and tipping back his head.

For this one instant, he wasn't thinking of any other woman but her. His expression of pure, pained pleasure burned through her, making her breasts ache, her thighs quiver, the longing in her burn hotter.

She pressed her hips forward again. Gregor gave a muffled curse, his hands tightening painfully on her arms. "Don't tempt me," he rasped out.

"Why not?"

He met her gaze solidly. "You know why not." His brows lowered, his mouth suddenly grim. "Venetia, you will have to stop this. I *can't*."

He wanted her to send him away. But the fact that it was so obviously difficult for him made her want to prolong it all the more. If she ended this now, she knew she'd never again feel his arms around her, his lips on hers.

It was heady, realizing that she had the power to make Gregor MacLean burn with passion. He'd conducted his affairs the same way he did everything else in his life, controlled and calm. Never had she seen him swept away by desire; he selected his mistresses with the same dispassionate interest with which he chose his horses.

A flash of pride rippled through her. And in asking her to regain control, Gregor had forgotten one little item: she was an Oglivie. She embraced life, and she wanted Gregor to kiss her, to touch her and answer the hunger in her body.

She slid her hands up his shirt, clutching the folds and drawing him closer. "Kiss me."

His gaze darkened, his hands tightening around her hips. "If I kiss you, I will not stop." His voice was harsh.

"I don't want you to," she said softly.

His jaw tightened, his green eyes bright. "Then we will have to live with the consequences. You understand that? We will have to marry."

Marry? The word dashed her passion with freezing-cold reason. She stepped away from him so suddenly that she almost tripped.

Whirling away, she crossed her arms over her chest as if to cover herself from his gaze.

Gregor was left with his arms empty, his objective accomplished. With one sentence, he'd cooled the wanton ardor that had simmered silver hot in Venetia's eyes.

It would have been laughable if she hadn't reacted so violently.

For a moment, he understood Ravenscroft's disappointment that his planned elopement hadn't occurred. Though Gregor didn't wish to marry, neither did he relish rejection. An instant sense of loss filled him, leaving him aching.

God, he wanted nothing more than to take this woman, press her against the settee, lift her skirts, and sink into her softness. She'd been willing and ready, the air still heavy with their mutual desire.

Damn the rum toddies and the snowstorm and the close proximity the inn had thrust upon him and Venetia. He wished he'd had a choice, but he hadn't. If he'd allowed this tempting moment to progress into mindless passion, it would have locked them into a course that would destroy their friendship forever.

Damn, it had been difficult to let her go, too. Venetia would have allowed them both to sink into the passion that threatened to swallow them whole. But afterward? What then? Gregor drew a deep breath, thrust his lust-laden thoughts away, and turned from Venetia in an attempt to collect himself.

The chill of the room seeped through his clothing as he walked to the window and opened the curtains, relieved to see that Ravenscroft and Chambers had left. He leaned one hand over the window and rested his forehead against the cold glass, his body still thrumming with awareness of the woman who stood silently behind him.

When Gregor's hands no longer trembled and his loins allowed his brain to function, he straightened and turned. "Venetia, I —"

The door swung open. Ravenscroft stood swaying in the opening, snow covering him from head to toe. Behind him, Chambers hovered anxiously.

Venetia frowned. "What do you want?"

Ravenscroft stepped into the room, his face contorted with fury. When his foot caught on something, he stopped and looked down.

His foot rested on Gregor's discarded waistcoat.

Gregor started forward. "Ravenscroft, do not —"

Ravenscroft roared with fury, his voice ringing throughout the inn. "MacLean, you blackguard! You have seduced her! I demand satisfaction!"

Far to the south, London was slowly digging itself out from the unexpected snowstorm. After almost four days, people slowly made their way back onto the streets. Horses, carriages, and carts rattled and slid down the avenues, past mounds of snow, the roads a mess of packed ice and muddy puddles.

At exactly half past five, a neat coach-and-six pulled up to the front stoop of White's, a gold-etched crest glimmering in the fading sunlight. The butler, Mr. Brown, clapped his hands and sent a footman to inform the cook that the final member of the private party in the dining room had arrived. Then, smoothing his coat, Mr. Brown threw open the huge oaken doors.

Lord Dougal MacLean paused on the portico, flicking an infinitesimal piece of lint from his sleeve. Mr. Brown waited patiently. MacLean was an acknowledged leader of society fashion, and it was easy to see why. His waistcoat was a deep red damask shot through with silver thread and adorned with exquisitely wrought silver buttons. His cravat was tied in an intricate weave that Lord MacLean had refused to name, to the chagrin of those who wished to ape him. Black breeches molded his powerful legs, while a single emerald, matching the green of his eyes, flashed on one finger.

Every bit of his attire set off his muscular form and blond hair to perfection. Many ladies in London had been heard to sigh whenever Dougal MacLean passed their way.

"Good evening, Brown," that worthy young gentleman said as he peeled off his gloves. "Have my brothers arrived?"

"Yes, my lord." Brown took Dougal's gloves and passed them to a footman. "They bespoke the dining room. Dinner is to be served within the half hour."

"Excellent." Dougal shrugged out of his multicaped coat, revealing an evening coat that fit across his broad shoulders like a loving hand.

Mr. Brown eyed the rose that adorned the gentleman's left lapel, wondering how many other blades of fashion would appear thus over the next few days. Every nuance of his lordship's clothing was studied and copied, sometimes within the same day.

"How long have my brothers been waiting?" MacLean drawled, looking around with that sleepy manner of his.

Some members of the ton had allowed

themselves to be fooled by his lordship's rather lazy manners, but Brown had heard that the men who sparred in Gentleman Jackson's Bond Street Academy had learned that those sleepy eyes hid the prelude to a powerful right hook.

"They have been here the last hour and then some. Except Lord Gregor MacLean." Brown paused significantly. "May I say that your eldest brother seems a bit out of sorts."

Dougal sent the butler a look from beneath his lashes. "Alexander is always out of sorts. It's his defining mark, as it were."

"I am glad to hear that, my lord. I thought perhaps we'd done something to make him angry."

"Oh, he rarely gets angry. But he is perpetually irritated." Dougal sighed sadly. "It is most boring."

He slid a gold coin into the man's hand. "I am sorry you've had to deal with the famed lack of MacLean humor."

"Thank you, my lord! I hope you enjoy your evening. Shall I escort you to the dining room?"

"No, no. I can take myself." Dougal smiled absently, then walked through the arch at the end of the entryway and turned left down a wide hall. Moments later, he paused beside a large mahogany door, one hand resting on the brass knob.

Inside, he could hear two deep voices murmuring. With a sigh, he fixed a faint smile on his face and entered the private dining room.

"There you are!" Hugh said from where he leaned against the mantel.

Dougal's eldest brother, Alexander, sat in a thickly cushioned red chair before the crackling fire. He regarded Dougal with disfavor. "Thank you for taking time from your social schedule."

"It was difficult," Dougal said airily, ignoring his brother's sarcasm, "but you *are* family after all."

Hugh almost smiled, but Alexander didn't so much as glint. "We've been waiting an hour."

"I was asleep when I received your missive and had to dress."

"It was two o'clock."

"I never rise before four during the season," Dougal said gently. "But to be honest, I am still a little pressed. I only have" — Dougal slipped out a large gold watch etched with silver swirls and regarded it — "twenty-one minutes." He returned the watch to his pocket and said apologetically, "I am engaged to dine at the Spencers'."

"The Spencers can wait." Alexander's

gaze flicked over him with disdain. "You have become a damned dandy."

Dougal took a seat, crossing one leg over the other as he withdrew his quizzing glass from a pocket and regarded his Italian leather boots. "I am certain you did not travel all the way from Scotland to critique my clothing." He dropped the quizzing glass, which swung from a ribbon against his waistcoat. "At least, I hope you did not. A letter would have sufficed had that been the case."

Alexander's jaw clenched.

"That's enough, the both of you," Hugh said. "We've had enough weather already." Tall, broad-shouldered, and dark-haired like most of the MacLeans, Hugh was distinguished by a streak of white hair over his right temple and a playful temperament. If there was mischief to be made, Hugh was in the middle of it.

Today, Hugh did not have his normal twinkle. He met Dougal's gaze grimly. "We are worried about Gregor."

Alexander nodded. "People are talking. I don't like that."

Dougal raised his brows but made no comment. Alexander was the tallest of his brothers, towering over them all. Dougal, at six-foot-one, was the shortest of the lot.

Since he was the only one also to possess their mother's blond hair, he'd taken more than his fair share of ribbing from his siblings, with the exception of his sister, Fiona. With such tall brothers, he'd learned the value of attacking first and fast.

At the time, it had seemed a hardship to be different from his brothers and sister, but now he rather enjoyed it and was even glad. If he'd been as huge as his brothers, it would take an entire calf every time he ordered a new pair of boots.

Dougal shrugged. "Don't worry about Gregor. He can take care of himself."

"Do you know where he is?"

"He went to assist Venetia Oglivie. He should be somewhere on the North Road, probably held by this storm. Why?"

Alexander and Hugh exchanged glances before Alexander said, "I received a letter from Mr. Oglivie."

Dougal winced. Gregor had asked him to keep an eye on the old gent, a more difficult task than one might suppose. Oglivie had been an emotional mess, weeping one moment, threatening Ravenscroft with horrible death the next. Worse, he refused to stay home, dashing here and there so that Dougal had been hard pressed to keep up with him.

Dougal had been glad when Oglivie had finally decided to stay out of town with an old friend for a few days. "What did this letter say?"

"He told us about Venetia. He thinks something might have happened to Gregor."

Dougal made a face. "Oglivie is a fool. Alexander, you know Gregor. Do you think anyone could keep him from getting in touch with us if he wished?"

"What if he cannot?" Hugh asked. "What if Gregor is ill or injured, or worse?"

"What is worse than injured?"

"Married," Alexander said promptly.

Dougal laughed. "Gregor would never marry anyone, much less Venetia Oglivie. She is like a sister to him."

"No, she's not," Hugh said, a thoughtful look in his eyes. "You've seen how Gregor talks to Fiona. He speaks to Venetia Oglivie in a very different manner."

Alexander nodded, his gaze hooded. "Gregor cares for Venetia."

"Just as she cares for him, but they are not interested in each other in that way."

Hugh shifted from one foot to the other. "Dougal, that doesn't matter. Since Gregor does care for Venetia, his sense of chivalry might force him into extreme action."

Gregor's greatest flaw was his rather

antique sense of values, and a faint sense of unease began to grip Dougal. "Have you spoken to Mr. Oglivie?"

"We can't find him."

"He's with Viscount Firth. I drove him there myself yesterday."

Alexander nodded. "We need to talk to him." His gaze darkened. "This evening; the Spencers will have to wait."

Dougal frowned. "I will fetch him, though I still don't see why —"

"Dougal, it has been four days since Gregor contacted anyone." Alexander steepled his fingers, regarding Dougal over the top. "I believe that means Gregor has failed in his first mission, which was to return Miss Oglivie to London with her reputation intact. Everyone seems aware of her absence and that something untoward has happened."

Dougal scowled. "That is Mr. Oglivie's fault. I tried to keep an eye on him, but it was impossible."

Alexander's jaw tightened. "He is a fool. And now Gregor is in a precarious situation. He is fond of Venetia, and he will feel honor-bound to protect her."

Dougal sighed. He hated becoming involved in this. "Very well. I will fetch Mr. Oglivie this evening. Should I bring him here?"

"No," Alexander said. "We'll stay at Gregor's town house until we hear from you."

"And then?" Dougal asked.

Alexander's gaze burned with intensity. "We will ride to Gregor's aid."

"He won't like that."

"I don't care if he likes it or not," Alexander retorted. "If he wishes us to stay at home, he should do a better job keeping us informed of his whereabouts."

"Or at least contact us when something this significant has occurred," Hugh said.

Dougal shook his head. "I think you are both being precipitous. For all we know, Gregor could have the situation well in hand."

Alexander's jaw tightened. "You don't have to come with us; we can manage without you."

Dougal stood, smiling slightly. "Oh, I'm coming — if only to witness Gregor's expression when we arrive, ready to rescue him. *That* will be worth seeing indeed."

CHAPTER 14

'Tis a pity we canna see ourselves the way others do. If we could, we might act a wee bit differently. Sometimes it takes a distant eye to see a thing that's too close to our own hearts.

Old Woman Nora from Loch Lomond
to her three wee granddaughters
one cold evening

"That's enough!" Gregor snapped. He grasped the furious Ravenscroft by the cravat and hauled the younger man off his feet. "Keep your voice down, you fool! People will hear you."

"I —"

Gregor tightened his grip, lifting Ravenscroft even higher, until his toes didn't quite touch the floor.

Ravenscroft gasped, his face turning red.

Gregor shook him. "There is a lady involved. You don't even deserve to say her name."

Ravenscroft clutched at Gregor's wrists, his toes shuffling madly for purchase. "Awk!" was all the sound he could make.

Venetia raced over, grasped Gregor's arm, and pulled. "Stop! You are strangling him!"

"He deserves no less." Gregor gave Ravenscroft another hard shake, then released him. Ravenscroft tumbled to the floor, where he lay gasping.

"What is going on here?" the squire asked, coming into the room.

Behind him, Venetia could see Mrs. Bloom, Miss Platt, and Elizabeth racing down the staircase. Her face burning, Venetia whirled on her heel and went to the window, her hand pressed to her forehead. How had things come to such a pass?

"It's nothing, squire," Gregor said grimly. "A little disagreement between Mr. West and myself."

Ravenscroft gurgled something, but his voice seemed to have disappeared along with his breath.

"Oh, my *dear* Mr. West!" Miss Platt said, sinking to her knees beside Ravenscroft.

Elizabeth and Mrs. Bloom came to stand with Venetia.

"My dear, what happened?" Mrs. Bloom's gaze passed from Ravenscroft to Gregor, then back. "What did Mr. West say to upset

Lord MacLean so?"

Venetia rubbed her forehead. "They were just talking, and —"

"Goodness!" Elizabeth exclaimed. "Mr. West is holding Lord MacLean's waistcoat. How did he lose that?"

Gregor yanked the waistcoat from Ravenscroft's weak grip. "I was in the barn, and one of the buttons came off my waistcoat. Miss West was kindly sewing it back on when her brother walked into the room and mistakenly assumed something improper was occurring. He protested, and I was forced to protect myself."

"A mill!" the squire said, his eyes bright. "I would love to have seen that!"

Ravenscroft attempted to rise, but Gregor moved his foot slightly, trapping the young man by the edge of his coat and holding him to the floor. To the others, it appeared as if Ravenscroft was too weak to rise.

"You tried to defend your sister's honor!" Miss Platt pulled Ravenscroft's head into her lap and pressed a handkerchief against his head. "You brave, brave man!"

Ravenscroft slapped the handkerchief away, but Miss Platt refused to allow him to slip from her lap, holding him down with surprising ease. "Rest, poor man."

Mrs. Treadwell entered the room, her eyes

wide. "What's happened? I was with poor Elsie, who's feelin' quite low, when I heard the commotion."

Mrs. Bloom put her arm around Venetia and glared at Gregor and Mr. West. "Poor Miss West was forced to witness a brutal display!"

For once, Venetia was glad for the older woman's forceful personality. She found herself leaning a bit and realized that her knees were still weak, though not from seeing Ravenscroft so summarily disposed of. "I believe I should lie down," she murmured.

Mrs. Bloom went into action. She admonished the squire to help Mr. West to the settee, as he was blocking the doorway, then bustled Venetia from the room, declaring she was going to have Miss West rest in a darkened room with some smelling salts. As she passed Ravenscroft and Gregor, Mrs. Bloom said in a rather challenging tone that if anyone had a problem with that, they would have to speak to her, for Miss West would *not* be available.

Just as Venetia passed the doorway, Gregor turned his head and met her gaze.

As if drawn toward a flame, Venetia's steps veered toward him, but Mrs. Bloom's firm hand urged her past Gregor and out of the room to the peaceful quiet of her bedchamber. There, Mrs. Bloom, showing surprising restraint, asked her no questions but tucked her comfortably into bed, a lavender-scented cloth upon her head.

Venetia slept late the next morning, far past the time for breakfast. Pleading a headache, she sent word through Elizabeth that she was staying in bed and didn't wish to be disturbed.

Elsie brought a tray at noon and set it on a small table by the window. "Sorry to hear ye are feeling poorly, miss."

"I'll be better once this snow melts."

Elsie smiled, then winced, putting a hand to her jaw.

"Are you well? Mrs. Treadwell said you'd taken to your bed."

"I've a bit of a toothache, but I'm feeling better," the girl said stoutly, though her paleness belied this. "Mrs. Treadwell was going to send for the surgeon to take out m'tooth, but I told her it wasn't necessary. It'll stop hurting on its own."

"I'm so sorry you're in pain. I believe Mrs. Bloom has some laudanum if you need it."

"I'll be fine. See?" Elsie pulled out a small bag suspended around her neck on a piece of twine. "Beet root. My mam dug it up under a full moon, so it's potent." She tucked the bag back into her gown. "I'll be right as rain in no time."

Venetia wasn't certain she believed in the curative powers of beet root, but all she said was, "I hope it works swiftly. If it doesn't, let me or Mrs. Bloom know, and we'll get you some laudanum."

"Thank you, miss. You're very kind." Elsie crossed to the door. "I'll come to pick up your tray in an hour."

Venetia ate, then retrieved her book on the Roman Empire and settled into a chair by the window. She tried to read, but it was difficult to concentrate. Sunlight shimmered through the wavery glass, warming the room deliciously, and the faint murmur of voices rose from the common room below. Venetia strained to make out any specific words, but she couldn't.

After a nap, she began to feel restless. She couldn't stay in her room forever. She'd managed to hide away last night, claiming a headache, and then she'd slept in this morning, pretending not to waken when Elizabeth went about her morning toilet.

Venetia glanced at the door wistfully. Everyone would be gathering for dinner soon, talking and laughing while she was here, confined to her room like an invalid.

She should go downstairs and face Gregor and the others. She'd have to do it eventually.

Reluctantly, Venetia dressed. She noted with envy that two of Elizabeth's gowns were already pressed and hanging over the chair, ready for their mistress. Venetia looked at her own crumpled pink gown and yearned for the comforts of her home, her own bed, the service of her own maid, the luxury of going for a ride. Perhaps Ravenscroft had deserved being choked after all.

Pushing aside her uncharitable thoughts, Venetia pinned up her hair, pausing when a commotion arose in the innyard. She got up to look outside. The snow was almost gone, the innyard a mass of mud except for a few lingering icy drifts. As she looked, Chambers arrived, driving Ravenscroft's carriage. Mr. Treadwell was riding with him.

Now that the snow was almost gone and the carriage repaired, they could leave. Sadness and relief quivered through her. What would happen to her and Gregor then? She didn't know. All she knew was that she wished to leave *now.*

She finished dressing and headed downstairs. She had no answers, and the more she thought, the more questions she came up with. There was much more involved than just her and Gregor's inexplicable passion.

When she'd first arrived at the inn and had realized the extent of Ravenscroft's deception, she'd somehow blithely thought they'd find a way to mitigate the damage to her reputation, and all would be well. But the snowstorm had confined them for a longer time than she'd expected, the situation further complicated by the arrival of the squire and his daughter, whose connections in London could not be denied.

She was in serious trouble. If she returned to London now and saw the squire or his daughter at some event, and they realized she'd been traveling under the name Miss West with two unmarried men, she'd be dropped from society before she could count to ten.

She didn't relish the thought of becoming a pariah. She loved London and her life there.

The murmur of voices inside the common room told her that everyone was already there, Gregor's deep voice distinctive over the others. Blast it, she didn't want to face him in a crumpled gown. Why was it that fate rarely allowed one to dress properly for major events in one's life? It wasn't fair.

Best to get it over with quickly. Venetia

took a deep breath and opened the door.

Ravenscroft rushed forward, taking her hand tightly between his. "Venetia! I must speak with you — apologize for —"

Miss Platt gripped his elbow and tittered nervously. "Miss West — Venetia — I'm so glad to see you're feeling more the thing!"

Turning his shoulder toward Miss Platt, Ravenscroft mouthed to Venetia, *We must talk.*

She nodded and pulled her hand free, then turned to curtsey to the squire, who was gruffly asking her if she had slept well.

As she murmured a polite reply, she glanced toward Gregor, who stood by the table. For the first time since their arrival, he looked less than perfectly put together. His cravat was slightly askew, his coat rumpled at the elbows, his hair mussed, his eyes dark. Of course, on Gregor, slightly mussed still looked delectable, and Venetia's heart ached slightly at the sight of him, as if she were missing something important.

Miss Platt slipped her arm through Ravenscroft's. "You should rest! Come back to the sofa." She half dragged him away, much to Venetia's relief.

Mrs. Bloom was there at once, tucking Venetia's hand into the crook of her arm and leading her to the table. "There you are, my dear! I'm not surprised you took a nap, after such a difficult day."

"I'm feeling much better," Venetia said, painfully aware that Gregor was now standing beside the squire, his dark gaze watching her every move.

She'd managed not to look directly at him, but it didn't matter. Whether she looked at him or not, she couldn't quell this *awareness.* She could feel his gaze as surely as she'd felt his touch yesterday.

Gregor watched Venetia bend her head to listen to something Mrs. Bloom was saying. She looked as tired as he felt. She was worried; he could see it by the way she shifted in her chair and clasped her hands together.

Gregor sent a glare toward Ravenscroft, who flushed and looked away sullenly. The fool had avoided him all morning, which suited Gregor very well.

Damn his loose tongue! In one stroke, he'd almost ruined everything.

Of course, Gregor had to accept his share of the blame. He'd come damned close to crossing the line with Venetia. He hadn't counted on how delectable he'd find her. Or how drawn to her he was now, as if their unfinished scenario were still there, unplayed but inevitable.

Though he tried not to pay attention to

her, he couldn't help but notice when she lifted her hand and brushed away a strand of silky hair from her cheek. Her hair was a complete mess, and the sight made him smile. She no longer seemed to have enough pins to keep it controlled at all, for long tendrils had escaped here and there, wispy and full about her face. It was much longer than he'd originally thought, perhaps even to her waist.

That was an interesting thought — one he forced himself not to consider. But as he turned away, he caught Ravenscroft staring at Venetia, his gaze rapt and admiring. Gregor looked across at her again, noting how the warm sun soaked across her. Her skin was creamy and faintly tanned, the pale freckles over the bridge of her nose almost begging for a kiss.

He suddenly realized with a sinking feeling that she was worth every admiring gaze Ravenscroft turned her way.

He'd spent a long time last night thinking about what had happened between them. He could no longer pretend that things had not come to a head. Even without his lamentable lack of control yesterday, Venetia was a ruined woman. Gregor had little doubt that the squire's daughter would take London by storm. Her beauty and connections would make her the debutante of the season, and she and her father would be invited everywhere. It would be impossible not to run into them eventually, which meant that it was only a matter of time before Venetia's exposure.

She deserved better. In addition, he knew that inevitably he'd be drawn into the outcry, as would Ravenscroft — if the fool hadn't yet fled the continent to keep from meeting Lord Ulster on the field of honor.

They were all in the suds now, and there was little he could do to change the unappealing fact that there was only one way to save Venetia now — he had to marry her.

Even now, after hours of consideration, Gregor's heart tightened at the thought. He'd never thought to marry in such a way, but there were no other options.

He needed to inform Venetia of his decision and decided to find her alone after dinner.

"Lord MacLean?" The squire stared at him expectantly.

"I beg your pardon. My mind was wandering."

The squire glanced from him to Venetia, then back, a shrewd look in his eyes. "So I see. I mentioned that if we combined our resources, we might be able to travel in a day."

Gregor forced himself not to look back at Venetia. "That is a capital idea. I'd like to leave as soon as possible."

"My thoughts exactly. We can leave some of the baggage behind and have the gentlemen ride outside the one carriage that is functioning."

Gregor nodded. "Then we could ride to a larger town, somewhere where we might hire another carriage to fetch the luggage and then go our own ways."

"My thoughts exactly."

Mrs. Treadwell burst into the room. "Law, but the whole world has done ended!"

"What's happened?" Mrs. Bloom said.

"Elsie's tooth has taken a turn for the worse, and she can't cook dinner."

"Oh, dear," Venetia said. "Perhaps I should go to her."

"Whist, Miss West, there's no need fer that. I done dosed her up with some laudanum and wrapped a warmed onion against her stomach to scare off her ails. She'll be right as rain in the morning, see if she's not."

Venetia hoped the onion wouldn't interfere with the purported benefits of the beet root. "Is she sleeping now?"

"Aye. It wasn't until just now that I realized that with her gone, there's no one to make dinner."

Ravenscroft frowned. "What about you, Mrs. Treadwell?"

Mrs. Treadwell laughed heartily. "Why, I can't cook at all, which has been a sad disappointment to Mr. Treadwell, let me tell ye, especially on account of him having this inn and all."

Venetia caught sight of Gregor's sudden grin, a humorous light in his dark green eyes as he said, "I wonder if Mr. Treadwell was aware of that sad fact before he married you?"

"Indeed he was not," Mrs. Treadwell said cheerfully. "He didn't ask, and I didn't say." She looked at Venetia and said in an undertone, "I don't call that a lie, as I never said a word. Then once't we was married and he found out I couldn't cook, he seemed to think all I had to do was step into the kitchen and it would come to me. Well, I tried it, I did, and 'bout near burned the house to the ground. That's when he got me Elsie and had her do the cooking, which has worked quite well ever since."

Gregor's lips twitched, and Venetia hastily said, "Perhaps I should go and see what can be made with the stores in the kitchen."

"What? Let a guest cook her own dinner? Not at the Blue Rooster." Mrs. Treadwell shook her head. "Don't ye worry none, Miss West. Mr. Treadwell is in the kitchen now. He said if'n he had gentry to feed, then he'd guess he'd have to cook somethin' hisself."

"He can cook?"

"In a manner of speakin'," Mrs. Treadwell said cheerfully.

"What manner of speaking is that?" Gregor inquired in a painfully polite tone.

Venetia pretended to cough to hide her chuckle.

"Oh," Mrs. Treadwell said airily, "he once tried to cook a partridge, but he burned it to a cinder."

The squire looked disappointed. "Blast it!"

"So now he's making a nice porridge. That's what he was fixin' when I come in here."

"Porridge?" Ravenscroft said, blinking. "That's all? Just *porridge?*"

Miss Platt immediately added, "There has to be something more than porridge for dinner."

"Well," Mrs. Treadwell said uncertainly, "Mr. Treadwell says 'tis porridge or naught."

"Mrs. Treadwell," Gregor asked, curiosity plain on his face, "have you had the privilege of eating Mr. Treadwell's porridge before?"

"Me? La, no! But me da did once, afore he died."

"How *long* before he died?" Gregor asked.

Venetia sent him a warning stare. "Mrs. Treadwell, don't mind him. He is just funning."

"Mr. Treadwell's sister says 'tis fine stuff and swears it will stick to yer ribs for a fortnight."

"Lovely," Gregor said.

"I can't have just porridge for dinner!" the squire said, coming forward.

"I'm certain there must be some other options. I should go and see what's to be done," Venetia said.

"Nonsense," Ravenscroft said, waving his hand imperiously. "You cannot cook." He seemed to remember he was supposed to be her brother and added lamely, "I mean, I know you can cook, but, ah, not well enough for company."

Miss Platt tittered. "Mr. West, you are so kind to your sister! Miss West, I'm sure you're exaggerating. What do *you* know of cookery?"

"I know enough to fix dinner," Venetia said.

A faint burning smell floated into the room, accompanied by a puff of smoke from under the door leading into the kitchen.

Mrs. Treadwell turned to Venetia, a worried look on her face. "If'n ye don't mind, miss. Would ye help with the meal?"

"Of course." Venetia stood.

Miss Platt blinked in amazement. "Miss West! You cannot be serious! Helping in the kitchen?"

Mrs. Bloom frowned. "What's wrong with assisting where assistance is needed?" She favored Miss Platt with a stern gaze. "It's our duty, isn't it?"

Ravenscroft snorted. "For servants, perhaps."

Miss Platt firmed her chin. "Yes! Exactly what I think. For *servants.*"

Mrs. Bloom sniffed and went to join Venetia, but Mrs. Treadwell's voice halted her. "Mrs. Bloom, I hate to ask, but if ye don't mind, perhaps you could help get the table ready whilst Miss West helps Mr. Treadwell?"

"Of course," Mrs. Bloom said. "Do not let it be said that *I* have forgotten my position. I do not mind working in the kitchen." She glared at Miss Platt, who remained in her seat, then followed Mrs. Treadwell to a cupboard tucked to one side of the common room. A twist of a knob revealed an assortment of crockery. Mrs. Treadwell gave a few instructions to Mrs. Bloom, who immediately began gathering dishes and carrying them to the table.

Miss Platt turned to Ravenscroft to say in an arch voice, "You need never worry about *me* not knowing my place. I shall stay right here beside you."

Ravenscroft hurried to stand. "Venetia! I think I shall join you."

"No, thank you," Venetia said smoothly. "I am certain you'd be better help here, assisting Mrs. Bloom."

"But I —"

"Mr. West," Mrs. Bloom said. "Here are the spoons." She held out a handful of cutlery.

Realizing he'd been outmaneuvered, he went to assist her.

"I'll help, too!" Miss Platt said brightly.

Ravenscroft winced.

"Mrs. Treadwell," Venetia asked, "what sort of stores do you have?"

"Oh, all sorts! We've that brace of partridges, some nice venison, and some fat hens behind the barn, if it gets to that."

Ravenscroft choked. "Hens? Still alive?"

"Indeed they are. And fat as can be, too. 'Tis a wonder they can walk. I daresay they'd braise up right juicy."

He shuddered. "I cannot eat meat that is

just blooded! That's — that's —"

"Too much for your delicate stomach?" Gregor suggested.

The squire choked back a laugh.

"Uncivilized!" Ravenscroft finished, sending a black look at Gregor.

Mrs. Treadwell looked confused. "Ye liked my ham pie yesterday, did ye not?"

He gasped. "That was fresh?"

"O' course! We killed the pig just the morning afore we cooked it up." She brightened. "Which reminds me, we also have fritters and a nice hock left, as well as the innards, which we can tie up in a sack and make —"

"Mrs. Treadwell," Venetia said hastily, catching sight of Ravenscroft's sudden pallor, "let's see what Mr. Treadwell has already accomplished." She took the older woman's elbow and led her to the kitchen.

There, she and Mrs. Treadwell coughed at the smoke. "Heavens!" She waved at the thick air. "Open the door to the yard!"

Mr. Treadwell, wrapped in a large, messy apron, turned to do her bidding. Venetia went to the spit, where a brace of partridges were charred to a crisp, a large pot boiling noisily to one side. She lifted the lid, and more smoke poured out. Venetia grabbed a hook and lifted the pot from the fire, set it on the table, and used the poker to tip off the lid. Bubbles roiled through a thick, black mass.

"My porridge!" Mr. Treadwell exclaimed, peering into the smoking pot. "Do ye think we can save any of it?"

Venetia thought they'd be hard pressed to save the pot. "Perhaps we should just begin again."

"But the gentlemen are hungry."

"They'll survive." She reached for an apron hanging on a hook and swiftly tied it on. "Mr. Treadwell, perhaps I should take over."

"Can ye cook?"

She smiled, rolling back her sleeves. "Heavens, yes. I've even cooked a partridge that the prince swore was the best he'd ever had."

"The prince?" Mrs. Treadwell looked impressed.

Looking relieved, her husband unlaced his apron. "Very well, then. I'll leave it to you, Miss West."

"Thank you. While I'm doing this, can you open a new bottle of port and tell the gentlemen it will be at least thirty minutes before dinner is served."

"That's a capital idea!" Mrs. Treadwell said. "Perhaps I should make some tea for the ladies, too?"

"That would be lovely," Venetia said as she ran an expert eye over the large and well-appointed kitchen.

A wood-burning oven sat to one side, a neat stack of logs ready for use beside it. A long table ran down the center of the room, its much-marked surface proclaiming it to be both preparation area and cutting board. A variety of spices sat beside a stack of crockery bowls.

"This is a lovely kitchen," she said.

Mrs. Treadwell looked around, blinking. "Why, so 'tis," she said as if seeing it for the first time.

Mr. Treadwell gave Venetia a proud smile. "I spared no expense for Mrs. Treadwell's kitchen, though she'd never stepped more'n a foot in it."

"Why would I do something as ninny-hammered as that? You'd be expecting me to fix all of the meals then." She winked at Venetia. "I may not be the smartest woman there is, but I know a trap when I see one, I do."

"A trap?" Mr. Treadwell protested. "I thought you wished to help me run me inn!"

"And so I do, but not from the kitchen," she said, fists planted on her hips. "I help as I can, greetin' the guests and such."

"Runnin' yer yapper is more like," Mr. Treadwell said, humor in his eyes.

Mrs. Treadwell grinned. "We all have our gifts."

Chuckling, they departed on their separate errands, leaving Venetia alone.

She filled a pan with water from the cistern and hung it on the hook over the fire, then gathered potatoes, four rather dried-out carrots, a slab of bacon, some salted pork, a bundle of dried fish, some onions, and several bags of wheat. Further digging unearthed a small store of dried blueberries, a crock of sugar, and some yeast.

Venetia decided to make a nice stew, followed by scones. "And maybe a comfit, if I can get the fire hot enough," she said thoughtfully to herself. "That will be a nice touch."

"Yes, it would be," came a deep voice.

Venetia turned. There, just inside the door, stood Gregor.

CHAPTER 15

There comes a time in everyone's life when they have t' decide whether they wants t' be right or if they wants t' be happy.

Old Woman Nora from Loch Lomond
to her three wee granddaughters
one cold evening

Venetia turned away, hot tingles making her breasts tighten in a most inexplicable way. She busied herself filling a bowl with water and setting it on the table in order to wash the vegetables. "I thought you'd be drinking port with the gentlemen."

He held up a half-filled glass, his eyes glinting with amusement. "It was, of course, delightful hearing Ravenscroft tell of his gambling woes, much to the squire's disapproval, but I thought I'd be more entertained here." He watched as she deftly chopped a potato. "I had no idea you possessed such a skill."

"How do you know I do? You may dislike my dishes."

"Because I know you. You wouldn't have offered if you didn't."

The praise sent a real smile to her lips. She picked up a potato and began scrubbing it in the water.

"The real question is," he said, "how did you learn to cook, and when?"

"Who do you think prepared all those meals when my mother quarreled with that horrid French cook of ours?"

"The fat one who could not speak a word of English?"

"He could say 'I quit' well enough." She took a folded cloth and lifted the burned porridge from the table.

"Allow me." Gregor placed his glass on the table and came to stand beside her.

A prudent woman would have sent him away. But a prudent woman would also have ended up cooking the entire meal by herself. Venetia handed Gregor the folded cloth. "Thank you."

It wasn't as if she could force him to leave, anyway. He was far too big to push around, she thought, eyeing the rippling of muscles in his forearms as he lifted the heavy iron pot.

It always amazed her how Gregor managed to keep from becoming as soft as all of the other men in London. It was but one of the things that kept the women of London panting in his wake.

Blast it, I wasn't going to start doing this again! Venetia picked up Gregor's glass and returned it to his hand. "Thank you for your assistance. I believe I have it now."

There. That was certainly direct. But all he did was take a sip, then lean against the table, his gaze never leaving her.

Venetia chopped another potato. "Really, Gregor, I don't need any assistance."

"I would rather stay. Ravenscroft is brooding."

"Miss Platt must find that exceedingly attractive."

"Oh, yes. I believe the word she used was *Byronic*."

"Goodness! No wonder you wish to escape." Venetia glanced around. "If you must help, you could chop the carrots." She gestured with a knife over her shoulder. "They're in the storeroom."

In that moment, Gregor had to face a rather uncomfortable fact about himself. In the many months since he'd first gone to London, he'd gotten a bit spoiled. Somehow he'd become accustomed to being treated . . . not differently, exactly, but definitely with more than the usual deference.

He'd thought he hated the fawning obsequies, the eager attentions, and the obvious invitations. Yet now, facing Venetia's pragmatic orders to chop carrots, he found he rather missed the attention he'd once scoffed at.

"When you are done with the carrots, you can also chop a few onions," Venetia said, setting aside the scrubbed potatoes and finding a bright blue bowl. She poured in a measure of flour and then a little cream from a pitcher and began to mix it vigorously with a wooden spoon. "You *do* know how to chop an onion, don't you?"

Despite his irritation at being ordered around, Gregor grinned at her audacity. "No, I don't know how to chop an onion, as I've never done so before, though I feel reasonably certain I will manage the intricacies on my own."

"I knew I could count on your excellent understanding."

Gregor wrinkled his nose at her and headed to the dry room. It was a small area, barely large enough to stand in, packed to the ceiling with barrels of salted pork and crocks of honey and lard and lined with bags of flour.

The air was pungent with the scent of dried herbs and various vegetables that hung from the corners.

He brought the carrots and several large onions back to the table and set them down, grimacing at the dirt on his coat. He was not a fastidious man, but he had already been reduced to blacking his own boots and brushing his own clothes.

He took off his coat and hung it on a peg by the door, rolled up his shirt cuffs, and returned to the table to begin sorting the vegetables.

Venetia kept her gaze on the table before her, but if she tilted her head ever so slightly, she could see his hands. The man had amazing wrists, thick and strong and faintly tanned.

She found it difficult to swallow. He was all man, from his black hair to his booted feet. She turned a bit so she could see more of him without openly staring. His knitted breeches were molded to his muscular thighs, tucked into high-top boots that ensconced large, masculine feet.

Hmmm. Didn't they say a man's feet echoed the size of his manhood? Of its own accord, her gaze darted up Gregor's legs to where his deliciously tight breeches caressed his —

"Knife."

She blinked, her gaze jerking up to his face, her skin flushing. *Please, God, don't let him know what I was thinking.*

"Knife," he said again.

"Knife?" she repeated dumbly.

"Good God, Oglivie. I will need a knife if I'm to cut these vegetables. I can't do it with my bare hands."

"The knives are in the block behind that red crock," Venetia said hurriedly. Heavens, what *had* she been thinking? She hoped he didn't notice her cheeks were as hot as the fire.

To keep him occupied, she added in a rather breathy voice, "Please make certain you wash those before you cut them. We cannot eat dirty carrots."

His gaze narrowed. "And the onions?"

"You peel the skins from those, so they won't need washing."

"Ah." Gregor lifted a brow. "I want to point out that I am not the finicky sort of man who pales at the thought of eating freshly blooded meat."

Venetia had to fight a grin at that. She didn't appreciate Ravenscroft's softer side, either. Yet neither did she relish Gregor's less than sympathetic character. The perfect man would be somewhere in the middle.

She cast another glance at Gregor from beneath her lashes. No, the perfect man would be Gregor, with his black hair and lopsided smile, looking so intriguingly and deliciously male, and yet he'd possess . . . a touch of empathy, perhaps. Something that made him less stern.

For all his handsomeness and breath-stealing maleness, he lacked passion. Oh, he had lust, but did he have the ability for love? Didn't that take something more?

Venetia realized Gregor was holding the dripping vegetables in his large hands, and she gestured to the other side of the table. "You may cut them there."

He lined the carrots in a row, watching Venetia as he did so.

She was thinking about something serious. He could see it in the way her brows were lowered, her mouth set in a straight line. She dipped a finger in the batter and lifted a large dollop to her mouth.

Gregor's breath stopped. Knife suspended, he watched her pink tongue flick out to taste the batter. Her gaze narrowed, then she took another delicate lick.

It was all Gregor could do not to groan. She had no idea how tantalizing she was. Gregor forced himself to look away from her plump lips as she added a large dash of cinnamon from a small tin.

Gregor lifted the knife and slammed it down. The tops of the carrots rolled across the table, some hitting the floor.

Venetia jumped, her gray eyes wide. "What on earth are you doing?"

He slammed the knife again, more carrots scattering. "I'm chopping carrots." He lifted the knife again.

She reached across the table and grabbed his wrist, her fingers warm on his skin. "Gregor, they are carrots! Not tree branches."

"I fail to see the difference." He shook his wrist free and slammed down the knife once more, the tip biting into the wooden table this time.

He went to lift it, but it would not budge.

"Here." She walked to his side and twisted the knife free. Then she placed a carrot before her and, rocking the knife back and forth, deftly cut the carrot into tiny pieces.

"Oh." He watched as she picked up another carrot and did the same. "You really do know how to cook."

She made a face. "So would you if your parents had a tendency to argue with the cook before every dinner party."

His lips twitched. "I can imagine."

"Mama would get in a tizzy thinking something hadn't been done, and before we could stop her, she'd be in the kitchen, berating the poor cook." Venetia sighed, her full breasts pressing against the thin material of her dress. "Mama can be quite demanding, especially about justice."

Gregor forced himself to look away from her breasts, wondering about the color of her nipples. "I'm sorry?"

"She felt the cooks were cheating her of their salary when things did not turn out as she wished."

He shook his head. "I've known for the longest time that you were the only sane member of your family, yet I still keep trying to make sense of them."

"I just accept and love them as they are." She laughed, her white teeth flashing between her rosy lips. "Otherwise, I'd go mad with them."

He laughed, too. Even when he was at his sourest, Venetia had a way of making things seem brighter, her humor contagious, her unusual beauty appealing. That damned young upstart, Ravenscroft, had recognized her value all too well.

Damn Ravenscroft. Gregor's hand tightened on the knife.

"If you do not stop massacring those carrots, I'm going to have to ask you to leave the kitchen."

Gregor looked down. He'd chopped the carrots, tops and all, into minutiae.

Venetia frowned at the mess. "Those are the last carrots, too."

"I can pick out the greenery." He used the tip of the knife to flick little bits out.

"Gregor! That went into my scones!" Venetia walked around the table, sending him an irritated glare. "Stand back; I'll do it."

As she bent over the table and began to remove the leaves from the carrot pile, Gregor eyed the exposed nape of her neck. Of all the sensitive places on a woman, it was his favorite. What would she do if he nuzzled her there, tasting the sweetness of her skin?

He knew what she'd do. She was a tinder box of passion, ready to burst into flame at the smallest strike. He shoved his hands into his pockets to keep from reaching for her.

Now was the time to tell her of his plan to save her reputation, and explain how marriage was their only recourse. Yet as he opened his mouth to do so, she moved to one side, still bent over the table. He found himself looking down at her skirts as they curved over her lush bottom, so perfectly rounded to fit his hands.

His mouth went dry and he was suddenly unable to speak a word. Bloody hell, what was wrong with him? This was Venetia, not some ladybird who knew lust and how to use it to her advantage. Venetia's allure was completely unconscious and he'd damn well better remember that. His lack of control had caused them enough trouble as it was.

He closed his eyes. He supposed he should just be thankful that he'd only recently discovered Venetia's dangerous combination of vitality and sensuality. If he'd discovered it sooner, their friendship wouldn't have lasted.

He wondered how many men other than Ravenscroft had noticed Venetia's attractions? His jaw tightened at the thought. Thank God she'd never shown any interest in any of the men her parents had paraded before her. They were determined to see her wed, though as the years passed and she remained steadfastly unattached, they'd been less aggressive in their efforts.

"I am surprised your father countenanced Ravenscroft," he said.

Venetia looked over her shoulder, surprise in her expression. "Why wouldn't Papa countenance him? He is a gentleman in every sense of the word."

"Except in abducting you."

She straightened, her hips brushing him in a very uncomfortable place. Unaware that she'd just sent a jolt of awareness through him more potent than any brandy, she said, "Gregor, I was picking stems from your carrots. What made you say such a thing about poor Ravenscroft?"

"He abducted you. I find his presence more and more onerous." He paused, then said in a deliberate voice, "Once we are married, I will not countenance that puppy in our house."

Venetia turned to face him, her eyes wide with disbelief. *"What* did you say?"

He reached over and removed the knife from her hand. "You don't have any choice," he said grimly. "You are ruined."

"But that's — I don't know why you —" She put her hands on her hips and leaned forward, unwittingly giving him a direct view down the front of her gown. "Gregor MacLean, how much port have you had?"

Her bosom rose and fell in outrage, the very bosom he was staring at as if he'd never seen one.

Her breasts were remarkably full and ripe, the tops curved enchantingly against the material of her gown. Her chemise was plainly visible where it held the tantalizing curves together, pressing them upward as if offering them to him. The delicate scrap of lace at the top of her chemise seemed to be straining with the weight.

Gregor's mouth watered as if he'd just been offered a piece of his favorite cake. No wonder Ravenscroft had been so demented as to face possible ruin. Well, Gregor would make certain that neither Ravenscroft nor any other man besides him received such a view again. Once he married Venetia, he'd purchase a whole new wardrobe of high-cut gowns. Red ones and green ones and pink ones and —

"Gregor?" Venetia followed his gaze. She gasped and crossed her hands over the top of her gown. *"Gregor!"*

He grinned wickedly. "Sorry, my love. You were saying?"

"You shouldn't look at me that way!"

"You are my intended. I can look at you any way I wish."

"Even *if* we were engaged, which we are *not,* I wouldn't countenance that!"

His brows rose. "No? I think you'd enjoy it."

She opened her mouth to retort but could find no words. Venetia passed her hand over her eyes. She couldn't believe Gregor was asking her to marry him.

Actually, he was *telling* her. "You said you would never marry."

He shrugged. "I see no other solution."

His words flicked across her like hot ash on bare skin. *"No."*

Gregor frowned, disbelief in his gaze. "I beg your pardon?"

"I said no." She went back to her side of the table and began to stir the scone batter. "I would rather be ruined than married to a man who didn't care for me."

"I care for you."

She looked him straight in the eye. "Oh?"

"I do," he said stiffly. "I have always been fond of you."

"Fond is not enough."

He knew, then, what she wanted. Love. After a moment of silence, he said, "It's all I have."

They looked at each other a long moment. Disappointment filled her eyes with tears.

Gregor's chest ached. "Venetia, be reasonable. I am fond of you, and I'm also attracted to you. Most marriages are based on less."

"Not *my* marriage. And if I have to explain that to you, then you definitely are not the man for me."

Gregor raked a hand through his hair. "Do you realize what is going to happen once

311

the squire sees you in London? You will be shunned, abandoned."

"That is my problem. I will deal with it on my own." She wiped her eyes and then pointed to the onions. "Please cut those; I need them for the stew." She went to the fire and removed the lid of a large pot, sprinkling an assortment of herbs into whatever bubbled there.

Gregor couldn't absorb her refusal. He'd never thought she would say no. He'd assumed her arguments would be about when and how rather than why. He'd been prepared to be magnanimous about those things, to let her plan whatever sort of service she desired and spend a ridiculous amount of his money if she so desired.

But to say no in such a way? He didn't know what to say. Gregor grabbed an onion and raised the knife.

"Peel those first," Venetia said, her voice tight as she returned the lid to the pot over the fire.

Gregor peeled and sliced the onions, the strong odor stinging his eyes. He cut as much as he could, then turned away, his eyes burning almost as much as his pride. "Bloody hell, these are strong!"

"They get stronger as they age." She tossed a rag across the table. "Dry your eyes before someone thinks I've stepped on your toe."

She had stepped on his pride. That was what ached so badly now. He wiped his eyes, the burning subsiding a bit, and replaced the rag on the table. "Thank you."

She gathered the onions and carrots and carried them to the pot.

Gregor watched silently. He'd botched everything. His attempted rescue had achieved nothing, and now his attempt to settle her future had put yet another barrier between them.

He should have found a better way to present his proposal — though, eventually, she'd have to agree to it. There was no other solution.

Venetia removed the lid from the pot and added a pinch of something.

"That smells wonderful. What's in it?"

"Some ham from yesterday, some broth, rosemary, and garlic." She gave him a brief impersonal smile before she turned away. "Thank you for helping, Gregor."

She was dismissing him. Gregor stiffened, his pride bruised. But then, so was hers. He watched her for a moment, noting the high color in her cheeks and the way she avoided his gaze.

Perhaps it was better if he left, for now.

Once she'd had time to think things through, she'd come to the same conclusion he had. All she needed was a little time for reflection.

Gregor washed and dried his hands, then shrugged into his coat. Damn it, this was not the way he'd thought this would go. He paused by the door, trying to find words to explain what he thought and why, but none would come.

Instead, he said, "We should be able to leave tomorrow. You will need to pack your portmanteau. I suppose you will wish to return to London right away."

She replaced the lid on the stew and returned to the table. "No. I have decided to go to my grandmama's as I originally intended."

"Fine. I will escort you."

"No, thank you. I can travel on my own."

"Don't be ridiculous."

She smiled thinly. "Why shouldn't I travel alone now? I'm a ruined woman, remember? In a way, I am certain I will find it very freeing."

"Venetia, I —"

She lifted her eyes to his, a hopeful expression burning there. "Yes?"

Gregor heard the hope, the hint of wanting, and for an instant, something deep inside him responded to that hint of *more.* Then his good sense returned. "I will escort you, and I won't take no for an answer."

She shrugged, wiping the table as if her life depended on it. "Do whatever you will. By this time tomorrow, things will return to normal."

But things wouldn't, and they both knew it.

Gregor left, torn by the desire to explain — what? That he didn't love her and therefore couldn't say so? That he respected her more than any other woman, and that should be enough?

Scowling, he grabbed his overcoat from a peg by the door and headed out to the sanity of the stables.

CHAPTER 16

There's no bond like that betwixt a mum
and her wee ones. No one can make yer
heart sing louder, or yer knees quake
more.

Old Woman Nora from Loch Lomond
to her three wee granddaughters
one cold evening

The squire set his napkin on the table.
"Miss West, that's the best stew I've ever
had! And to think we were afraid we'd
starve to death."

Venetia offered the squire a faint smile.
"Thank you. I enjoy cooking." She turned
her gaze back to her own bowl, studiously
avoiding Gregor's gaze. He'd come in late
and had taken a chair, growling at everyone
who attempted to draw him into conversation.

Ravenscroft looked up from where he'd
been ravenously gulping the stew. "I say,

Venetia, can you cook anything else?"

Miss Platt tittered. "Oh, Mr. West! Surely you know what dishes your sister can prepare."

Ravenscroft blinked. "Oh. Well. I might except that, ah, well . . ." He swallowed noisily, then said in a rush, "Venetia lives with, ah, our parents whilst I have a set of rooms off St. James. She didn't know how to cook back when I lived at home." He sent a wild glance at Venetia. "Isn't that right?"

She sent him an approving smile. "My skills have only recently been proven. After Ravenscroft moved into his own apartments, Mama hired a temperamental French cook who delighted in quitting hours before any given entertainment."

Mrs. Bloom nodded. "That is very good of you to assist your mama, my dear. What are your favorite dishes?"

"My favorites are Cornish hens stuffed with crab dressing, duck in mint sauce, and an especially savory liver pâté."

"That," Ravenscroft said, spooning in another mouthful, "is just another reason why you should have run away with me to Italy."

"Run away with you to Italy?" Elizabeth looked at Ravenscroft with surprise. "Why were you and your sister planning on run-

317

ning off to Italy?"

"My sister? Oh! Well . . ." Ravenscroft's cheeks burned a bright red.

"My brother is such a tease. He is forever suggesting we should run away from home to Italy."

"Just so," Ravenscroft said. "Venetia could marry an Italian, and I could write a novel or some such thing."

Mrs. Bloom clucked her tongue. "Mr. West, you and your sister are too old to be running away from home. What would your parents say?"

Ravenscroft opened his mouth, then closed it, then opened it again. "Our mother is a saintly woman who —"

"I am certain Mrs. Bloom does not wish to hear that particular story." Venetia sent Ravenscroft a warning glance. He'd tangle them up in a story so wild they wouldn't be able to remember the details.

Ravenscroft flushed and obediently busied himself with his stew.

Satisfied he would cause no more harm for the moment, Venetia told Mrs. Bloom, "My brother is forever imagining he will start a new life in Italy with me to wash his clothes and take care of him, though I have informed him that I will take no part in such nonsense."

"I don't blame Mr. West for wishing to have a cook with him." Miss Platt forced a laugh and said in a plainly critical voice, "Although I must admit I've never known a *lady* who could cook at all."

Elizabeth sent a hard glance to Miss Platt. "I am glad Miss West can cook, or else we'd have been forced to eat cold bread and cheese for dinner."

"Indeed," Mrs. Bloom said, eyeing Miss Platt with disfavor. "I hope none of us is so ungrateful as to describe Miss West's talents as anything other than wonderfully fortunate for us all."

"Yes," Gregor said, surprising everyone, as he'd not said a word the entire meal. He stood and bowed in Venetia's direction, his mouth still turned in a straight line. "Miss West, you have taken simple stew to a new level."

Venetia didn't know where to look. She wished she'd approached their conversation in the kitchen in a different manner. It was arrogant of Gregor to have assumed she would marry him as a matter of expediency, but now that her emotions were a bit cooler, she had to admit that the offer was quite chivalrous.

If only he'd worded it with some finesse. She had been so outraged at his assumption that she should blindly allow him to fix all of her problems that it wasn't until she was alone in the kitchen that the other aspects of his offer had sunk in.

She wished she had the chance to apologize for her hot temper, but looking at his expression, she rather doubted it would do much good.

Gregor told the squire, "Mrs. Bloom has offered us the use of her coach after dinner to see if we can find a horse in town to replace your injured one. The road is clear enough to travel."

The squire nodded. "Excellent. Thank you, Mrs. Bloom."

"It's nothing." Mrs. Bloom waved her plump hand. "Miss Platt and I plan on leaving first thing tomorrow morning. It'll be good to get the coach out of that musty barn and into the fresh air."

The squire raised his brows. "It's still kind of you." He stood as well. "Elizabeth, have your maid pack your bags this evening. We should be off at first light as well."

"I should pack, too," Mrs. Bloom said. She gathered her shawl and stood. "Miss Platt, come with me."

Miss Platt tore her gaze from Ravenscroft, blinking in surprise. "But . . . I, ah —" She snatched up her spoon. "I have not yet finished this delicious stew."

Mrs. Bloom sent a knowing look at Ravenscroft, who appeared miserable, but she only said, "Very well, Miss Platt. When you finish, pray come to our room, and let's pack our things. As charming as this inn is, it is time we go to London." Mrs. Bloom left and was soon heard making her way up the stairs.

Gregor sent a glance at Venetia. "I daresay you and your brother will wish to leave at the same time?"

She nodded. "I will pack this evening, too."

"Good. I will be accompanying you and Mr. West to your grandmother's." He turned to the squire. "Arc we ready?"

"Wait!" Ravenscroft jumped to his feet, tossing his napkin onto the table. "I will help you!" He hurried to join the other two men by the door.

"Good," Gregor said. "We could use someone to carry the broken wheel from the Higganbothams' carriage."

Ravenscroft gawped. "But I'll get dirty."

"So you will," Gregor said with obvious satisfaction as he followed the squire from the room.

Ravenscroft sighed. Miss Platt half stood, her hand outstretched, a hopeful expression on her face. Ravenscroft gulped, then almost ran from the room.

"Did you see that?" Miss Platt said, dropping back into her chair, almost glowing. "Oh, Miss Elizabeth, he *looked* at me!"

"Did he?" Elizabeth frowned. "I missed it."

"He looked *directly* at me!" She waved a hand to fan herself. "I think . . . he must . . . is it possible that he cares for me? Oh, Miss West, please tell me what you think? He is your brother, after all."

"I don't think Mr. West is capable of truly caring for anyone," she said. "He's much too young."

Miss Platt's face fell.

Elizabeth sent the older lady a quick look of compassion. "Which only means he's not capable *yet.*"

Miss Platt attempted to smile.

Venetia felt as if she'd just kicked a puppy. "I'm sorry, Miss Platt. Perhaps I'm not the best person to ask about Mr. West's feelings."

Miss Platt tried to take heart, squaring her shoulders. "That's true, though I know what I saw. Miss Elizabeth, perhaps we should go upstairs and pack our things?"

Elizabeth nodded absently. "Of course. Go ahead. I will be up in a moment."

Miss Platt looked from Elizabeth to Venetia, then back, plainly unsettled by Elizabeth's implied dismissal. "But, Miss Higganbotham — Elizabeth — I thought that while we were packing, we could discuss romance, as *we* are both veterans of that joyous state."

"Yes, well, I have something I must discuss with Miss West first. You may go ahead and I will arrive shortly. This will not take long."

Miss Platt sniffed her disapproval and flounced out of the room, closing the door with a decided snap.

Elizabeth rose and went to the door. She opened it a crack and peeked out. Apparently satisfied, she closed the door and came to sit beside Venetia, her eyes unusually bright as she took one of Venetia's hands and held it tightly. "I must speak with you!"

"Of course."

Elizabeth leaned forward. "Miss West, there is no one else I can trust. Mrs. Bloom is too judgmental, and Miss Platt — well, there have been times in the past few days I have thought her not a nice person."

Venetia had been thinking the same thing. It was odd, but she'd first thought Mrs. Bloom a horrid person who sadly tromped upon Miss Platt's pride. Since then, though, Venetia had witnessed the many kindnesses

Mrs. Bloom conferred upon her fellow travelers, while Miss Platt seemed more and more selfish.

Elizabeth sighed heavily. "I have no one else to turn to. Miss West — Venetia — promise you will not fail me!"

"I will do what I can," Venetia said cautiously.

"Elizabeth!" Squire Higganbotham called out.

The girl sent a harried look at the door. "Miss West, I have thought a lot about what you said to Miss Platt about being independent and keeping your opportuni—"

"Elizabeth!" The squire was almost at the door.

She stood, still clinging to Venetia's hand, her expression serious. "Miss West," she said urgently, "can I trust you?"

"Of course you can, though I don't know —"

The door opened, and the squire entered, bundled in his coat and hat, carrying a large portmanteau half stuffed with shirts and waistcoats, most of which were falling out. "Ah, there you are!" The squire set the portmanteau on the table, and a waistcoat immediately fell to the floor. "MacLean is having the broken axle removed from our carriage, so I thought I'd pack my things, only it wasn't as simple as I'd thought. I need that silly maid of yours to see if she can get all of my clothes back into this blasted thing."

Elizabeth forced a smile. "Of course! As soon as she's done with my clothes, I shall have her organize this for you."

"Excellent. I'll carry it to your room."

Elizabeth sent Venetia a long, meaningful look and reluctantly followed her father out the door.

Venetia sighed. What on earth had Elizabeth meant about being able to trust her? And when had Mrs. Bloom become so generous and Miss Platt so difficult? Had Venetia misjudged them both?

But none of that mattered in the face of what had happened in the kitchen with Gregor. She placed her elbows on the table and dropped her face into her hands, succumbing again to the quicksand of reliving those kisses over and over. She couldn't stop thinking about how fathomless Gregor's eyes had been, how absolutely tasty he'd appeared all during dinner, even when glowering at her.

More to the point, she couldn't stop wondering what would happen to all the members of their little party when they rejoined society.

■ ■ ■ ■

The next morning broke sunny and warm. The snow had melted off the roads, and only the icy drifts by the side of the barn reminded them of the blanket of white that had covered everything only a day ago.

Venetia folded a pair of stockings and carefully tucked them into her portmanteau, the faint scent of lavender making her long for the orderliness of her bedchamber in Oglivie House. She sighed and snapped the lock closed.

After so much excitement, last night had been woefully uneventful. Gregor, Ravenscroft, and the squire had not returned from Eddington until well after dinner, leaving Venetia at the mercy of the other members of their party.

Following her cryptic comments Elizabeth had spent the evening sending Venetia looks brimming with unspoken meaning. When Venetia tried to question her, the girl merely gave her a secretive smile and said in an arch voice, "All in good time, my dear Miss West! All in good time!"

Soon tired of it all, Venetia escaped to her bedchamber. She'd just donned her night rail and had unbound her hair when she heard Gregor and the men returning. The plank floors had done little to muffle their voices, and somehow she found herself pressed to the floor, trying to hear what was said.

Eventually, this cold and futile effort palled, and she climbed to her feet, brushed off her knees, and climbed into bed. There she stayed, wishing she felt even a little sleepy.

Elizabeth eventually came in, her maid following. Between the two of them, they made enough noise to wake the dead. Venetia had pretended to be asleep; she could not handle another drop of drama.

The younger woman had sighed, rolled over, and fallen into a deep and immediate slumber. Venetia lay awake most of the night, thinking about Gregor's words. He was right, of course; there would be a scandal. People would talk, and some would openly refuse to speak to her. Then the invitations would cease coming. Only the very, very wealthy could break with propriety without harming their social standing, and Venetia was not one of that select group.

The situation would be horrid from beginning to end, a fact Gregor had realized. No wonder the poor man had felt so sorry for her that he'd resigned himself to marrying her.

But Venetia didn't want a bridegroom who was resigned. She wanted a bridegroom who was excited, thrilled, ecstatic to be married to her. Not one who would casually mention it "had to be done" while chopping carrots.

Her heart heavy, Venetia plumped her pillow and rolled to her side, away from Elizabeth's loud snoring. Eventually, exhaustion lured her to sleep.

When morning finally dawned, Elizabeth's maid arrived with a breakfast tray and informed them in an annoyingly cheerful voice that the gentlemen were already having their breakfast in the common room. Grumbling about people who woke up in a good mood and how annoying such a trait was, Venetia arose, exhausted, listless, and thoroughly blue-deviled. She dressed quickly and was soon tucking her gloves into the pocket of her pelisse, ready to go downstairs.

Meanwhile, Elizabeth and her maid whispered to one another, their voices strident even when hushed.

A knock sounded on the door. Elizabeth paused in giving her maid endless instructions and raced to the door. "I'll get it!"

There, her manner changed instantly. Instead of a wide-awake young lady of fashion, she sagged listlessly against the doorframe, one hand over her brow. "Good morning," Venetia heard her say in a low, husky voice. "Lord MacLean is here." She followed the words with a feeble cough.

"Good morning, Miss Higganbotham." Gregor's rich voice seemed to fill the room. "I was going to wish you a good morning as well, but I can see you're not feeling well."

She pressed her fingers to her throat. "No. I fear I am catching something, as is my maid."

From behind her, the maid managed a feeble cough.

"I am sorry to hear that."

Elizabeth smiled bravely. "I can only hope it does not settle in the lungs." She turned from him, stumbling a little as she moved back from the door.

He caught her arm, holding her upright. She leaned against him with a grateful sigh, smiling weakly up at him, much in the manner of a very poorly acted Drury Lane drama.

Venetia met Gregor's gaze, and for an instant, amusement quivered between them.

Then his expression tightened, and he abruptly turned away.

Venetia turned back to her portmanteau, fighting the urge to burst into tears. Never again could she and Gregor be friends. Their relationship was far too damaged.

As Elizabeth allowed her maid to assist her to the chair, Venetia tried to focus on her irritating chamber mate instead. What mischief was she into? Was she trying to capture Gregor's attention?

The thought burned through Venetia. She rammed her silver comb into her reticule, almost tearing the delicate stitching. *Blast it, blast it, blast it!* She wished she could stop reacting every time Gregor was nearby — yet another thing that had changed during the last five days.

"Miss Higganbotham, the squire wished me to inform you that he will be ready to leave shortly," Gregor said. "He is sending up a man to collect your trunks."

Venetia's skin tingled at the rough sound of Gregor's voice, but she forced herself to continue placing items in her reticule — her favorite watch, a handkerchief, her silver mirror. *Act calm, and you'll feel calm,* she told herself firmly.

"I hope to be ready soon," Elizabeth said unconvincingly, her voice soft and shaky. "I'm sorry if I seem indecisive, but I didn't sleep well last night."

Venetia turned an amazed glance on the girl. She had snored so loudly last night that Venetia had fantasized about placing a pillow over those delicately shaped lips.

"I am certain you'll feel better once you are under way," Gregor told her.

"I hope so," she said softly. She took a shimmering blue opera cloak from her maid and pulled it over her shoulders. "There. I believe I'm ready now."

Venetia wondered at the odd choice of cloak. Far too fine for traveling, it would afford very little protection from the weather.

"Venetia?"

She found Gregor looking at her, his expression dark and unreadable. "Are you ready?"

"Yes, thank you." Venetia yanked the strings on her reticule and placed it over her arm. Gregor's gaze fell on her portmanteau, and he stepped forward, his broad shoulders and towering height making the bedchamber seem suddenly small and airless.

Venetia grabbed the leather handle of her portmanteau, but he was quicker, his fingers brushing hers.

A jolt of heat surged through her. Her chest ached from the lack of air before she turned away to gather her pelisse and bonnet. "I must settle with the Treadwells for the bedchamber and —"

"It has already been taken care of."

She frowned. "You didn't need to do that."

"Yes, I did. Ra—" He scowled, shooting a glance toward Elizabeth, who was too busy whispering with her maid to hear. "*Your brother* was even more underfunded than I thought."

"Then who fixed the carriage?"

Gregor shrugged.

Yet something else she owed him, blast it. As soon as they returned to London, she'd repay him.

She pulled on her pelisse and buttoned it to her neck. "I'm surprised the wheelwright could fix our wheel in so short a time."

"He replaced it with one from another carriage. Fortunately, West's equipment is rather plebeian, so it wasn't difficult. The squire wasn't so fortunate."

Elizabeth turned a suddenly concerned face toward them. "What happened?"

"The axle was beyond repair. Fortunately, Mrs. Bloom has offered to allow you and your maid to ride with her and Miss Platt to London. The squire will accompany you on horseback."

A frown appeared between Elizabeth's eyes. "I see."

Her maid watched her mistress with wide eyes, her habitual smile missing. Finally, Elizabeth nodded, spots of color high on her cheeks. "I suppose I shall have to ride with Mrs. Bloom, then. I hope Jane and I don't give her the ague."

Venetia eyed the maid, who didn't seem ill.

Gregor turned to Venetia and started to speak, then glanced at Elizabeth, who was adjusting the hood of the bright blue cloak so that it framed her face. Frowning, he merely said, "I shall see you downstairs, then."

He hefted her portmanteau and was gone.

Venetia waited until she couldn't hear Gregor's footsteps anymore before she walked down the stairs. Perhaps it would be better if she and Gregor just had a good, loud row and got all of their frustrations out. The trouble was, this time it might take much, much more than a mere argument.

Venetia found Ravenscroft standing in the doorway to the innyard, his bags about him. She noted sourly that while she had been told she'd only need "a few things" to travel to grandmama's, he'd apparently brought everything he possessed.

He brightened on seeing Venetia, rushing up to her with both hands outstretched.

"There you are! I asked MacLean when you'd be down, but he was damnably vague."

Venetia glanced past Ravenscroft to the carriage and large traveling coach awaiting them. Apparently, Mrs. Bloom believed in comfort, for the traveling coach was huge and would easily accommodate several additional passengers.

A door slammed upstairs, followed by the pounding of booted feet upon the stairs. Venetia and Ravenscroft looked up to see Miss Platt storming down. Her thin face was lined in outrage, her chin jutted out at a rebellious angle. She paused on the bottom step and said in a dramatic voice, "Miss West, I have left Mrs. Bloom! I throw myself on your mercy."

"What?" Venetia said, blinking. Twice.

Mrs. Bloom came downstairs next, dressed in a black pelisse, a large fur-lined bonnet trimmed with purple velvet, and a long lavender scarf. Her lips were folded in disapproval, her eyes snapping angrily. She saw Miss Platt at the foot of the stairs and pointed a gloved finger. "There you are, you ungrateful wretch!"

Miss Platt notched her chin higher, crossing her thin arms over her chest. "I am not ungrateful! I am merely asserting my right to — to — to —" She looked at Venetia as if asking for the word.

Venetia just blinked at Miss Platt.

Mrs. Bloom reached the bottom stair, her extra chins quivering. "Miss Platt, I wash my hands of you. Now, please move, for you are blocking my way!"

Miss Platt sniffed. "I will be glad to let you leave. You have not treated me well, has she, Miss West?"

Mrs. Bloom turned an accusing glare on Venetia.

Venetia opened her mouth, astonished to be brought into the conversation. "I can't possibly say. I mean, that's for you to decide and not —"

Miss Platt put her hands on her hips. "Mrs. Bloom, I am not your servant."

"I never said you were!" Mrs. Bloom snapped. "I was paying you a wage, which I didn't have to do, after all I did for you and that worthless brother of yours."

"Bertrand is not worthless!"

"He is a scoundrel," Mrs. Bloom said firmly. "If you don't believe me, ask the people he stole money from, running that fake investment company!"

Miss Platt's cheeks burned. "He made some bad choices —"

"No," Mrs. Bloom said firmly, "he *is* a bad

choice."

Ravenscroft cleared his throat. "I think I'll take my bags to the carriage." He scooped up the closest two and dashed for the safety of the innyard, abandoning Venetia without a backward glance.

Mrs. Bloom snorted. "To think that I helped your good-for-nothing brother because I felt pity for you and your circumstances! I have gotten you out of trouble for the last time, Miss Platt. From now on, you are on your own!"

"I want to be on my own! I have *options,* plenty of them, and I don't have to settle on you. I know, because Miss West told me so."

Venetia's heart sank. She *had* said that.

Mrs. Bloom's outraged gaze rested on Venetia for a startled moment before color flooded her cheeks. "Fine, then! If Miss West thinks you have options, than let *her* be your first one. I wash my hands of you *and* your brother!"

"Good!" Miss Platt said, marching smartly to Venetia's side and taking her arm. "From now on, I am Miss West's companion! The next time Bertrand needs assistance getting out of prison, I shall ask her to help him and not you!"

Mrs. Bloom tossed her scarf over her

shoulder and sailed past them into the innyard.

"Good riddance!" Miss Platt said, fixing a bright smile on her face. "Miss West, I suppose that means that I will be traveling with you." She sent a delighted grin toward the innyard, where Ravenscroft was instructing the Treadwells' man.

"Miss Platt . . . I don't know how to say this, but I don't need a companion!"

Miss Platt's face fell. "But you said I had options, that I didn't need to put up with Mrs. Bloom's ill tempers!"

"And I'm certain you do have options. Only I am not one of them."

"Oh, dear." Miss Platt's thin lips began to tremble. "What am I to do, then? I cannot go back to Mrs. Bloom. Not after the horrid things she's said." She looked at Venetia pleadingly.

Venetia could feel her resolve melting. In the back of her mind, she could hear Gregor telling her not to meddle in the affairs of others.

She sighed. "I suppose you may come with us. I can find you a position once we reach Stirling."

Miss Platt grasped Venetia's hand between her own. "Thank you! This will work out beautifully, wait and see." With a glowing smile, Miss Platt ran upstairs to fetch her things.

Venetia looked up the stairs, her hope for things to improve slowly draining away. Good God, what had she done? Now she was saddled with Miss Platt, who would annoy them all by fawning over Ravenscroft and tittering like a madwoman.

"There you are."

Venetia turned to find Gregor standing behind her. He looked at the bags still blocking the entryway. "Good God, Ravenscroft. These can't all be yours!"

Ravenscroft, who had just returned from the innyard, grabbed two more. "I thought I was leaving the country, so naturally I packed a few more things than normal." He nodded to the remaining two bags. "If you'll just get those, I can have them all loaded in a trice."

Gregor folded his arms over his chest.

Ravenscroft sighed. "Oh, never mind." He tromped out to the waiting coach, passing the squire, who hurried inside to say jovially, "There you are, Miss West! I was worried I wouldn't see you to say my good-byes."

"I couldn't allow that," Venetia said lightly, though she felt anything but. "In fact, I was just getting ready to tell Lord MacLean that Miss Platt will now be traveling with us."

Gregor's gaze narrowed. "Oh?"

Venetia lifted her chin in the air. "Yes. She and Mrs. Bloom have decided to part ways."

"No surprise there," the squire said, "though I do think Miss Platt is making a mistake. There aren't many women who'd put up with a companion who puts on such airs."

Gregor quirked a brow. "Miss Platt is not wholly to blame for her attitude. She had some assistance in thinking herself better than her station."

The squire glanced past Venetia to the steps. "Ah! Elizabeth, my child!" He rushed forward to where the girl was coming downstairs, the blue cloak swirling about her. "I hear you are feeling poorly."

"I'm not as badly off as poor Jane. Father, I don't think she should travel with us today. She's coughing and coughing. I told her to stay in bed. We can send one of the coachmen to fetch her once we reach London."

"Yes, but —"

"Mrs. Treadwell can see to Jane until she's better."

"But if your maid stays here, who will attend you on the road?"

"Oh, I shall be fine by myself. Miss West hasn't had a maid all week, and she seems to do well."

The squire eyed Venetia's hair before he replied in a doubtful voice, "I suppose you're right."

"It's either that or you'll have to sit in the carriage and hold a bowl for her."

"A bowl?"

Elizabeth turned a wide, guileless eye toward her father. "Didn't I mention that not only is she coughing but her stomach is upset, too?"

The squire looked a little queasy at the thought. "No, you didn't. I will speak with Treadwell, and we'll leave the girl here."

"Thank you, Father." She reached down to brush off one of her lavender half-boots. "If you'll send one of the men to fetch that final trunk from my room, we'll be ready to go."

The squire frowned. "Another one? I don't know how we'll get another on the coach."

"You can't," Gregor said shortly. "Chambers said it was overloaded as it is."

"Wonderful," the squire muttered.

Elizabeth coughed a bit. "Pardon me, Miss West. If there's no room for my trunk on Mrs. Bloom's carriage, would you be willing to take it on yours?"

Venetia blinked. "On mine? But —"

"If you'll let us know when you've arrived

in London, Father will send a servant to collect it."

The squire brightened. "That's an excellent idea! I say, Miss West, would you mind?"

"No. Not at all. Though it may be several weeks before I arrive."

"Oh, that's no problem," Elizabeth said. "Thank you! I knew I could count on you."

There was something odd about the way she said that, but Venetia couldn't fathom what the girl could possibly mean.

"It's time we were on our way," the squire said. "Mrs. Bloom is already in the coach, Elizabeth. We've just been waiting for you."

Gregor caught Venetia's eye, a question in his gaze. She nodded. "I'm ready, too."

Within a short time, she and Ravenscroft and Miss Platt were ensconced in Ravenscroft's carriage. Gregor stood by with his mount while they waited for Chambers and Mr. Treadwell's man to bring the forgotten trunk.

Meanwhile, the squire assisted his daughter into Mrs. Bloom's handsome carriage.

The girl coughed again. "I shall sleep the entire way — oh! I forgot my gloves." With amazing agility, she whirled from her father's side, the blue opera cloak swirling about her. "I shall be right back!" she called as she hurried toward the inn.

The squire shook his head. "She's sadly shatter-brained."

"The young are like that," Mrs. Bloom said, sending a glare toward Miss Platt. "I hope we shall not have to wait for Miss Higganbotham very long, as I —"

"Ah!" the squire said, satisfaction in his voice. "There she is now."

Miss Higganbotham dashed from the inn door through the puddle-strewn yard, her brown boots hopping between the puddles with assuredness, one gloved hand tightly clutching the hood around her face.

She climbed the carriage steps and slid into the far corner.

The squire stepped back to allow the coachman to put up the stairs and close the door.

Mrs. Bloom leaned out the window. "Miss West, Mr. West, Lord MacLean. I daresay I shall see you in London."

Venetia didn't think so but nodded anyway. Ravenscroft, apparently having forgotten that once he returned to London he had a duel to face, promptly agreed. Gregor merely bowed.

The great coach creaked to a start and left, the huge wheels cutting deeply in the mud. Moments later, Chambers and Treadwell's man staggered out, carrying the forgotten trunk.

"Good God," Gregor said, coming forward to assist the two men. "What does that woman have in here?"

"I have no idea," Chambers said, "but we're wagerin' 'tis bricks."

"Or gold." The other man gasped.

Eventually, the trunk was lashed to the back of the carriage, and they, too, set out. Gregor rode behind; Ravenscroft pretended to sleep to avoid conversation with Miss Platt. Venetia, meanwhile, leaned back on one corner, miserable and exhausted.

And Miss Platt, blissfully unaware of the currents that swirled about her, chattered on and on, delighted with events.

Venetia could only hope they'd reach Grandmama's house before any of their tenuous relationships unraveled even more.

Chapter 17

Och, me wee lassies! 'Tis important ye
learn to say what ye mean. 'Tis the greatest gift ye can give yerself and the ones
ye love.

> Old Woman Nora from Loch Lomond
> to her three wee granddaughters
> one cold evening

Gregor urged his horse to a trot. It was
wonderful to be on horseback, the air cool
and moist, heavy with the scent of damp
earth, the trees whispering. It was a pity
Venetia hadn't brought her riding habit; this
was precisely the type of ride she loved, one
that tugged at all the senses.

He could imagine her now, riding ahead,
her horse prancing, that mischievous half
smile on her face as she laughed back over
her shoulder at him.

Gregor smiled for the first time since their
conversation yesterday.

He glanced back at the carriage, which lumbered slowly along, Chambers meticulously avoiding the deeper ruts and muddier spots. Even from this distance, he could hear the murmur of Miss Platt's incessant chattering. Venetia and Ravenscroft would be ready to murder the woman by the time they reached Venetia's grandmother's house.

The carriage's leather curtains were pinned open. If he dropped back, he could catch a glimpse of Venetia, her brown hair haphazardly pinned, the thick curls hanging down around her neck, doubtless a pained expression on her face as Miss Platt tittered on.

Venetia couldn't walk down the sidewalk without some story of woe attaching to her skirts. He supposed he should sympathize with her. In the past — last week, though it felt like years ago — they would have laughed at the silly creature.

He would have ridden beside the carriage and met Venetia's look, and she would have instantly known his thoughts, and he hers. Now, she avoided his gaze, avoided him.

All desire to smile left Gregor. He missed those times, and part of him feared they'd never be again. He hadn't realized how much he loved to hear Venetia laugh until these last few days, when she'd done so little of it. She had the most endearing gurgle of humor, her eyes lighting to a sparkling silver, her lips curving in an entrancing way.

Damn, damn, damn! It was unfair that Ravenscroft's thoughtless gesture had led to such an estrangement. Gregor's hands tightened on the reins, and he urged his mount farther ahead of the carriage.

Now, he couldn't stop being aware of her, noticing a thousand things that had been hidden to him before. How her hair curled at the nape of her neck, how she always smelled so sweetly, how she tilted her head when listening — all things that suddenly made her more than a mere friend.

It was as if all these years, he'd seen her through a dark glass, and now the shades had been ripped aside, and the brilliant sunshine was illuminating her for the first time. Venetia Oglivie, his best friend in the entire world, the one woman he'd never thought of in a sensual manner, was beautiful. Not the flamboyant, skin-thin beauty of the ton but the deep, rich, earthy beauty of a real woman.

That realization had thrown him off-balance and had caused him to be cow-handed in his dealings with her. Though she was too stubborn to admit it, she would be far better off marrying him than anyone else. He knew her, appreciated her, and cared for her. He was well established and could take good care of her. He could easily add new stables to his Lancashire estate to hold the horses he knew she'd wish to purchase. What more could she ask for?

He grimaced, remembering her outraged expression when he'd announced that she would marry him. Though she didn't really have a choice, she deserved to be asked. That was what a woman would want.

Gregor sighed. Perhaps in the peace and quiet at her grandmother's house, he could begin anew, explain to her the advantages of a match with him. She wasn't ready to admit how dire things were, but once she was, he was certain she'd reconsider his offer. She had to.

The thought cheered him, and it was with a lighter heart that he rounded a bend. *"Whoa!"*

A light phaeton was mired deep in the mud at the side of the road, the driver and his coachman standing beside it. The driver, a middle-aged man in an olive drab coat, lifted one well-shod foot and kicked the wheel of the phaeton.

Gregor laughed.

The man looked around, appearing embarrassed when he saw Gregor. "I'm sorry you had to witness that," the man said, coming forward to proffer his hand. "I'm Sir Henry Loundan."

The man's handshake was firm and solid, his gray eyes clear and direct. There was a touch of gray at his temples, and his eyes crinkled at the corners as if he laughed a good deal.

Gregor smiled. "Good afternoon. I'm Gregor MacLean. I hope you don't mind if I remain mounted; the ground looks uncertain."

Sir Henry shook his head ruefully, indicating his muddied boots. "I should have brought my own mount and not the chaise, but in any event, I'm glad to see you. We've been here for the last hour, and not a single person has passed. I was beginning to think we'd have to walk the four miles to Eddington."

Gregor eyed the mucky road with disfavor. "It's damnably soft here, isn't it?"

The man nodded. "There's a firmer strip on the other side of the road. Wish we'd known that before we sank."

"I wonder if it is wide enough for both wheels of a carriage." Behind him, Gregor heard the carriage approaching. He nudged his mount to the center of the road just as it lumbered around the corner. Chambers took in the situation at a glance and pulled the carriage to a halt.

The door opened, and Ravenscroft came barreling out, regardless of mud and muck.

"Mr. West!" Miss Platt stuck her head out the window. "Do be careful! I vow you'll get your feet wet if you stand there. Are we stuck? I hope we don't have to get out and walk, for I have no walking boots with me, and it would be ruinous for my skirts. Mr. West, don't you think walking would be horrid in this weather?" She sat down again, her voice continuing, presumably now addressing her comments to Venetia.

Ravenscroft walked toward Gregor, a haunted look in his eyes. "MacLean! We should change places. Let you have a warm, toasty carriage ride, while I brave the elements in your place. It must be damnably cold here, and —"

"No." Gregor turned back to Sir Henry. "If you'll assist us through this mud, I'm certain we can take you as far as Eddington. You might be able to hire a mount and continue your journey from there."

"That would be wonderful." Sir Henry gave Gregor a rueful look. "I am in the greatest of hurries, which always seems to necessitate some sort of breakdown, doesn't it?"

"Every time," Gregor agreed.

"My lord?" Chambers called down from his perch on the carriage. "Should the ladies alight? If we were to slide down off the road, we might overturn."

"You're right. I shall help them." Gregor went to the coach and opened the door.

The light slanted inside, turning Venetia's eyes to silver. Gregor held out his hand. "You will have to stand aside for a few moments while we guide the coach over this section of road."

She hesitated, then nodded, placing her hand in his.

The light pressure of her fingers sent a wave of heat through him. He tightened his grip as she stepped forward to the edge of the door, and for a startled instant, her gaze met his.

Without thought, he slipped an arm around her waist and lifted her from the carriage, holding her flush against him, every inch of her form molded to his.

Her cheeks pinkened, her eyes widening. "Gregor!" she breathed, sending an embarrassed look around.

Her unease reached through his lust, and he set her down, stepping away reluctantly.

A strained silence held those nearby. Ravenscroft was scowling, Chambers and

Sir Henry's groom were suspiciously busy with their duties, and Sir Henry was looking away, though there was a hint of sympathy in his gaze.

Gregor made a faint bow to Venetia. "I didn't want you to muddy your feet on the mud. It's, ah, less dirty here."

She looked down. Gregor's gaze followed hers. She was standing in an inch of water; he'd placed her squarely in the middle of a puddle.

Venetia lifted her skirts and walked to one side, her boots making sucking noises as she walked. "I appreciate your efforts, Mac-Lean."

"Yoo-hoo, Lord MacLean!" Miss Platt stood in the carriage door, apparently ready to jump into his arms. "I'm ready to climb down!"

Venetia gurgled with laughter, which she tried to cover with a cough.

Gregor sent her a glare before saying over his shoulder, "Mr. West, be so good as to help Miss Platt from the carriage."

"Me? But —"

Gregor sent him a look.

The younger man gulped. "Oh, very well." He made his way through the puddles to the carriage, then stood far, far away, merely offering the tips of his fingers for Miss Platt to hold on to.

She blinked. "I can't step out there. It's *muddy.*"

He dropped his hand. "Very well." He turned to Gregor. "Miss Platt would rather stay in the carriage and be overturned."

"I didn't say that!" she huffed.

He held out his hand, still as far away as before.

Forced to make do, Miss Platt was soon standing beside Venetia by the edge of the road, their feet muddied and wet.

Gregor turned to Chambers, Ravenscroft, and Sir Henry. "If we keep the carriage moving slowly but push a bit from this side, we should be able to keep it from slipping off the road."

"That might work," Sir Henry said. "When my carriage began to slip, I foolishly halted the horses and the wheels sunk into the mud. There was nothing to be done after that."

Gregor nodded. "Then we have a plan."

"I beg your pardon," Venetia said from the side of the road. "I wouldn't do it that way."

Ravenscroft smiled. "My dear Venetia, I am certain we know how to get this carriage over this stretch of road without —"

"How would you do it?" Gregor asked, ignoring Ravenscroft's startled glance.

"If you go slowly, it will allow the carriage's wheels to sink. I'd take it faster."

Sir Henry looked impressed. "She's right. The momentum might carry the carriage over the mud."

Gregor nodded thoughtfully. "We'll take Venetia's advice. Chambers, drive quickly and evenly across this stretch. Sir Henry, perhaps your man can run by the leader and encourage him on? Ravenscroft, you and Sir Henry and I will push from the low side to make certain the carriage doesn't slide off the road."

As soon as Gregor, Ravenscroft, and Sir Henry positioned themselves, Chambers set the horses in motion.

The large carriage rumbled forward, Sir Henry's man holding the lead horse by the bridle and urging him forward. The road slanted a bit as they entered the turn.

"Now," Gregor said, pressing his shoulder to the back panel of the carriage.

Ravenscroft and Sir Henry pressed as well. The carriage moved smoothly forward . . . then hung a moment and slid a bit to one side.

"Push harder!" Gregor ordered, gritting his teeth as he struggled to keep the carriage from slipping into the muck.

Thank God for Venetia's suggestion. With

the help of the horses, the carriage continued on. Within moments, they were out of the muck and on the firmer ground ahead, and Chambers pulled the carriage to a halt.

Gregor caught sight of Venetia's relieved expression. Without thinking, he tossed her a wink.

She winked back without pause.

Gregor grinned, suddenly feeling better about life in general.

Sir Henry blew out his breath, leaning against the back of the carriage. "That was something!" He grinned. "I wish you all had been here when I was trying to get over that same ground. The —" He shoved himself from the carriage. "Is the carriage sliding? I felt it move."

As if in answer to his words, the carriage rocked a bit.

"Chambers!" Gregor yelled.

The groom turned around and looked back over the carriage. "My lord?"

"Are you moving?"

"No, my lord. We're firm as —" The carriage rocked again, and this time, a muffled cry came with it.

"Good God!" Sir Henry said, stepping away from the rocking carriage. "What in the hell is that?"

"Oh, no!" Venetia ran forward, grabbing

the straps at the back of the coach and frantically trying to undo them.

Ravenscroft frowned. "Venetia, what on earth are you doing?"

Gregor grabbed the top strap and quickly undid it. With a crash, the trunks came falling off the carriage in a heap. The one Venetia had offered to carry to London for Miss Higganbotham rolled to one side and then fell open. Out spilled a mound of silks and gowns, flailing slippers, and a glimpse of petticoats, as Miss Elizabeth Higganbotham rolled out head over heels, into a large puddle.

"Elizabeth!" Venetia and Sir Henry exclaimed as one.

Then they looked at each other, eyes wide.

"I — I — I'm muddy!" Miss Higganbotham wailed. Mud streamed from her golden curls and soaked her gown from neck to hem. Thick clots clung to her white skin and smeared her chin.

To everyone's shock and surprise, Sir Henry Loundan fell onto his knees in the puddle, scooped her into his arms, and breathlessly kissed her.

Much later that afternoon, the squire realized the depths of his daughter's determination to, as he put it, "ruin her life." He had followed Mrs. Bloom's heavy coach for most of the day, frustrated at the lack of speed. At this rate, they'd have to spend another night in an inn, which distressed the squire no end. He'd been dreaming of staying in his own town house, with its fresh sheets and thick mattresses and the services of a cook directly from York, where he'd been born and raised. Soon he'd have Elizabeth safely tucked away from her ill-conceived passion, and life could resume normality.

Mrs. Bloom, for all her irascible ways, had shown herself to possess a generous heart. The one time they'd stopped, Elizabeth had remained huddled in her corner of the carriage, the hood over her head, a hand pressed to her forehead as if pleading a headache. The squire thought she was merely engaging in histrionics, but Mrs. Bloom was inclined to believe she was suffering from overexcitement, first at being removed from her "fiancé," then by their accident and the days of being confined to the inn. Elizabeth had eventually fallen asleep, her head drooping, the cloak hood covering her face and blocking the unwanted light. Mrs. Bloom had become quite protective and had refused to allow anyone to awaken her.

A wooden sign proclaimed another inn ahead. The squire sighed when Mrs. Bloom's plump hand extended from the window, waving a white handkerchief to signal that she wished to stop once more.

Good God, the woman must possess England's smallest bladder. Grumbling to himself, he waved agreement, hoping they wouldn't be long. The carriage turned smartly into the yard, and the squire followed, deciding to remain outside while Mrs. Bloom did what she must and sampled the tea dishes.

He informed Mrs. Bloom of his intentions as her groom opened the door.

"Very well," she said airily. "Although it's bad for your digestion to miss tea."

"I am certain I shall survive. Has Elizabeth been better company?"

"La, no! The child has done nothing but sleep. She sleeps as quiet as a mouse, too. Why, if I couldn't see her breathing, I wouldn't know if she was alive or not. I do hope she'll feel better for her nap." With that, Mrs. Bloom went into the inn, where she was welcomed by the innkeeper and his wife, both heartily hoping she would leave a pot of vales in her wake.

The squire leaned in through the coach window and peeked at his daughter. She was exactly as Mrs. Bloom described, covered head to foot in her blue cloak, sound asleep, not a sound emanating from her but deep, even breathing. Poor child. He had been a little rough on her, but it had been for her own good.

He had led his horse to the front of the carriage, checking the wheels and equipment, when the sound of approaching horses made him turn.

Three men rode into the courtyard on horses that made the squire envious. The first two men were very large, dark-haired, and dressed in somber black. The last was blond and more slender, his clothing of a dandified cut, his coat and boots clearly from London.

They pulled up at the inn door, and one of the dark-haired men swung down, removing his hat as he did so. The late sunlight filtered over him, highlighting the streak of white in his hair and outlining the planes of his face.

The squire blinked. He knew that face, that defined nose and chin.

The squire moved forward. "Good afternoon, gentlemen! I don't wish to intrude, but are you perchance related to Gregor MacLean?"

The man standing by his horse sent a

quick glance at his companions before nodding. "Yes, we are." His voice was thick with a Scottish burr. "Gregor is our brother. I am Hugh MacLean. These are my other brothers, Alexander and" — Hugh nodded toward the blond man — "Dougal."

"Actually, I know Dougal MacLean from a business endeavor. I am Squire Higganbotham. I was hoping to learn Lord Gregor MacLean's address so that I could thank him for the service he did for me and my daughter."

Dougal swung off his horse and came forward, his green eyes bright. "Did you say our brother had performed a service for you?"

"For us all. We were stuck in an inn because of the snow. He assisted us in getting the carriages repaired, he and his man healed the injured horses, and he helped make certain our luggage was well tied. He was quite helpful."

Hugh rubbed his forehead as if struggling to understand something. "Helpful? Are you certain it was my brother? He has a scar —"

The squire traced a line down the left side of his face.

"Hmm." Hugh shook his head in wonderment. "I cannot believe 'twas him."

"Why not?" the squire asked, puzzled.

"It is rather out of character for Gregor to be so helpful."

Dougal edged forward. "Did Gregor appear injured in any way? A wound to the head, perhaps?"

"No."

"Hmm. I thought that might account for such a change, but perhaps it was Miss Oglivie's influence."

"Oglivie? Who is that?"

Dougal's brows rose. "A woman about this high?" He held out his hand to his shoulder. "Brown hair? Gray eyes? A bit plump? She would have been with Gregor, along with a man named Ravenscroft."

"Why, yes! You are talking about Lord MacLean's charges, Mr. and Miss West."

A tense silence ensued.

Alexander scowled so heavily the squire took a step back. "I beg your pardon," Alexander growled, "but did you say the Wests?"

The squire nodded.

The men exchanged glances once again, sending a ripple of unease through the squire. "You seem surprised, and I don't understand. Who is this Ravenscroft? And who is Miss Oglivie? I've never heard of her, yet you seem to think she looks exactly the same as Miss We —"

"Och, good squire!" Dougal smiled, coming forward to shake the squire's hand mightily. " 'Tis just a piddly little family matter. I don't suppose you know where our brother was heading?"

"Mr. West said they were to visit Miss West's grandmother in Stirling."

"We know the estate," Alexander said, appearing less than happy.

"Good." The squire paused, his thick brows drawn. "That's odd. I don't know why it didn't dawn on me before, but Mr. West spoke of the grandmother as if he wasn't related to her."

Dougal shrugged as he turned to remount, his brother Hugh doing the same. "I happen to know Mr. West very well, and he's a bit of an idiot."

"Thank you for your assistance," Alexander rumbled, turning his huge horse toward the road. His brothers followed suit.

"Good evening to you!" Dougal called over his shoulder.

"Wait!" The squire hurried forward, but the men were gone, the thunder of hooves proclaiming their hurry.

What was going on? Why were MacLean's brothers in search of him? And why had they seemed surprised to learn of his wards? Surely, if they were his brothers, they would know of his wards?

The squire glanced at the inn, wishing Mrs. Bloom had been there. She had spoken with Miss West quite a bit, as had Elizabeth — Ah! His daughter might know something about the now-mysterious Miss West. They had shared a bedchamber, and women tended to tell one another things.

He hurried to the carriage and opened the door. His daughter was still deep asleep, her breathing quiet —

The squire's own breath caught in his throat. No sound? Elizabeth had snored since she was a small child. Even sitting upright, she snored and gasped as if fighting for breath.

He reached for her cloak. If he didn't know better, he would think —

Mrs. Bloom heard the bellow from where she sat before the fireplace in the inn, lifting her first cup to her waiting lips. Regretfully setting down her tea, she gathered her pelisse and hurried to the innyard.

Standing by the carriage, his hands clenched in fury, face almost purple with rage, was the squire.

And before him, swathed in a familiar blue cloak, was not Miss Elizabeth Higganbotham but her brown-haired maid.

"You — you — you —" The squire couldn't seem to find the words.

Mrs. Bloom hurried to his side. "Really!" she said to the wretched girl. "How *could* you? Where is Miss Higganbotham! Tell us this *instant!*"

Though terrified, Jane was also sincerely attached to her mistress and wholeheartedly agreed with the dramatic Miss Higganbotham that her father was cruel and a beast to try to separate her from her beloved Henry.

Jane thought it a cold crime indeed that anyone should cause the lovely and amazing Miss Higganbotham to cry.

No one could cry as prettily as Miss Higganbotham. Her skin remained unblotched, her eyes clear, her nose lacking the pink tone of those of other weeping misses.

Jane was abjectly and completely under her mistress's spell, especially once Elizabeth had tearfully revealed that the squire intended on hiring an older, more staid individual to wait on his daughter in London. Jane's days with her beloved mistress were numbered.

With nothing to lose, Jane had agreed to take Elizabeth's place in the carriage. It was the one way she could prove her love for her beautiful mistress before being banished back to the country, and she was prepared for the squire's red-faced threats and blustering yells.

Mrs. Bloom, however, interrupted the squire in mid-tirade with an abrupt "This is getting us nowhere."

The squire, rendered speechless, stood glowering.

"Squire Higganbotham, with your permission, I should like to speak to Miss Jane" — she fixed a steely eye on the now-quaking maid — *"alone."* She reached over, grabbed Jane by the ear, and led her forthwith into the inn.

What happened after that the squire was not to know. From the innyard, all he heard was a loud squall and the babbling of a weeping girl.

Finally, Mrs. Bloom came marching out, the innkeeper and his wife watching her with newfound respect. "Squire Higganbotham, please instruct the coachman to take us to Stirling."

"Of course, but —"

"Ride with me, and I will tell you what that silly daughter of yours has done. But hurry, for there's not a moment to be lost." A martial light in her eye, Mrs. Bloom added, "We will rescue both your daughter and Miss Platt, for I fear that she, too, has fallen in with a band of common adventurers!"

CHAPTER 18

Livin' well is the best revenge. Those as wish ye harm will find nothin' more bitter t' swallow.
Old Woman Nora from Loch Lomond
to her three wee granddaughters
one cold evening

Mrs. Oglivie was going to die. Oh, not in a *corporeal* sense, but rather on an *emotional* level — which was much, much worse than a mere bodily death.

They would find her here, in her bed, dressed in her best pink silk, alone, her eyes staring blankly at the ceiling, her expression empty of emotion . . .

She frowned thoughtfully. Her expression might have *some* emotion. An indescribable aura of suffering, perhaps. Yes! That was what they'd see. Endless suffering.

If Viola closed her eyes, she could almost see it — the weeping servants, the perplexed look on the doctor's face, the penitence in her mother-in-law's eyes. *That* one made Viola smile, for the dowager was going to be the cause of her demise. Viola was sure of it.

She'd come to Stirling to assist her mother-in-law, who had succumbed to an especially horrid case of the ague. The dowager had regarded Viola as an angel, a reaction Viola knew would last only as long as the dowager needed her.

And indeed, the second the dowager was out of bed, the not-so-subtle criticisms began. Unfortunately, the snow started at the same time, and Viola was stuck. Stuck in a house with a woman who believed Viola wasn't "good enough for my Geoffrey."

With growing resentment, Viola watched the snow pile up outside the damp old house. She missed the comfort and elegance of her own home, the presence of her beloved Geoffrey and her beautiful daughter, Venetia.

Actually, Venetia had been the subject of Viola's last argument with the dowager. The old bat had commented one time too many that Venetia was "wasting away" without a husband, implying that it was somehow Viola's fault.

Nothing could have been further from the

truth. Viola simmered even now thinking about the unfair comments, the hints that she'd somehow raised Venetia incorrectly or (worse) had selfishly kept Venetia at home to run the household instead of making a respectable match.

Viola clenched the sheets, wishing her hands were around the dowager's scrawny neck instead. If the old bat only knew of the countless efforts Viola had made to interest Venetia in the veritable *swath* of eligible men she had invited to Oglivie House, of the *numerous* entertainments she had sponsored, the *endless* events she'd escorted Venetia to, all in the hope that Venetia might show interest in at least one young man.

And all for naught.

It wasn't that Venetia wasn't cooperative. She wasn't ungrateful, nor did she refuse to participate in events, but neither was she excited about them or about the men she met. She was simply impervious.

Viola had her own opinion about why her daughter was so difficult to please. His name was Gregor MacLean, and he'd been a blasted inconvenience from the beginning. It was difficult to expect Venetia to pay attention to an ordinary mortal man when Gregor MacLean was about. Even Viola found herself staring at Gregor. It was ludicrous, but the man was simply too handsome to be stood.

So now Venetia was far past the marriageable age, and Viola wished more than life itself to dandle at least *one* grandchild on her knee before she died.

Thus, the accusations from her mother-in-law were especially painful, and were directly responsible for the fact that Viola was now lying upon her bed, a bottle of smelling salts within easy grasp.

She lifted her head from her pillow and regarded the clock on the mantel. It was five minutes after four. She'd been in her room for more than three hours, and *still* no one had come to see why she hadn't appeared for tea. Viola threw herself back on the pillow, her stomach rumbling uncomfortably. Surely the dowager would soon send someone to see if she was well. Unless that had been part of the evil woman's plan, to encourage Viola to starve herself and then —

A soft knock sounded at the door.

Finally! Viola smoothed the covers, then pressed herself back into the pillow and crossed her hands over her chest.

Another knock sounded, this one a bit louder.

Viola waited, holding her breath. She

closed her eyes, cracking one open the slightest bit so she could see the door.

The knob turned, and the door opened. From the crack between her eyelids, Viola saw Liza, the dowager's maid, tiptoeing across the room.

Viola closed her eyes tightly and waited.

There was a hesitant step, then another.

Viola imagined how she must look, her long blond hair (light enough to hide most of the gray that threaded through it, thank goodness!) tucked neatly beneath her white lace cap. Her pink silk gown draped to the floor in a graceful slant. Her face in repose, elegant yet proud . . . oh, yes. It would be a sight to behold.

Hope swelled in Viola's breast. Perhaps the dowager regretted her hasty words. The old woman must have been horridly worried when Viola had not come to tea, had finally realized that she should treat her daughter-in-law with some respect, and had sent her maid with regrets for her boorish behavior.

Seeing Viola's still form, the maid would grow concerned, perhaps even frightened. She would gasp and run from the room, yelling for help. Others would come, and the dowager would be notified of Viola's possible death. The old biddy would be so sorry she'd probably burst into tears, frightening the servants with the unexpected display of emotion. Then everyone would realize how wrongly the dowager had treated Viola.

The maid's footsteps disappeared. There was a thick rug near the bed, so she must be approaching. Viola forced her face to remain perfectly expressionless, her body relaxed, her breathing deep and slow.

"Mrs. Oglivie?" The voice was directly beside the bed now.

Viola allowed her eyes to flutter, but she did not open them.

"Mrs. Oglivie?" Liza placed a tentative hand over Viola's on top of the coverlet. "The dowager sent me to fetch ye."

Viola fluttered her eyes again but did not move.

"Ye ain't havin' yer woman time, are ye?"

Viola almost gasped. How dare the maid suggest such a thing!

"If ye are, I can fetch ye some bitterroot, which will kill off the ill humors."

Viola did not deign a reply. Really! How unfeeling of the woman to say such a thing. She wondered if the dowager had suggested it.

"The dowager said ye might be feeling a bit out of sorts because o' yer woman time.

She said that if ye were, I was to toss the water from yer washbasin on ye. I don't like to do such a thing, meself, but if it'll rouse ye . . ."

Despite her best intentions, Viola's eyes flew open. "That *woman* told you to throw water on me?"

"Aye. Actually, she wished me to throw water on ye and *then* tell ye to get up, but I didn't think that a sportin' thing to do."

Viola's temper exploded. She sat upright and glared. "Please inform the dowager that I am *not* in the mood for tea."

"I daresay ye aren't," Liza said, unperturbed by Viola's icy voice. "But ye needs to come anyway. There's guests, and the dowager isn't too pleased, as she only had four scones readied for tea."

Viola's gaze went to the window. The snow was finally melted, but the roads were a river of mud. "Who would come on a day like this?"

"Yer daughter is one o' the guests. Some of her acquaintances seem a bit ragtag to me, though one o' them is as beautiful as Lucifer!" Liza shivered deliciously. "He even has the devil's own scar across his face!"

"Sweet roses!" Viola hopped off the bed so suddenly the maid jumped back. "Get my blue morning gown! And don't waste another moment, you foolish girl! We must hurry!"

Viola was dressed in a remarkably short time. She heard the dowager's quavering voice as she flew down the steps, along with several other voices. What had occurred to send Venetia here? And who was with her?

Viola stepped into the sitting room, her gaze immediately finding her daughter. Venetia, who was elegant even under the most strenuous circumstances, was sadly crumpled and tired-looking. The entire group appeared to be out of sorts, muddied, mussed, and wrinkled.

"Mama!" Venetia rushed forward and threw her arms around Viola.

Venetia had always been an affectionate child, but there was something almost desperate in the way she hugged Viola. "Venetia! What are you doing here? Not that you're not welcome, but goodness, what has happened?"

Over Venetia's shoulder, Viola caught Gregor's gaze. He returned her look evenly, but she had the fleeting thought that something was different.

Something significant.

A flicker of hope lifted in Viola's breast. She patted Venetia's shoulder. "There, there. You must tell me everything."

"I will. It's a long story. Meanwhile, allow me to introduce my traveling companions. This is Miss Platt."

A thin woman with mousy brown hair bobbed her head nervously.

"And this is Miss Higganbotham, and Sir Henry Loundan." An exceptionally beautiful girl, who was unfortunately covered in mud, blushed and nodded a greeting. The distinguished gentleman beside her, who had risen to his feet on Viola's entrance, bowed.

"And you know Ravenscroft."

He bowed from where he stood by the window, away from the main group.

Viola eyed him with interest. Lord Ravenscroft seemed somewhat sullen, his usually carefully disheveled locks now not so carefully disheveled. He appeared to have slept in his clothes, for his cravat was oddly knotted, his coat rumpled, his hair standing on end, and mud streaking one leg.

The thin, angular woman cleared her throat and said in a painfully arch voice, "This is an interesting house. The exterior is so morbid and the interior quite dark. I cannot help but think we've all stumbled into a Gothic novel of some sort. One of us might wake up dead before morning!"

The dowager was not pleased. Dressed in

her habitual black and lavender, her hair covered with a huge, improbably red wig that was stuck with a mass of glittering jeweled pins, she sniffed loudly. "Miss Flat —"

"It's Miss *Platt.*" The woman tittered again.

The dowager's thin brows snapped down. "Miss *Flat,* I do not like the implications of your words. If you find my house offensive, feel free to leave. The door is over there." The dowager pointed to the wall to one side.

The entire group looked at the wall. There was no door there, only a large window that opened an entire story above the garden.

Viola stifled a tired grin even while she admitted that Miss Platt was right about the house; she wouldn't be a bit surprised to discover a dead body in one of the lesser-used rooms, along with a set of clues pointing directly to the owner of the house.

"My lady," Miss Platt said, looking nervously at the window. "There is no door there. It's —"

"Venetia!" The dowager glared at her granddaughter. "Did I invite you?"

"No. However, you have told me many times that I don't visit you often enough."

"I didn't mean for you to arrive like this, unannounced and with a group of scoundrels!"

"Grandmama!" Venetia said, her eyes flashing. "Please don't be rude."

"It's not rude to speak plainly." Her grandmother squinted at Gregor. "You there! You've the look of the MacLeans about you."

He bowed. "I am Gregor MacLean."

"Humph. Are you the scalawag who keeps flirting with my Venetia but won't come up to snuff and marry her like a godly man?"

Venetia covered her eyes with both hands.

To Viola's surprise, Gregor smiled faintly. He crossed to the dowager's side and took her gnarled hand from the arm of her chair and kissed it with a gallant air. "I am that same MacLean; both a scoundrel and rogue. But not because I won't marry your grand-daughter. I *have* asked her to marry me, and she has refused."

Viola gasped.

"What?" Ravenscroft cried.

Miss Platt crossed her hands over her heart. "Miss West! You never said a word!"

Miss Higganbotham and her beau appeared confused.

Viola wondered who Miss West could be while Venetia dropped her head, her eyes still covered by her hands, a moan escaping her.

The dowager stomped a foot. "Why won't

she have you?"

"Because I botched my proposal in the most ham-handed way possible. I am hoping to persuade her to give me another chance, for I feel we are eminently suited."

Viola's heart leapt. She never had seen MacLean give her daughter such a heated look before. Something had definitely changed. But why wasn't Venetia responding?

The dowager eyed Gregor. "I'm surprised you're letting a mere gal tell you no."

"Grandmama!" Venetia said, dropping her hands. "Please stop this. And do not call Gregor names."

"Huh!" The dowager hunched her shoulders. "Any family that's been given a weather curse is scoundrelly in my book."

Gregor grinned. "In my book, any woman who was able to torment my great-grandfather to the point of madness is a sad romp."

"Ha!" she said gleefully, her wrinkled cheeks pink. "Told you about that before he kicked off, did he?"

"You are a legend in my family. Your portrait is still hanging in the grand hall, facing his — much to the fury of my long-deceased great-grandmother. They say she still walks the halls, gnashing her teeth and wailing, almost fifty years since she died."

"That was Pauline for you. Cried at this. Wept at that. Reminds me of other people I know." The dowager looked directly at Viola.

Viola opened her mouth to protest, but the dowager was off again. "I may lose my temper now and again, but I never waste my time weeping. If something is wrong, then you fix it. This namby-pamby generation won't address their problems. They just dance around them and wring their hands." She eyed Gregor a moment, her gaze lingering on his legs. "You may sit beside me."

Gregor bowed. "I shall do just that, once all of the ladies have taken their seats."

Venetia visibly gathered herself. "Grandmama, everyone has had a long and difficult journey. I believe it would be best if we all retired to have baths and to rest awhile."

The dowager shrugged. "Do as you wish. I don't nap. Never have, never will." She looked sharply at Viola. "See to the guest rooms. I don't give a damn where these others stay, but put MacLean in the Pink Room, where Bonnie Prince Charlie once stayed. Then put Venetia in the Blue Room."

Viola met the dowager's gaze, a smile quivering on her lips. The Blue Room and the Pink Room were adjoining. In that moment, Viola could have hugged her prickly mother-in-law. "Of course. I shall take them there now, and —"

"No, thank you," Venetia said in a firm tone. "I would much rather have my usual bedchamber in the east wing, if you please."

Viola frowned. "Venetia, your grand-mother has kindly offered you the Blue Room, which is much nicer."

"I said no, thank you, Mama. And I mean it."

The dowager scowled. "Still obstinate, eh?"

Venetia returned her grandmother's gaze evenly. "I am an Oglivie."

The dowager's thin lips cracked into a smile. "Yes, you are, by God. Very well, I will allow your insolence this time. Just don't expect me to be patient forever. Viola, take these hooligans to their rooms. I don't nap, but I do like my quiet."

Viola agreed, though she was disappointed with the dowager's capitulation. The old bat had no compunction in ordering Viola about — why couldn't she have done the same for Venetia, especially when it concerned something as important as Viola's future grandchild?

Viola collected the group, who made their formal (and unappreciated) good-byes to the dowager, and led them into the mazelike, dimly lit corridors of the Dowager House.

Viola was certain they all longed for hot baths and soft beds, neither of which they'd receive. The servants were so old and the rooms so far removed from the main part of the house that the bathwater would be tepid by the time it made it to the respective tubs, and the beds were all lumpy from lack of turning.

Viola kept Gregor and Venetia with her to the last, bursting with curiosity about Gregor's proposal. They reached the Sun Chamber first, the room Venetia traditionally enjoyed while at her grandmother's. It was as far away from Gregor's room in the west wing as possible.

Venetia hugged her mother. "Thank you, Mama."

"I shall deliver Gregor to his room and return so we can have a long, comfortable chat."

Venetia's expression grew guarded. "Not now, Mama. I am too tired. I think I shall sleep until dinner."

"Won't you want some tea? Or some lavender water to —"

"No, thank you. I just wish to sleep." Venetia dipped a frigid curtsey to Gregor, who bowed deeply and winked.

Venetia's cheeks pinkened, and she disappeared into the room so quickly Viola was left speechless in the hallway.

Gregor eyed the firmly shut door for a long moment, his gaze considering. After a moment, he turned back to Viola. "Mrs. Oglivie, I am going to marry your daughter."

"That would be nice," Viola said bracingly, though she couldn't shake the thought of the sad, determined turn of Venetia's mouth. Viola patted Gregor's arm. "I wish you luck."

His jaw tightened, and it dawned on Viola that perhaps Gregor MacLean was just as hardheaded as Venetia. The thought gave her hope.

"Come, you must be exhausted. Let me show you to the Pink Room. It's quite isolated, as it's the more formal part of the house, and the dowager rarely allows anyone there. It's quite a compliment to you."

Gregor offered Viola his arm and smiled in such a way that her heart fluttered. "Lead the way, madam. I assure you that I am prepared for the worst."

Venetia ordered a bath and washed and combed her hair, letting it dry before the fire. Afterward, she donned her night rail and, tossing her robe over a chair, sent word to her grandmother that she had a headache and would not be joining the party for dinner. This impertinence earned her a tersely worded reply that Venetia ignored and a visit from her mother, who arrived carrying laudanum, a cup of herbal tea, a cold cloth soaked in Egyptian milk for her forehead, and a hot brick for her bed.

It soon became apparent why Mama had come; every question she asked had to do with Gregor's proposal. Venetia refused to cooperate and directed the conversation toward her adventures, how Ravenscroft had tricked her into leaving London, and how the others had come to be at the inn. She left Gregor's name out of her recital almost entirely.

When the dinner bell rang, Mama gathered the empty tea cup, kissed her on the forehead, tucked her into bed with the hot brick at her feet, and left.

Surprised at her mother's unaccustomed tact, Venetia snuggled beneath the covers, hoping sleep would come.

Of course, that proved a vain hope. After tossing and turning for a good half hour, Venetia eventually rose and went to sit before the fire.

It was so tempting to think that marrying Gregor would not only save her reputation, but might also bring them closer. Perhaps love would grow between them.

But what if it didn't? Did she want to start a marriage on such a poor basis? What if, one day, Gregor looked back at their marriage and felt cheated somehow? What if she did?

She couldn't do it. She couldn't take the chance that —

The door flew open.

Venetia whirled around, half expecting to face deep green eyes, but found her grandmother, dressed in a formal evening gown of lavender trimmed with black ribbons, a huge red wig on her head that made her seem amazingly tiny, and diamonds winking from pins and brooches, necklaces and bracelets.

The old woman limped in, her butler hovering behind her. She pointed with her cane to the small table before the fire. "Set the tray there, Raffley."

"Yes, madam." The butler did as he was told. "Will there be anything else, madam?"

"No. That's all." She waved him out.

Venetia blinked at the tray, which held a teapot, two cups, a small dish of tarts, and stiff linen napkins. "Grandmama, this is so nice of you, but I am not hungry."

"This isn't for you. It's for me." Grandmother limped to the tray and picked up a tart. She popped it into her mouth and said around it, "Couldn't eat at dinner with that Miss Flat woman yapping like a drunken sailor."

Venetia had to smile. "I see." She went to the tray and took a seat across from it. "Come and sit. I'll pour the tea."

"Can't sit; my hip's been giving me fits. But I will have some tea. Extra cream, please." She took the cup offered, her bright eyes fixed on Venetia's face. "Well, Miss West? What do you have to say for yourself?"

Venetia sighed. "I see you know every-thing."

"Most of it. From what your mother was able to tell me — which wasn't easy to understand, the way she mealy-mouths everything — and from what those ram-shackle travelers of yours had to say over dinner, I think I pretty well know what's what."

"Oh?" Venetia doubted the old woman could know everything.

A brow went up over the shrewd eyes. "That fool Ravenscroft went over the line, and MacLean is willing to throw himself on the fire. You won't have him on those terms, so you told him no. That about sum it up?"

Venetia nodded, a lump in her throat. "I

can't allow Gregor to do so, of course."

"Why not? He's a man. He ought to take responsibility."

"For someone else's mistake? No. It would be different if —"

"If what?"

If he loved her. Which he didn't. The lump in her throat grew. She took a sip of tea, hoping she wouldn't choke on it.

Grandmama's gaze never left her. "You are being silly, my dear. If your mother was the woman she should be, you'd be done with these die-away airs and on the way to the altar."

"I don't wish to go to the altar with Lord MacLean."

"Of course you do! He's a damned fine-looking specimen. Sort of man I went after myself, way back when. There's nothing shameful in wanting, Venetia. There's only shame in not getting."

Venetia set her cup back in the saucer with a loud *clack*. "Grandmama, every woman in London has thrown herself at Gregor's head. I won't be one of them."

"Forget his head. That's not the part that's the most interesting." Grandmama cackled when Venetia's cheeks heated. "Don't play your missish airs on me, young lady. I saw how you were looking at him, and he at you.

There's good, healthy fire there. The kind that makes marriages last and brings big, healthy boys into the family line."

Venetia almost laughed. "It's a wonder Mama hasn't taken to her bed, the way you talk."

"She takes to it every other day, but I know how to roust her." Grandmama limped toward the window, her teacup in one hand, her cane in the other.

"Come and sit by the fire," Venetia said, rising to follow her grandmother. "You'll spill your tea."

"I can hold my own cup, thank you," Grandmama said testily. "It's hot in here. Open a window."

"But —"

"I feel a bit faint. Open a window before I drop dead."

Venetia sighed and opened the window. A cold breeze swept into the room, banging the shutter open.

"Much better!" Grandmama said while Venetia shivered. The old woman limped toward the bed. "What did MacLean mean when he said he'd made a mull of his proposal?"

Venetia rubbed her cold arms. "It doesn't matter. I won't marry under such circumstances. If he . . . if he'd really wanted to marry me, then perhaps — But that doesn't matter, because it's not the way things are."

Grandmama fiddled with the tassel on the bed, the teacup held precariously over the mattress. "I never liked this color. I meant to have green tassels hung from the corners, but that demmed seamstress talked me out of it. Said it wouldn't go with the yellow."

Why on earth was Grandmama talking about bed tassels? "Grandmama, why —"

"Oops!" The tea sloshed on the bed, a brown splash hitting the pillows and cover. "Blast it all! Looks as if I ruined your bedding." There was a faint hint of satisfaction in her voice.

Venetia sighed, suddenly too tired to figure out anything other than the fact that she longed to be alone. "Don't worry about it. I'll have one of the maids dry the bed as well as she can. I'll sleep on the other side." It was a huge bed; four people could sleep in it without touching one another.

Grandmama hobbled to the bellpull. "My granddaughter will not sleep in a damp bed. You'll catch your death of a cold, especially with that window open."

"Really, Grandmama, it's nothing. I can —"

A soft knock sounded, and Raffley entered.

"There you are." Venetia's grandmother made her way to the door. "I've spilled tea on the bed. My granddaughter will need a new room."

Venetia said, "I don't —"

"Put on your robe, child. You can't walk through the hallways dressed like that." Grandmama paused in the doorway. "Raffley knows where to take you. I'd take you m'self, but I'm too tired."

"Grandmama —"

"Good night, my dear. I will see you at breakfast."

Venetia sighed. There was no naysaying Grandmama; she wasn't sure why she even tried. A maid appeared, who briskly repacked Venetia's portmanteau and carried it to the hallway to a waiting footman. Venetia thrust her arms into her robe and followed the butler down the hallway. They wound past various bedchambers, finally passing the Pink Room, where Grandmama had placed Gregor.

Venetia couldn't help wondering what he was doing. Had he retired already? She had an instant image of him sliding between the sheets and would wager her last groat that he slept without a stitch on. A delicious tremor went through her at the thought.

Raffley stopped by a set of doors farther

down the hallway and threw them open. The room was twice as large as her usual bed chamber and cozily warm, both fireplaces burning brightly. The bed was turned down, the heavily brocaded cover decorated with a mass of blue flowers, a pile of blue and gold pillows luring her forward, candles lit on either side of the bed casting the crisp sheets in a beguiling light.

Chairs and a settee were placed before one of the fireplaces, thick rugs scattered. Wide double doors led to a balcony that overlooked the gardens behind the house. Long, thick draperies of heavy navy silk pooled on the floor, and gold pillows were placed here and there.

Raffley unpacked Venetia's belongings while a footman brought in a new tea tray filled with fresh strawberries, raspberries and cream, cinnamon scones, and a chilled decanter of sherry. Venetia supposed her grandmother was apologizing for spilling her tea on the bed.

Finally, Raffley took one last look around the room, nodded his satisfaction, bid her a quiet good night, and closed the great doors behind him.

Venetia took off her robe and threw it over a chair, then went to the tray and poured herself a glass of sherry. This would be just the thing to help her sleep. She sipped her way through one glass and naughtily decided to have another.

She stretched her toes toward the fire, wiggling them in the delicious heat. Tomorrow, she'd see what she could do to help her companions. Sir Henry might actually make a good match for the romantically inclined Miss Higganbotham. He was steady and stable and had impressed Venetia with his attentiveness.

Miss Platt was another matter. She would have to find a position for the woman soon; perhaps Grandmama knew someone who needed a companion.

And Ravenscroft needed to return to London and apologize to Lord Ulster. Her mother might be able to help, since she knew Ulster's grandmother rather well. The old lady held her grandson's purse strings, so it was entirely possible she could nudge him into accepting Ravenscroft's tardy apology. Yes, that plan had merit.

She frowned a bit, sipping her sherry. That only left herself. Her companions had to know by now that she wasn't Ravenscroft's sister, that they'd been together under improper circumstances, and that Gregor wasn't her guardian.

Venetia sighed. What could she do? She

loved living in London and couldn't see becoming a recluse, but that was exactly what she'd have to do. She could live down the censure if she married Ravenscroft, but nothing could persuade her to take that step.

She lifted the sherry glass to her lips again and was surprised to find that it was empty. She refilled the glass and stretched, the bottoms of her feet delightfully warm. The firelight played off her skin in the most flattering way, gilding it to match the silk bed hangings.

Venetia let her mind wander to the way Gregor had looked at her that evening. If only she could believe he felt more for her than mere responsibility. Something . . . significant.

She sighed, so deep in thought that she didn't hear the handle turn on the balcony door.

Didn't notice the shadow of a person walking toward her across the thick rugs.

Didn't realize someone was standing there, watching her, until the faint scent of his cologne made her nipples peak beneath her thin night rail.

She closed her eyes and whispered, *"Gregor."*

Chapter 19

The difference betwixt women and men is this: if they're in love, one will tell ye what ye want t' hear, the other will do it.

Old Woman Nora from Loch Lomond to her three wee granddaughters one cold evening

Gregor smiled down at Venetia. "Mind if I join you? You look quite comfortable there." *And damned sexy, too.* He'd plainly seen the outline of her legs through her night rail as she'd held them to the fire, and it almost stopped him in his tracks. By God, but she had beautiful legs, curvy and sensual. He wanted to trace their length with his hands, rub his cheek over the curve of her hip —

His body tightened uncomfortably. *Stop thinking like that, or you won't be able to talk.*

Her gaze flickered to the balcony doors and back, her brows knitted in confusion. "My balcony doesn't connect to yours."

"I jumped." He grinned at the flash of concern he saw in her eyes. "At dinner, your grandmother informed me that you'd be moving to the room beside mine. She also mentioned how close my balcony was to yours; so close that even an old lady like herself could leap between the two without the least effort."

Venetia's cheeks heated and she pulled her nightgown closer. "Grandmama is anything but subtle."

"Almost as subtle as your mother."

"Oh, no! Not Mama, too."

Gregor paused beside a small table to pick up a silver tray holding a cut crystal decanter and matching glasses and set it on the table before Venetia. "Your mother was concerned I might be afraid of heights. She told me that if *she* were thinking of jumping between the balconies and couldn't bring herself to make the leap, it might be possible to pick the lock on the connecting door with, say, a cravat pin."

Venetia blushed. "I'm surprised they aren't in here now, throwing rose petals before you as you walk."

"I would never countenance petal tossing. Too showy." He took the chair opposite hers, trying to keep his eyes from wandering, which was damnably difficult, as she was wearing the most intriguing night rail. "How did your grandmother get you to move to this suite?"

"She 'accidentally' spilled tea on my bed." Venetia sent him a look from under her lashes. "Gregor, it . . . it would be best if you would go."

"Do you wish me to?" He held his breath, not wanting her to see how much her answer meant.

"No." The word came out in a breath, as if she could no longer hold it. Her gaze traveled over him, lingering on his open shirt. She closed her eyes, then opened them with a rueful smile. "I'm sorry for staring. It's just that I'm tired and . . ." She gestured lamely.

He laughed softly at her blush. "I've never seen you wear so little . . . or look so lovely."

Her cheeks were truly flaming now. She crossed her arms over her chest. "This is Mama's night rail. Mine isn't as revealing."

"More's the pity." He wanted to lift her into his lap and sit with her sweetly rounded behind nestled against him. His manhood stirred at the thought. *Not yet,* he told himself. He'd come to see what could be done to persuade her to marry him. *Keep focused,* he told himself.

He lifted the decanter and filled a glass,

then handed it to her before pouring one for himself. He took a sip and grimaced.

She sipped a bit herself. "I've never had such delightful sherry."

He set his glass back on the table. "I prefer my sherry dry." He let his gaze drift over her delicious form. "It's my women I like sweet."

Delicious color raced over her face and neck, and he burned to follow it with his lips.

She took a nervous gulp of the sherry.

Gregor lifted his brows when he saw the empty glass. "Would you like some more?"

She nodded thankfully. "Yes, please."

He poured her half a glass.

Venetia frowned. "There's plenty more in the decanter."

"I don't wish you to wake up with a headache, which will happen if you keep gulping it down like that."

"I am not gulping," she said in a lofty voice. "I was savoring it quickly. That is a different thing altogether."

"I see," he agreed gravely. He could tell from the glitter in her eyes that she was already a bit bosky from the sherry. A true gentleman would have refused to serve her more, but Gregor couldn't help but think that if she was relaxed and warmed by a glass or two of sherry, she might be more willing to listen to his proposal. He was determined to make it again, only this time, he'd do it right.

He'd realized one thing during the long ride here and that was that Venetia was too important to him for him to merely accept her refusal. "Very well, then. You may have more." He filled her glass to the top. "But don't blame me if you awaken with a headache."

Like a rainbow bursting from a storm-dark sky, she smiled. "Thank you. It's nice that we're talking again."

It *was* nice. "I've missed you." The words were past his lips before he knew that he'd said them.

"I've missed you, too." She set the glass down and leaned forward, the thin night rail stretched over her full breasts. "Gregor, I don't know what's happened to us, but I want things to return to the way they used to be." She frowned, her gaze locked with his. "I don't know if that's possible, but now I wonder if perhaps . . ."

He lifted his brows. "Perhaps?"

She took a fortifying drink, her lips moist from the sherry. "Gregor, I have been thinking that perhaps you had the right idea about exploring this attraction between us."

She met his eyes and whispered, "It's not going away. I — I find myself thinking about you and . . . I still want you."

His hand tightened about his glass. This was what he'd wanted and hoped for. He sat still, afraid that any movement, any word might ruin this moment, yet his heart thumped against his ribs like a wild animal in a cage.

Still he couldn't help but let his hungry gaze roam over her.

If there was one part of a woman's body that Gregor loved, it was her breasts. He loved them full and rich, creamy white with large, rose-colored areolas. As Venetia leaned forward, her breasts were clearly outlined, her erect nipples pressing against the thin material. Gregor heard her voice and knew he needed to listen, for he was almost certain he agreed with what she was saying. But all he could do was stare at her breasts, wondering . . . imagining . . .

Venetia gasped and crossed her arms over her chest, standing uncertainly. "Gregor, I —"

He grinned. The thin lawn of her night rail was like gauze. Her arms might be covering her lovely breasts, but the rest of her body was fully outlined for his pleasure.

She was all woman, his Venetia. Her calves

were pleasingly plump, just the size to fill a man's hands. Her sweetly curved hips begged to be held, explored, enticing a man to passion. Her hair fell in long, sweeping curls around her shoulders, her rounded arms dimpled and womanly. God, she was beautiful!

She stomped one foot, her breasts bouncing at the movement. "Gregor, say something! Were you even listening to me?"

Gregor realized she was growing angry with his lack of response. If only she knew how much he *was* responding to her. Like a banked volcano, he boiled beneath the surface. Any movement might send his thinly held control flying.

"Oh! Never mind!" She whirled away, her night rail shifting at her hips, tugging across her thighs, and lifting at her ankles.

One thought tore through the red mist of lust. She was leaving, and he had to stop her.

The next moment, he was standing, cradling her in his arms.

She blinked up at him, shock and uncertainty flashing across her face, turning her silver eyes to dark gray. "What — what are you doing?"

He looked into her eyes, and suddenly he knew this was right. That this moment was meant to be. "I am making your grandmother's dreams come true."

Excitement and nervousness warred in her eyes as he bent to capture her lips.

That touch ignited the banked passions that had been simmering inside Gregor for this last week. A raging desire not just to make love to her, but to possess her, body and soul, flared through his veins. He *would* have her; whether she knew it or not, she was his.

Their marriage was inevitable. Not because she had to marry or face a life of ostracism, but because Venetia was his and no one else's. And the sooner she realized it, the better things would be for them all.

Without another thought, he broke the kiss and lifted her in his arms. She gasped, her eyes meeting his, and that was all it took. Gregor kissed her to brand her. He kissed her because every sinew of his body cried out for her. He kissed her because she was dear and beloved and the only woman who had ever sent his senses tumbling, caused his heart to ache, made him crazed with wanting.

She moaned against his mouth, tasting of sherry and desire, her arms slipping around his neck as she pressed forward. Gregor deepened the kiss, plundering her sweetness. She filled his arms, and his groin ached with the need to bury himself in her.

God, but she was amazing, every delectable inch. He strode the three steps to the bed and paused there, his breath harsh in the stillness of the room, a question in his eyes.

Venetia's breathing was just as ragged, her nipples pressing against the thin night rail, her lips moist and swollen from his kiss. "Gregor."

It was only one word, but the timbre said so much more. Gregor placed her on the bed, her hair splayed across the silk pillows. He slid beside her, placed one hand on her gently rounded stomach, and traced a kiss from her temple to the corner of her lips. Had she been more experienced and less precious, he would have disrobed first, but he didn't wish to scare her. Venetia deserved to be cherished. And though he ached to possess her, after he did so, she would remember not just the passion of the moment, but the care he'd taken as well.

Gregor nipped at her ear as he ran his hand across her stomach to her hip. Venetia stirred restlessly, tugging him closer, her hands tight around his open shirt, her legs pressing against him, driving him mad with want.

He had to regain his control. He pushed himself back and looked into her eyes. "Do you trust me, Venetia?"

Her eyes were the dark of a stormy sky. "Yes." The passionate whisper warmed his heart.

Gregor slowly reached down and slid her night rail up her leg. She gasped when the fine lawn material reached her knees, and he paused, looking up at her questioningly.

Her hands clenched on his shoulders, but she didn't ask him to stop. If anything, her hungry look urged him on.

He pulled the night rail higher, to the middle of her thighs.

Her skin danced with goose bumps, her toes curled, her chest rose and fell rapidly. Gregor noted the curve of her dimpled knees and thighs, revealed to his hungry gaze. He lifted her leg to expose the soft, sensitive back of her knee, then kissed her there. She gasped and arched wildly, grasping his hair.

Gregor grinned. "Easy, sweet. That hair is attached, you know."

A trembling smile lifted one corner of her mouth. She released his hair, sliding her fingers to his cheek. "I'm sorry. That spot is ticklish."

"I know." He flicked his tongue over the

spot once more and blew softly over the dampness.

"Oh!" She grasped the sheets, her hips lifting from the bed.

Gregor slid up a bit, his tongue laving a path from the back of her knee to the inside of her thigh. There he let his tongue dance upon her tender skin, enjoying her delighted gasps and shivers. Her breath quickened; her hips began to move with wild recklessness. Then her hands were back in his hair, tugging.

"Gregor," she gasped. "I — I can't — *don't.*"

He stopped immediately, holding statuestill. *I must be gentle. God help me, but I must.* He placed his hand on hers. "If you say not to, then I won't," he said simply.

Her gaze flicked to his. For a long moment, she just looked at him, her breathing returning to normal, her eyes dark with thought. Then slowly, ever so slowly, she bent her knees and moved them apart, opening for him.

The gesture was delicate, perfect, delicious. Gregor's heart pounded against his throat as he bent forward to press a kiss on the inside of her thigh.

She quivered but held completely still, her thighs still parted, her feet planted firmly on the bed. Gregor slowly slid all the way up her thigh . . . and delicately ran his tongue across her womanhood.

She gasped his name as she writhed against him.

Gregor slid his hands beneath her thighs and pulled her closer. He took her with his mouth, worshiping her sweetness, teasing and tormenting her until, with a cry, she arched upward, crying out his name.

Gregor pulled her against him, cradling her in his arms. She panted into his chest, clutching him to her, her hair tickling his chin. "Gregor!" She pressed her face against him, deep quivers still racking her body.

He held her tightly until her breathing slowed to a normal rate. He was so hot he ached. But still he held her, her warmth enclosed in his arms.

Venetia began to regain her sanity. Was that what lovemaking was like? Good God, why hadn't anyone *told* her? She was well past thirty, and she'd waited? What had she been thinking?

The problem was, all she'd been doing *was* thinking. This was about feeling, and, oh, how marvelous those feelings were. She wanted more. Now.

She tilted her head back and met Gregor's eyes. Now that her heart had stopped thudding, she was aware of how loudly his beat in his chest. She could feel his manhood against her thigh and knew that he was holding back for her, waiting for a sign that he could continue.

Venetia placed her hands on either side of his dear, dear face, tracing a light path down his cheek as she pulled his mouth to hers. She opened beneath him, rolling to her side and pulling him with her. He exploded in passion, his mouth hot and possessive, his hands moving and never stilling.

In no time, his pants were undone, and he was shoving out of them. With eager hands, she tugged his shirt over his head and tossed it off the bed with a soft laugh.

He rolled atop her, his body naked against hers. The feel of his skin and the roughness of the hair on his chest and legs abraded her deliciously, sending welcome shivers through her. His hands, large and warm, touched and stroked, his mouth following.

He cupped her breasts, looking at them as if amazed. Then he bent to capture her nipple, laving it with his tongue until she thrashed wildly beneath him. A deep, hungering ache built, and she welcomed it, loving the sensations that flooded through her.

Gregor moved against her, and she felt the tip of his manhood poised between her thighs. Venetia's breath caught in her throat. Oh, yes. This was what she wanted, more than anything.

"Venetia?" His voice was harsh with restraint.

She opened her eyes.

An unspoken question blazed in his, his mouth white with the effort to remain in control.

She slid her hands to his and laced her fingers with his, then gently lifted her hips, pressing against him, welcoming him.

He groaned as he slid inside her. She gasped at the fullness of him, at the new sensations that rippled through her. Suddenly, he paused, still pressing, but more gently now. A deep pang caused her to wince and gasp. His hands tightened over her, and he pressed deeper still. "Easy, my love," he murmured against her hair.

He moved again, sliding back. The pain was gone now, and in its place was a quiver of something new, something just out of reach. Venetia moved beneath him, searching for that something.

He gasped once, and then he was moving, faster and faster, stroking her inside and out. She moved with him, lifting to meet each thrust, as desperate now as he was. They strained together, every moment sending them higher and higher. Suddenly, Gregor tensed, and Venetia's body exploded. She arched, lifting against him with a cry.

Unable to hold back a second more, Gregor tumbled over the edge of ecstasy with her.

CHAPTER 20

Och, me lassies! The fun ye'll have when
ye've a man of yer own to torment!
Old Woman Nora from Loch Lomond
to her three wee granddaughters
one cold evening

Venetia awoke slowly, her body feeling soft
and full. She and Gregor had made love two
more times last night, each time as passionate and demanding as the first. They
couldn't seem to get enough of each other.
They didn't speak much but met each
other's gaze with bemusement and a sort of
awe.

She stretched, wincing at the soreness
between her thighs, then reached for him . . .
but he was gone.

She sat upright, tossing her hair out of her
eyes.

A soft *clink* beside the fireplace drew her
attention. Gregor stood by a large tray. Fully

dressed, he looked calm and gentlemanly, unlike the wild rogue who'd so thoroughly pleasured her just hours before. Uncertainty trickled through her, but then his eyes devoured her with the same hunger that had kept them awake most of the night.

Venetia grinned. "I thought for a moment you had left."

"Just long enough to wash and dress. I requested breakfast here. I thought you might like that better than having to face everyone in the breakfast room."

Venetia slid to the edge of the bed, rolling her shoulders a little.

"Are you stiff?"

She sent him a humorous gaze. "A little. I would ask you the same, but I suspect stiff is the only thing you're not."

He laughed.

She tugged on her robe and was halfway to the tray when a thought made her stop. "Gregor, did Raffley bring the tray?"

"Yes, why?"

"The servants will talk, and —"

He waved a dismissive hand. "That doesn't matter. When we marry —"

"Gregor, wait. We made love, yes, but that doesn't change anything."

His mouth tightened. "Venetia, we have to marry. I won't let you face the future alone."

Her hands clenched. Was it just chivalry, then, and nothing more? Slowly, another thought intruded. "Last night, you thought that if we made love, I wouldn't refuse you."

Gregor's gaze darkened. "That wasn't the only reason."

Her heart sank. "What else, then?"

"Venetia, we've always gotten along better than any other couple I know. Now that this has happened" — he gestured toward the bed — "we should complete it."

She wrapped her arms around herself. "We've made love, Gregor, but nothing else has changed."

"Venetia, we could have a wonderful life."

"Until you find yourself interested in another woman. Or I meet someone and believe he could truly love me." She looked up at him, her heart aching. "Gregor, I've watched my parents through the years. Through all their trials and tribulations, they are as in love with each other, and as faithful, as the first day of their marriage."

"Our friendship has survived ups and downs. Our marriage would, too."

"Marrying without love would make that unlikely. But there's more. Gregor, I love people, and I love helping them. You don't. During this entire adventure, every time I've tried to help someone, you've told me not to, sometimes in a very angry tone of voice."

"People take advantage of you."

"Sometimes they do, but more have been happy for a helping hand. I like one myself sometimes. You just want to be left alone. We're too different."

Gregor was silent a long time, his brow drawn. Finally, he shot a hard look at her. "Love won't solve everything."

"No, but it's the most necessary ingredient of a successful marriage. Without it, nothing works."

He turned away, pacing a few steps, then turned back. "Do you realize what a good life we could have? We could build the best stables in the country; I know you'd like that. And we could travel, too." He glinted a smile at her. "Perhaps even Italy, though I promise not to ask you to take in laundry or tutor ill-behaved children."

She gave him a faint smile but said nothing. She crossed to the washstand and cleaned herself, then looked in the wardrobe for a gown.

Gregor watched her solemnly, his smile gone.

Venetia found it frustrating that they were so compatible in some ways and so different in others. She dressed in a pink morning gown and then sat before the gilt-edged dressing mirror. She found her silver-backed brush and tugged it through her hair. It took only a few pins, and the long strands were fastened back in place. She met her own glance in the mirror. She didn't look any different. No one who saw her would know she'd spent the night lost in passion. The thought brought tears to her eyes.

"Venetia, come and eat."

She glanced over her shoulder. Gregor was standing beside the table, his arms crossed over his chest, an angry expression in his eyes.

"And then?"

"I don't suppose there is any then. You have made your wishes very clear. If you'd like, I will see you back to London. I shall return immediately."

She winced at the bitterness in his voice. "No. We brought Miss Platt and Miss Higganbotham and Sir Henry here. I have to get them settled before I leave."

"Blast it, Venetia! They can take care of themselves, and —" He clamped his mouth closed.

"They're people, Gregor. Just like you and me."

"They are not like you and me. When *we* have a problem, we fix it. They all want *you* to do it for them."

"Some people don't have our gift for finding answers."

"Some people won't know what gifts they have if you keep doing things for them."

"I can't just let them fail!"

His eyes narrowed, and his voice was low and fierce, almost a growl. "You arrogant woman."

She blinked at him, shocked. "Arrogant?"

"Arrogant," he repeated, looking at her with . . . distaste?

"What do you mean by that?"

He gave a harsh laugh, then shook his head. "Your tendency to get involved in everyone's life, even at the expense of your own — it's not about helping other people. It's about your desire to prove that you're better than they are, that you are smarter and more capable. You don't believe they *can* help themselves, do you?"

"That is not fair!"

"Isn't it? If I were some poor fool who couldn't put his shoes on straight, you wouldn't refuse me. But because I am a capable adult, a strong man, you won't make room for me in your life."

Her cheeks burned at his accusations. "I am sorry you have such a poor opinion of me."

"And I am sorry you have such a poor

opinion of the world in general."

Venetia fisted her hands until her nails bit into the palms, furious tears gathering in her eyes.

Damn it all, she wouldn't cry. Some people became blazingly eloquent when they were angry, but she just cried, loudly. She *hated* it, yet could not stop once she began.

A sob lifted in her throat. She spun on one heel and made a mad dash out the door.

"Venetia!"

She heard his voice as she fled down the hall. She just wanted to get away and never see him again.

To think she'd begun to believe that she loved him! He wasn't even worth being friends with if he could accuse her of such —

Venetia slid to a stop in the great hall as two footmen came to sudden attention.

Raffley, the butler, asked, "Miss? Are you —" His gaze moved past her, and he looked suddenly confused.

Gregor came forward, taking Venetia by the elbow. "Miss Oglivie and I have something we must discuss. Is anyone in the sitting room?"

"Yes, my lord. Some visitors just arrived, and I was —"

"I must speak with Miss Oglivie now. Who is in the breakfast room?"

The butler looked pained. "The dowager and Lord Ravenscroft. They had a disagreement about a game of whist they played last night. The dowager thinks his lordship might have, ah, cheated, so she's determined to —"

"The library?"

"Miss Higganbotham and Sir Henry Loundan, my lord." The butler added in an undertone, "Miss Higganbotham is upset over something Sir Henry said about her father. They are having quite an argument."

Exasperation flickered across Gregor's face. "Are there any other rooms?"

The butler appeared to consider this. "Well, there is a small sitting room, but Miss Platt is there now, with Mrs. Oglivie." He brightened. "I believe Mrs. Oglivie is anxious to escape, though, so if you wish to interrupt them —"

"No, no. Who are the new visitors?"

The butler inclined his head. "Your brothers arrived only moments ago. I was getting ready to send word to you when you and Miss Oglivie appeared."

Gregor scowled. "My *brothers* are here?"

"Yes, my lord. Three of them."

"Damnation! What the hell do they want?"

"I couldn't say, my lord," Raffley said in a reproving tone.

"I will see them after I speak with Miss Oglivie." He glanced at Venetia. "If we wish private speech, we might end up in the kitchen."

Raffley appeared offended. "The kitchen, my lord? Surely you jest! I will see if —"

A loud banging sounded on the front door, followed by a gruff, "Open up before I knock this door down!"

Gregor recognized the squire's voice immediately, as well as Mrs. Bloom's higher-pitched tones in the background, urging the squire on.

"Good God!" Gregor grabbed Venetia by the wrist and turned down the hallway.

"My lord!" Raffley's astonished voice called.

"Answer the damn door," Gregor called back.

The door to the library swung open ahead, and Gregor halted so suddenly that Venetia was thrown against him. He turned and looked back at the entryway, where the squire's voice now mingled with Mrs. Bloom's outraged tones.

Cursing beneath his breath, Gregor reached for the closest door, yanked it open, and thrust Venetia inside. He stepped in with her, then closed the door behind him, entombing them in darkness.

The scent of starch and fresh linen rose to tickle Venetia's nose. As her eyes slowly adjusted to the crack of light around the door, she blinked in amazement. "MacLean, we're in a linen closet!"

CHAPTER 21

La, child! Ye can't capture love! But it'll
capture ye, will ye, nill ye.
Old Woman Nora from Loch Lomond
to her three wee granddaughters
one cold evening

Gregor looked around. "So it is. And we'll
stay here until we finish this discussion."

"This is not a discussion. It's an argument. You are completely —"

"Irresistible? Devastatingly handsome?
Right?" He smiled grimly. "Even though you
don't agree with everything I say, you must
admit I make sense."

"Gregor, we can't stay here. The squire
and Mrs. Bloom sounded angry. This situation —"

"Which is of your own making."

"No, it's not!"

"Did you or did you not encourage Miss
Platt to leave Mrs. Bloom's employment?"

"Mrs. Bloom is a difficult woman."

"So is Miss Platt. It seems to me that they were made for each other."

Venetia wished the closet were larger, for she had to tilt her head all the way back to meet Gregor's gaze. "You might be right about that. But I didn't encourage Miss Higganbotham to run away from her father!"

"No? Didn't you show her sympathy, encourage her to feel sorry for herself, when perhaps you should have gotten a bit more information first?"

"Sir Henry seems perfect for her."

"He might be, but that is not a decision for us to make. The squire is not a stupid man. He wants what is best for his daughter —"

"He was taking her to London, tearing her from the arms of the man —"

"Whom she was trying to persuade to elope with her. Did you ever wonder if perhaps the squire just wished to keep his daughter from ruining herself? That once in London, he might allow Sir Henry to visit and perhaps even court his daughter, but in a more formal and safer setting?"

Venetia hadn't thought that at all. "What makes you think so?"

"Because the squire let it be known where

he was taking his daughter. He even wrote a note to Sir Henry, which is why we found the man desperately trying to reach London."

"You can't be certain about that."

"I am certain that the squire, for all his rough ways, has a good heart. He certainly showed it in his efforts to assist us all in leaving the inn."

That was true. Venetia bit her lip. "What about Ravenscroft?"

"Damn it, Venetia! Stop trying to fix all the ills of the world!"

"Gregor, don't you understand? That's what I *do*. I fix things. It's who I *am*." She met his gaze, her eyes swimming in tears as she whispered, "If you loved me, you'd understand that."

He *could* understand. She had been taught to take care of others, whereas he had been taught to control himself and never expect anything else. She was right, he finally admitted to himself. He had no right to expect her to give up something that obviously meant so much.

Outside the closet door, all hell seemed to be breaking loose. The squire was yelling, his daughter sobbing, Mrs. Bloom fussing, Miss Platt yattering, Venetia's grandmother calling for Ravenscroft's head on a platter, while that young fool demanded someone count the coins and prove he was telling the truth.

Venetia swiped at her eyes, wiping away her tears. "There's no more to be said. I can't stay here, Gregor; I have to go out there and help settle this."

She put her hand on the knob.

Gregor's hand closed over hers. In that moment, with Venetia's warm fingers clasped beneath his, Gregor knew what he had to do. Knew it with a crystal clarity that made him smile. "I'm coming with you."

She looked down at his hand, which clasped hers so warmly. "Why?"

"Because I love you, and I do understand."

Venetia's heart swelled. "You —"

"Love. You."

"Really?" she asked breathlessly.

He kissed her. Hard and passionately, lifting her off her feet and plundering her mouth. He told her in that kiss that they *were* right for each other, that they *did* belong together. And Venetia kissed him back, swept away by their passion as quickly as before.

It took all of his self-control, but he finally slid her back to her feet. "You were saying?" he asked huskily.

She swayed against him, her mouth parted, her eyes shimmering with desire. "I don't remember."

He laughed just as the ruckus in the hallway increased. He glanced at the door. "I suppose you want to go out there."

It wasn't a question, so she didn't answer.

"Very well. We'll take five minutes."

"Five?"

"Yes, so you can give them your opinion on how to fix things. But, Venetia, *they* have to do it. You can't be responsible for everyone, and I can't pretend I'm not responsible for you."

That seemed fair. She nodded. "Five minutes. I promise."

He grinned. "Good, because I can't wait longer than that to touch you again. If you go over the time, I can't be held responsible for what I do."

She chuckled. "Five minutes, then."

He threw open the door and stepped out, bowing. "After you, my love."

Venetia followed him into the hallway.

If it had sounded chaotic from inside the closet, it was more so outside. The squire and his daughter were yelling at each other in the hallway, Sir Henry trying unsuccessfully to intervene. Miss Platt and Mrs. Bloom were nose to nose as they accused each other of being unfeeling and selfish. Viola was trying to protect Ravenscroft from the dowager, who was attempting to smack his shins with her cane. And watching all this from the stairs with astonishment were Gregor's three brothers.

Dougal caught Gregor's eye and winked. Gregor grinned as Venetia stepped into the middle of the melee.

At the sight of her, everyone broke off and hurried forward, trying to tell their side of the story.

"Venetia!" Miss Platt shouldered Ravenscroft aside. "Mrs. Bloom has accused me of being a shameless flirt! A *flirt!* Can you believe it?"

"Oh," Mrs. Bloom said furiously, "you have done much worse! And after I arranged some special sewing for you, to help pay to get your worthless brother out of gaol! That's what I get for trying to help you, you ungrateful woman!"

Ravenscroft leaned around her, his face red. "Venetia, your grandmother says I cheated her out of two pence! Tell her I would never do such a thing!"

"Ha!" Grandmama snapped, waving her cane in the air. "I heard about that Ulster fellow who's waiting to gut you the second you return to town. Cheated him, too, didn't you?"

"Venetia," Mama said, leaning forward. "Where have you been? I went to your room, and there was no one there, and —"

Her blue eyes full of tears, Miss Higganbotham rushed forward to grasp Venetia's hand. "You must tell Father I am not going to London, no matter what he says! I won't leave my beloved Henry!"

"Who gave you permission to address Sir Henry by his given name?" the squire thundered.

"Don't yell at her," Sir Henry growled, his back stiff with outrage.

Venetia took a deep breath. "Everyone, please! I have only five minutes, so I'll have to make this fast."

"Five minutes?" Grandmama's wrinkled brow creased. "Why five?"

"Because it should be enough," Gregor said. "Venetia? Do you need any assistance?"

She flashed him a grateful smile. "No, I don't think so. I shall begin with Miss Higganbotham."

Which was a good choice, as Miss Higganbotham was tightly clutching Venetia's hand. "Father is so mean!" the emotional young lady said in a quavering voice. "He says I must go to London and cannot see Henry!"

Venetia looked at the squire. "Sir, I know I have no right to speak, but it does seem to me that completely cutting off all contact between your daughter and Sir Henry would only make her wish to see him more."

The squire scowled. "I never said he couldn't visit. It's not as if I'm burying her away from mankind! I want her to have a season before she makes any decisions like that."

"Just one?" Venetia asked.

Sir Henry looked at him expectantly.

Elizabeth frowned. "But that would be months!"

"Yes," Venetia agreed. "However, it would be well worth it if your father will allow Sir Henry to visit you while you are in London." She looked at the squire. "If Elizabeth agrees to an entire season and joins in as she ought and causes no more scenes and promises not to see Sir Henry except when you approve —"

"Venetia!" Elizabeth exclaimed. "I can't do all of that!"

"Yes, you can," Sir Henry said, looking at his beloved with a heartfelt gaze. "I would wait for you for a hundred years. What's one season, especially if I can see you?"

"Well?" Venetia asked the squire.

"I suppose so," the squire said. "But Sir

Henry is not staying at our house when in London!"

"I don't need to," that worthy gentleman said stiffly. "I have my own house in Mayfair."

The squire looked impressed. "Do you, indeed?"

"Henry has houses in London, Brighton, Bath, *and* York, don't you, Henry?" Elizabeth said.

"Actually, I have two in Bath. Both of them excellent rental properties."

The squire looked at Henry as if seeing him for the first time. "I thought you were a farmer."

Sir Henry offered a quiet smile. "I am, sir. A *gentleman* farmer."

Gregor grinned, his pride in Venetia swelling.

"There," Venetia said, turning now to Ravenscroft. "I believe you owe my grandmama two pence."

He huffed. "I do not! I won fairly and —"

Grandmama's cane smacked him in the shin.

"Ow!" He hopped up and down, his face contorted in pain.

"Grandmama, stop that."

"I don't like cheats!"

Venetia looked at Ravenscroft. "Do you

have two pence on you?"

"Yes," he said sulkily. "But it's a matter of principle!"

"It's a matter of saving your shins. I won't be here to stop her every time she wields her cane. And if you think she won't follow you to London, you're wrong. You'll be *praying* for Lord Ulster to shoot you."

"She's right," Grandmama said, shaking her cane at Ravenscroft.

He jumped back and fished in his pockets. "All I have is this guinea."

Grandmama snapped it from his fingers. "We'll consider it interest." Cackling, she pocketed the coin.

Ravenscroft's shoulders slumped, but he knew he'd been beaten.

"What about *me?*" Miss Platt stood with her bony arms crossed over her chest, her nose high. "Mrs. Bloom has not been kind to me!"

Mrs. Bloom stiffened. "Not kind? When I helped you find the money to pay your worthless brother's debts?"

"By making me sew!"

"I didn't make you do anything. I arranged for you to be paid very well for some specialty work, which is what *I* used to do before I married your uncle. There is nothing wrong with earning money, despite what my late husband might have told you."

Mrs. Bloom sighed and told Venetia, "Randolf was an excellent man in many ways, but he was never careful with his funds. I am afraid he encouraged Mr. and Miss Platt to be quite extravagant. They never learned the least economy and don't like the thought of earning a living. I fear it's ruined them both."

"We wouldn't need to make a living if you hadn't taken all of Mr. Bloom's money when he died," Miss Platt said in a sulky voice.

"Mr. Bloom didn't *have* any money when he died. I've told you that before, yet you insist on thinking otherwise!" Mrs. Bloom reached forward and took Miss Platt's hand. "I know you never thought I cared for you the way your uncle did, but over the years, you've become important." Mrs. Bloom's lip quivered. "When I thought you'd been misled by some hooligans, I couldn't get here fast enough!"

Miss Platt stared at Mrs. Bloom, tears filling her eyes. "Oh, Mrs. Bloom! Y-you came to *save* me?"

Mrs. Bloom nodded.

Gregor watched, amazed, as Miss Platt threw herself on Mrs. Bloom's neck and wept.

Venetia sighed happily, then glanced back at Gregor. "How much time do I have left?"

He pulled his watch from his pocket. "Thirty seconds. I'd say that's a —"

"One moment!"

Mrs. Bloom, her arm still around Miss Platt, eyed Venetia with disfavor. "Miss West, or Miss Oglivie, or whatever your name is, I believe you owe us all an explanation. You lied to us. You *and* your 'brother' and your 'guardian.' I demand an explanation."

"Yes," the squire said, blinking as if suddenly awakened. "Who are you, and why did you lie to us?"

Every eye turned on Venetia, who paled.

Her mother stepped forward. "Actually, I can explain everything."

"You don't need to," Gregor said, snapping his watch closed and replacing it in his pocket. "I am about to take my fiancée to a quiet, private place and propose to her in a proper fashion."

"What?" Dougal said, looking as if he'd choked on something.

"Demme, if you don't remind me more and more of your grandfather," the dowager said, cackling.

"Propose, hm?" Mrs. Bloom sent a hard look at Gregor. "I take it you are not her

428

guardian."

"No, he's not!" Ravenscroft cried, pointing a finger at Gregor. "He was *never* her guardian!"

"And you are not her brother?" Mrs. Bloom asked.

Ravenscroft reddened. "No." He stiffened. "I'm her —"

"Time's up." Gregor scooped Venetia into his arms.

She opened her mouth to protest but then met his gaze. A slow, warm smile curved her lips, and she sighed happily.

The feel of her in his arms was too, too tempting. Gregor cleared his throat and said, "If you will all excuse us, I refuse to wait another moment. I *must* propose to this woman."

"Again," Venetia pointed out.

"But this time, I shall do it right."

Venetia's eyes gleamed with passion.

"Excellent!" Viola clapped her hands. "Oh, I just *knew* this would happen one day!" She looked at the squire and said in a confidential voice, "They've been friends forever, you know. Such a good match."

The squire smiled reluctantly. "So long as they are getting married. I suppose he does need some privacy to make a good proposal.

Difficult thing to do in front of an audience."

Ravenscroft hurried forward. "Over my dead bod—"

Grandmama neatly hooked his leg with her cane, and Ravenscroft went flying to the floor.

He struggled to rise, but Viola was quicker. She rushed to his side.

"My hand," he groaned.

She stooped so her skirts covered where her slipper was firmly planted on his hand and looked at Gregor. "The sitting room is available. It's right there." She pointed.

"Perfect." Holding Venetia closer, he glanced at his brother. "Dougal, would you mind opening the door?"

"Of course."

Beside him, Alexander growled, "Gregor, I don't approve of any of this." He looked at the assembled company with disapproval. "It's very messy and chaotic."

Gregor shrugged. "It's a good thing, then, that it's not your life but mine." He looked into Venetia's face and grinned. "Personally, I am discovering that a little chaos can be a good thing."

Hugh chuckled and said to Alexander, "I fear you've been dismissed, brother. Come, let's find some port and let the happy

430

couple have their moment."

Dougal threw open the door. "I shall stand guard." He waited for them to walk through, and closed it firmly behind them.

As the door shut, Gregor heard Dougal say, "Mrs. Oglivie, I hate to be a demanding guest, but is there any port in this house? All of this has made me quite thirsty."

"Of course," Viola said. "Perhaps we should all remove to the dining room. Mother, do you think we might serve some refreshments to our guests?"

The dowager's answer was lost in the murmur of voices that arose as the guests moved away.

Against Gregor's shoulder, Venetia giggled. "I am going to like being related to your brothers."

"And I gain your mother and grand-mother, both of whom I now find perfectly delightful." He set her on her feet but held her close, cupping her intimately against him as he kissed her.

When they were both breathless, he raised his head, then rubbed his thumb over her full bottom lip. Eyes bright, he dropped to one knee, her hand held between his. "Venetia, I love you. I want to marry you. Will you have me?"

"Yes," she said breathlessly, tears shimmering in her eyes. "I love you, too."

Until that moment, he hadn't realized how closely he'd been guarding his heart. At her words, happiness, raw and pure, exploded through him, and he stood and swooped her back into his arms, swinging her around and around.

Life with Venetia would never be simple; there would be many messes to untangle. But with her at his side, it would all be worthwhile. After kissing her once more, he set her back on her feet.

She kept her arms around his neck. "I think we should celebrate properly upstairs."

He laughed softly and lifted her again. "Anything you want, dear heart. Anything you want."

ABOUT THE AUTHOR

Karen Hawkins is the *New York Times* and *USA Today* bestselling author of a dozen historical romance novels. When not stalking hot Australian actors, getting kicked out of West Virginia (thanks to the antics of her extended family), and adding to her considerable shoe collection, Karen spends her time warming her feet on her narcoleptic golden retriever while writing her next book. She lives in Florida.

Karen welcomes mail from fans and can be reached at 2511 East Colonial Dr. #146, Orlando, FL 32803. Please visit her Web site at www.karenhawkins.com.

The employees of Thorndike Press hope you have enjoyed this Large Print book. All our Thorndike and Wheeler Large Print titles are designed for easy reading, and all our books are made to last. Other Thorndike Press Large Print books are available at your library, through selected bookstores, or directly from us.

For information about titles, please call:
  (800) 223-1244

or visit our Web site at:
  www.gale.com/thorndike
  www.gale.com/wheeler

To share your comments, please write:
  Publisher
  Thorndike Press
  295 Kennedy Memorial Drive
  Waterville, ME 04901